Natasha Boyd is an autho[r] ... [mark]eting and public relations. She ... [scie]nce in Psychology from Royal Holloway, University of London and live[s] in the coastal Carolina Lowcountry, complete with [Spani]sh moss, alligators and mosquitoes the size of tiny birds. [She ha]s a husband, two sons and a host of internationally [sprea]d and scared relatives who worry the next book will [be abo]ut them. She is a member of Georgia Romance Writers, [Roma]nce Writers of America and Island Writers Network, [where] she has been a featured speaker. She has written two [full-le]ngth novels: the award-winning *Eversea*, and its much anti[ci]pated sequel *Forever, Jack*.

Praise for Natasha Boyd

'A [co]mpletely captivating read'   *Romfan Reviews*

'[H]ot [escapism!'   *Aestas Book Blog*

'Y[ou] will get lost in the characters and their stories. This b[ook] is escapism at its very best. A beautiful coming of age sto[ry] with lots of lovely romance mixed in'
                    Laura, *Bookish Treasures Blog* and Founder,
                    New Adult Book Club on Goodreads

'Y[ou] are a fool if you don't add this book to your "To Be Re[ad]" list. In fact, you should bump it right up to the top'
                                        Madison Says Reviews

'If [I c]ould give this book 10+ stars I would!'
                                        Luscious Literature

By Natasha Boyd and published by Headline Eternal

Eversea
Forever, Jack

NATASHA BOYD

eversea

headline
ETERNAL

Special thanks to Daniel Isaiah for permission to quote the lyrics
from 'High Twilight' (Secret City Records)

First published by the author in 2013

First published in paperback in Great Britain in 2014
by HEADLINE ETERNAL
An imprint of HEADLINE PUBLISHING GROUP

2

Cataloguing in Publication Data is available from the British Library

ISBN 978 1 4722 1965 7

Typeset in Sabon by Palimpsest Book Production Ltd, Falkirk, Stirlingshire

Printed and bound by CPI Group (UK) Ltd, Croydon CR0 4YY

Headline's policy is to use papers that are natural, renewable and recyclable
products and made from wood grown in sustainable forests. The logging and
manufacturing processes are expected to conform to the environmental
regulations of the country of origin.

HEADLINE PUBLISHING GROUP
An Hachette UK Company
338 Euston Road
London NW1 3BH

www.headlineeternal.com
www.headline.co.uk
www.hachette.co.uk

For Dorothy
Thank you for being my foundation

ACKNOWLEDGEMENTS

Thank you for reading *Eversea*. These characters would not leave me alone until I had them down. And even then, they would nag and nag until I had them and their story just right. They aren't done yet, though. Not by a long shot. Also, Nick, Jack and Devon did go for a drink after he got his turtle tattoo. The scene ended up on the cutting room floor – so to speak – but you will be able to read it on *BookishTreasures* blog. Also of interest, *Warriors of Erath* was a real story. It was a short I wrote three years ago and may revisit one of these days. Twin brothers M.A.X. and Damien – two dimensions of reality bleeding into one another. A girl . . .

Thank you to all my sweet friends and family who had to hear about Jack Eversea endlessly.

Thank you, in particular, to my husband for not getting jealous of Jack (or his pinterest page!) and encouraging me and supporting me every moment. I can always count on you to tell me what I need to hear – thank you for believing in me. Always. Doesn't Jack seem familiar to you sometimes? My kids for dealing with chicken nuggets from the freezer every other day (okay, every day). You guys are my life!

Thank you to my editor, Judy Roth. I am so grateful I found you! And you love Jack and Keri Ann as much as I do! Thank you for what you did for them, and me.

To my *Stormy Nights* girls: Not sure how I would survive without you, you keep it real – every day. Faith Martens and Karina Knowles – you fell in love with Jack along with me, thank you. Faith makes awesome book-inspired jewelry (I have an amazing seaglass Eversea-inspired charm bracelet! www.etsy.com/shop/HulaTallulah)

My beta readers: Ana D'Apolito, Angelica Dawson, Melvina Davis, Carole Ronneberg, Jenny Needham and, unofficially, Sarah-Kate Bozza; all of your feedback and supportive commentary was amazing. Words from my betas like "I can't believe this is your first book" and "I'm addicted to this story" kept me going many times when I wondered if I was deluding myself.

My sister, Cassy, who read an early draft with the view to designing the cover – I am so sad that your beautiful cover never got to see the light! Thank you for your time and care with Jack and Keri Ann. Cassy does amazing work: www.getocd.com

Thank you to Adrian Repasch who stepped in as my deadlines were approaching to take over the cover for the e-book edition. Isn't it beautiful? His website is: www.design-geek.com

My friends and supporters on FB who have cheered me on, and Laura Carter of *BookishTreasures* blog and the New Adult Book Club on Goodreads – it's champions like you that inspire people like me.

Thank you to my mother who showed me how to just be myself, and to always hold my head up high. You are beautiful.

Thank you to the mavens who paved the way in New Adult romance and who are breaking new boundaries every day. Thank you for inspiring me and giving me courage.

None of his would have happened though, if I hadn't over-heard and introduced myself to two gentlemen talking in a coffee shop about their writing. They invited me to share my work with them. Too embarrassed to show them the measly short stories I'd been experimenting with, I decided to start a story that had been teasing me all summer long. *Eversea* was born. Al Chaput and Dave McDonald, thank you for continuing to improve my craft and inspire me every week. You took me to the next level and beyond. I am honored that you let me join you. I wouldn't be here recognizing a lifelong dream without you.

Thank you to my 'nana' (Granny), Dorothy Magdalene Rosenfeldt. I miss you. Every day.

Finally – to all the teachers out there. There really was a teacher like Mr. Chaplin and he really did inspire a lot of children. It's the highest calling to be a teacher – thank you.

Keep in touch! I'd love to hear from you!

https://www.facebook.com/authornatashaboyd
http://www.pinterest.com/lovefrmlowcntry
Twitter @lovefrmlowcntry
Instagram @lovefrmlowcntry
Tumblr eversea.tumblr.com

Thank you.

eversea

CHAPTER ONE

You know you're in the Lowcountry when the steering wheel in your old red pickup is slippery from humidity, the news on the radio is all about the projected path of the latest Atlantic hurricane and the road kill you narrowly miss smearing further is a five foot long alligator.

I shuddered as I passed the sludgy reptile remains and held my breath. Lifting my ponytail off my neck, I hoped the hot South Carolina breeze coming through the window would at least feel cool against my damp skin.

The upside of fall was the tourists had gone home. The downside was the county stopped spraying for mosquitoes and no-see-ums, so the little fuckers got to gorge themselves in a type of 'eat local' frenzy. There was one inside the cab of the truck, and I tried very hard to ignore him as I went over the cross-island bridge. But, if he dared circle my bare ankles, I was going to have to pull over and hunt him down.

I checked the rearview mirror and started to change lanes, but a loud honking and growl of an engine made me swerve back. My insides lurched as a motorcycle emerged from my blind spot. I'd nearly side swiped it. The driver pulled up alongside and looked over as I raised my hand in a gesture of apology.

His helmet had a dark visor so I couldn't see in. After a few seconds he lifted a gloved hand in salute and took off ahead with a roar, his white shirt billowing out like a sail. California plates. Tourist. That figured.

I was late for my shift at the grill. Following the biker's example, I floored it too, assuming any police officer would pull over the out-of-towner before me, or at least only give me a friendly warning. When you live in a small town, you either went to school or church with just about everybody. Not that I'd been in either for a while.

Making it home with minutes to spare, I dropped off my truck and hotfooted it to work.

The small seaside town of Butler Cove Island had nine thousand off-season, full time residents, and some days it felt like they *all* had an opinion. I tried to paste on a smile and nod as I listened politely to yet another nugget of sage advice from Pastor McDaniel. The good pastor was pretending to drink plain iced tea, *not* laced from the little flask in his jacket pocket. *Seriously?*

His portly frame was wedged into a booth and the buttons on his dress shirt looked to be taking some serious strain.

I wondered if I would get a reprieve from him going on about my house again. The Pastor sat on the town council and seemed to think this entitled him to lay it on thick. "Now, Miss Keri Ann, yo' gran-mamma would fair turn in her grave to see the last remainin' bit o' real estate in your family turn so dog eared." *Nope*. He was on it again. "You need to keep that place up." He leaned forward conspiratorially. "Why don't I send my Jasper on up there on Sunday after church to give you a little hand?"

"That's very nice of you, Pastor." I hated to turn it down, truly. My family home was the last thing left for the Butlers of Butler Cove, and it was falling apart. I needed the help, but not at the price of the pastor doing me a good turn. And from the way his beady eyes shifted, I felt sure the idea of Jasper and me together had crossed his mind. What better way to get his hands on the house? Luckily, I was certain Jasper and I were on the same page of our platonic relationship. "I'd be glad to pay him, if he wouldn't mind some sanding and painting."

The Pastor puffed his chest out a little. "Well now, there'll be none o' that. My Jasper's a gentleman helping out a lady, is all. Did he tell you he was accepted into Charleston College of Law?"

I nodded.

"He's a smart boy that one, going places. Good with his brains and his hands. I'll send him over Sunday." He adjusted his gaze and seemed to peer down his nose at me, even though I was standing a good three heads above his sedentary frame. "I'll be seeing you at service, I hope."

How did he do that? There must be school for teaching pastors how to guilt people. I smiled slightly and set down the water I was holding right in front of him.

"How about some water, Pastor?" I asked, looking meaningfully at his spiked iced tea. I hadn't been back in church for six years. I might be struck by lightning if I went this Sunday.

It was a slow night; finally calm after the crazy tourist season. The only other people left in the dimly lit restaurant were up at the bar. One was my best friend Jazz, nicknamed for her love of the genre, and the other, a hunched-up guy with a ball cap and hoodie who'd just walked in five minutes ago and literally curled onto a bar stool in the corner. He was fishing a phone out of his jeans pocket.

It was almost closing time, I seriously hoped he wasn't going to stay long, I could really use an early night and closing the place down on time sounded like heaven.

"What can I get you?" I called over to hoodie guy as I went back around the bar. He mumbled something, not looking up from the phone he was busy texting on. I sighed and went further down the bar so I could hear him. People could be so rude. I'd had enough of them this summer, and I don't think I was the only one. Reportedly, there were a few cases of locals blowing their gaskets. Not a surprise. The county even had to post billboards reminding residents most of their funding came from tourism.

"A burger, medium, with fries. To go," Hoodie Guy repeated not looking up, the peak from his burgundy ball cap hiding his face completely. "And a Bushmills on the rocks while I wait." His accent was most definitely out of town. He went back to texting. I sighed and jabbed the order onto the touch screen. It was a good thing I had the patience of a saint. Ten seconds later Hector leaned out of the kitchen shaking his head at me.

"Sorry, Hector. Last one, then you can turn 'em off. I'll close it down out here." I smiled at his grumpy face. We both complained at times, but it was good-natured. We loved our jobs at the Snapper Grill. The salary and tips were huge all summer long, and in the off season, when most of the other seasonal employees moved on, we pretty much kept the place ticking. It was only really busy on the weekends when it became more of an islanders' bar than a restaurant. It helped that our owner, Paulie, had a subscription to the local sports games. Most residents took offense to having to buy a premium package on their cable contracts just to watch the Tigers or the Gamecocks. Hector ducked his dark head back in the kitchen muttering something in Spanish.

"Sooo, what's new in the world of entertainment?" I nodded at the magazine Jazz was devouring while I filled a glass with ice and some fine Irish whiskey.

Jazz looked up and groaned in happiness. "This is such bliss. I haven't been able to sit around and read a trashy magazine for months. You know my mom won't let me even have them at the house, says I'm liquefying my mind while she's paying my tuition. I can't wait to move out, as much as I'll miss her."

Jazz was going to college up at USC Beaufort, but living at home to save cash and working in a local boutique. I smiled in sympathy at my friend and delivered the stiff drink down the bar.

Hoodie Guy was still scrolling through his phone with his long fingers, mindless of the drink I set down with a napkin on the polished wood in front of him. I sighed and strolled back to Jazz.

"You know you can move in, Jazz. It's just me knocking around there while Joey finishes up med school." She pretended not to hear. I had made the offer a million times, but Jazz and my brother, Joey had dated briefly one summer when Joey came back from college. To say he broke Jazz's heart when he left was an understatement. I wasn't sure anyone realized how much Jazz cared for him, least of all Jazz herself. For my sake they had patched a makeshift and delicate friendship for when Joey returned for holidays. But now, between school and interning and an upcoming residency, he was home less and less.

"So McDaniel still trying to set you up with Jasper?" Jazz

asked, as she flicked the pages over. "You do need to have a date now and again, you know . . . stay in practice for when the real deal comes along." She winked.

"God, Jazz!" I quickly glanced at Pastor McDaniel to make sure he hadn't heard me taking the Lord's name in vain again. Oops. "You know I have too much on my plate to date right now. And who would be the real deal around here, for God's sake?" Wow, I was on a roll tonight. Luckily the good pastor was getting ready to head on out. I returned his wave as he left. It was a good thing he was walking home, I would have had to lift his keys otherwise.

"You won't believe it," Jazz exclaimed, totally dropping our topic and staring at the magazine in her hands. "Audrey Lane had an affair with her married director! That cow. I can't believe it. She's supposed to be dating Jack Eversea." Jazz looked horrified. She idolized Jack Eversea, along with possibly every girl in America.

I laughed at her. "Jazz, you do realize most of that stuff is made up, right?" I leaned over to look at the dubious and grainy photos she was tapping a lime green fingernail at, and then stopped at the abrupt sound of a stool scraping back.

We both looked over to see Hoodie Guy stand up and angle his back to us. He fished a wad of cash out of his jeans pocket, and peeling off a bill, placed it on the bar next to his unfinished drink.

I noticed Jazz's eyes roam down to rest on his extremely nice rear-end, encased in trendy denim.

I smacked her on the hand once, hard.

"Ow!" she yelped and I grinned.

Hoodie Guy tucked his chin down and walked out of the front door.

I met Jazz's eyes as she glared at me in mock outrage.

"What? He had a nice ass," she humphed and went back to her tabloid. She wasn't wrong, I was just more concerned with his weird behavior.

"Order's up," Hector barked from the kitchen pass-through, passing out a Styrofoam box. Great. Oh well, on the bright side, if he didn't return in five minutes, I was taking a burger home tonight. He better have left enough to cover his tab, I thought to myself. I walked down and grabbed the money off the bar. A hundred. Huh. I rang it up and pulled out the change from the register.

"Hector," I called back through the pass-through. "It was a good tip night." I passed eighty dollars in cash over the counter and into the kitchen. As much as I needed the money, Hector needed it more.

"*Madre*." I heard Hector chuckle.

"Shoot, I gotta scoot." Jazz hopped down from her stool and quickly came around to embrace me. "I'm opening up the shop tomorrow, I hate getting up early. See ya." And with that, my bubbly friend flew out the door.

Jazz and I had been best friends since Butler Cove Elementary when my family moved here to live in the family home and look after my grandmother. Making friends halfway through a school year in a new place was not high up on my list of skills. I wasn't sure how I lucked into Jazz, but somehow this blonde ball of energy with a round face of sunshine had turned her light on me one day in the fifth grade hallway, and I had been basking in the warm glow ever since. Even during the toughest moments of my life.

I turned the music down and followed in her wake to lock up.

It was a gorgeous night. Although the humidity still had a way to go, the heat had finally broken, and the stars were out in full. Standing in the doorway, I looked up and breathed in the fresh air. The cicadas were busy, the sound comforting in its endless and predictable rhythm. I knew a part of this place would always be in my soul. It was hard-wired in. As much as this town annoyed me at times, there was really nothing quite like this part of the world. I wanted to leave at some point in the future, I knew, I was just waiting for Joey to get done with school and trade places with me. That was the deal. That was one reason I didn't date. I really didn't want it to be harder than it had to be to leave. Another reason was I knew almost everyone in the eligible dating pool, and I was a choosy beggar.

My feet hurt. Tonight, I would probably sleep the sleep of a well-worked day and tomorrow, since I only worked dinner, I planned to continue the painting of the porch. Since funds were tight, I had to prioritize, and with Pastor McDaniel's less than subtle comments about the house's condition, I figured I better continue work on the outside.

Stepping into the restaurant's dimly lit courtyard to straighten some of the furniture, a movement in my periphery almost gave me a heart attack.

Shit!

Standing up from one of the tables in the shadows, like he'd been waiting for me, was Hoodie Guy. I slapped my hand on my chest, expelling a rush of air.

I judged the distance from where he stood to the door. Could I make it back inside before he got to me? How could I have been so careless? Joey was always telling me to have Hector do the lock up, and here I was not even knowing if Hector was still in the restaurant.

I stood still and tried to make out the guy's face under his hat. He was tall and looked strong, his dark jeans molding to his long straight legs. If he was going to attack me, at least I should try and remember what he looked like. Or wait— maybe that was worse. If I saw him, did that mean he would have to kill me?

I was aware I was frozen like a stunned rabbit, but it dawned on me slowly that he hadn't moved either, and I wasn't sensing anything menacing from him. Not that I was psychic. Unless you counted the times I was convinced Nana showed back up at the house to poke around and check on me. If anything, his stance and the way he hesitantly raised his hands caused me to stay put. Fear eased into curiosity. I still couldn't see his face. Why did the courtyard have to be so flipping dark?

I was about to speak when his long fingers reached up to his head, pausing for just a moment, like he was having second thoughts. Then he quickly grabbed his cap and whipped it and his dark hood off.

I found myself not being able to breathe for the second time in as many minutes. Standing in front of me was the most beautiful man I had seen in all of my twenty-two years on this planet. His rich dark brown hair, mussed up from the hat, stood up in a few places and framed a hard-planed face set with eyes the color of . . .

Well, I really couldn't tell the color of his eyes in the shadows, but I knew exactly what color they were, a deep gray-green. I hadn't been hiding under a rock for the last five years. And I certainly didn't need to double check the tabloid magazine Jazz had been reading, which definitely did not do him justice, to know that standing in front of me, Keri Ann Butler, outside the Snapper Grill in Butler Cove, population nine thousand, and hundreds of miles away from his expected location in Hollywood, was none other than Jack Eversea.

CHAPTER TWO

To my credit, I only gaped like a goldfish for a few moments before my prickly nature—always my 'go to' when I am nervous or caught off guard—made its presence known. I seriously cannot control myself sometimes.

"I suppose you want your burger now?" I'm sure that wasn't the first thing he expected me to say. Frankly, I surprised myself, too. It didn't seem to stop me from going on though. "First of all, don't lurk in the shadows, it's creepy. And second of all, you were so rude, give me one good reason I should let you in after closing?" Seriously. I said all that. To Jack Eversea.

"Rude?" He looked completely taken aback. "What the fuck?"

I arched a recently plucked eyebrow at him and spun on my sneakers back to the restaurant. I can't really explain my actions except I don't do weird encounters well, and this was way outside of my comfort zone. I definitely had a flight reaction setting in.

"Shit," he mumbled. "Okay, wait!" He strode forward, and reaching the door I was half way through in three long strides, wedged his foot in as it closed. Hard.

Oops.

"Ow!" he yelped. "Mother—" He stopped his expletive in the nick of time and wrapped his hand around the door-frame. "Wait." For a second, he looked really puzzled. "Wait, okay? I'm sorry about my language, but I paid for my burger." He paused, taking a deep breath and pitching his tone just right to appease me, this banshee of a girl. "May I please have it?"

I simply stared at him. Call it delayed shock setting in. Finally, I managed to snap out of it and stepped aside allowing him entry.

He looked at me warily and then walked past.

I closed the door behind him and locked it. It was a weird move, I admit.

"You taking me hostage?" he asked, his tone light.

"Can't be too careful with the kind of people who loiter around in the dark," I muttered. I honestly don't think he could tell if I was teasing. Hell, I wasn't sure. I mean, I was obviously, but I couldn't be too sure how things were coming out of my mouth. He looked like he was thinking the quicker he grabbed his food and got out of here, the better. Great. I get to meet Jack Eversea, *the* Jack Eversea, and I act like a complete imbecile. It was so good Jazz wasn't here, she would have clobbered me by now. For that matter, she would have clobbered him and dragged him back to her lair.

"So why did you say I was rude?" he asked. He shook his head slightly. In all likelihood at his idiocy in prolonging this weird encounter.

I stalked around the bar with a sigh, grabbing utensils and napkins as I did. Well, it couldn't get any worse, so I thought I might as well speak my mind. Or at least justify my odd behavior.

"Well, how about a list? You were so busy texting you didn't bother looking at me while I took your order. You mumbled it, didn't say please, and when I delivered your drink, you didn't say thank you. Did you not learn any basic courtesy growing up?" I delivered a plate to the bar counter and snapped open the Styrofoam box, sliding the contents out neatly, spilling nary a French fry on the way. Impressive. Even though I knew he wanted this order to go. What was I doing?

I continued, "Or are you so used to getting your way, because you look like God's gift to humanity? Maybe the fame has gone to your head a little bit?" My tone suggested *a little bit* was not what I meant.

"So I guess that answers my question about whether you know who I am?" He leaned forward against the bar and gave me a familiar furrowed-brow bad boy look. The same look that had been captured in *Vanity Fair* no less. Bad idea.

I huffed and rolled my eyes.

Jack Eversea finally looked stumped. Like he had no idea what to say and how to get his burger out of this place.

My nerves were subsiding. Not fully, considering I literally had some tabloid poll's sexiest man alive standing across the bar from me. But enough that I thought I might finally be able to converse normally.

"Sit and eat, you can keep me company while I shut this place down. It gives me the creeps after Hector locks up the kitchen and goes home." The fact that I didn't know whether Hector had left yet didn't seem to phase me.

I stuck out my hand and Jack took it warily. His hand was warm and strong, and if touching him didn't give me weak knees and a buzzing head, I was a monkey's uncle. "I'm Keri Ann Butler."

"Ja—"

"Jack Eversea, I know. Have a seat. Another drink?"

He nodded, still not releasing my hand. "Please."

I smiled at him then. The most natural smile I could muster despite the fact that holding his hand had launched a butterfly migration through my insides. I untangled my fingers from his after a few awkward beats, and Jack Eversea sat dutifully on the bar stool in front of his food.

He snapped open the ketchup bottle. "Can I ask you a favor?"

"Another one?" I winked to let him know I was teasing.

"Can you please not mention to anyone . . . I mean, anyone, including your blonde friend from earlier . . . that you saw me?"

I stayed quiet a few moments weighing the pros and cons. If anyone found out he was here, he'd never get his space to figure his shit out. And from what little I had gleaned from that tabloid article, he needed to. But this was Jack Eversea and Jazz was a huge fan.

"Please?" he asked again, quietly. Pleadingly.

"Of course." I inclined my head. "Your secret's safe. Not sure anyone would believe me, anyway." I laughed lightly.

He seemed to relax infinitesimally.

I delivered him a fresh Bushmills, and then set about wiping down the bar and closing out the computer, trying to look as relaxed as possible and not trip over my own feet.

Finally shutting the computer off, I calmly took a tray of plates through the swing door into the kitchen. As soon as it shut behind me, I put the tray down and sank against the refrigeration room door.

A flood of pent-up reactions ballooned inside me. *Holy shit!* Jack Eversea was on the other side of that door. *The*

Jack Eversea. Oh my God, Jazz was gonna tilt. Except, I couldn't tell Jazz. How was I supposed to keep something like this bottled up? *Okay, okay, breathe.* I was just a little star-struck, I would be fine in a minute. I mean, he was beautiful and everything, but he was also just a tad full of himself, and—I reminded myself—he was rude earlier. A spoiled celebrity. Not crushing material, at all. Well, maybe just a tiny crush. But only because I had seen him play Max from my favorite *Warriors of Erath* book series that made it onto the big screen.

I thought back to the movie and his bare, muscled torso with the medallion tattoo on his bicep. That was *his* body.

Jazz, literally his biggest fan, had watched every movie he had been in since she was fifteen, and had proudly declared he performed every one of his scenes with no stunt man or body double. It was natural a bit of her enthusiasm would rub off on me, right?

My face flamed as I remembered I'd just lectured Jack Eversea on his manners. Nice. He must think me a complete pain in the ass.

Hector was still there loading the last dishes. He turned and came for my tray, stopping as he saw me heaving for breath and clutching my middle.

"What's the matter, *Chiquita*?" he asked urgently.

I shook my head roughly and brought a finger to my lips. Oh man, I hoped Jack Eversea hadn't heard that. My eyes flicked to the pass-through and Hector did a quick head duck to look through before I could stop him.

He turned back to me, eyes wide. "Is that . . .?"

Shit. I couldn't keep a secret for ten minutes.

I nodded.

"*Dios mio!*" Hector whispered, crossing himself.

"Hector!" I hissed. "You can't say a word, okay? Not. One. Word." I bored my eyes into his crinkled gaze, willing him to get how serious I was.

"Okay, okay." Hector put his hands up in surrender.

"Seriously, Hector." I softened my whisper. "He's going through a bad break-up, I get the sense he's here to get away. Let's not invade his privacy?"

He nodded sagely.

I thanked my lucky stars Jazz had been in earlier, or I might never have known about his personal issues. I could tell Hector thought this a good enough reason not to tell his granddaughter about who he met at work tonight. He looked disappointed, though.

"Sorry, Hector. Maybe you can tell Maria in a few months? I don't know how long he's staying in town, or even *if* he is," I whispered.

"Can I ask him for an autograph, as proof, you know?" Hector looked so hopeful.

I sighed. "I guess we can ask him and tell him we promise to keep his secret until after he leaves."

I took a deep breath and went through the door followed by Hector.

"I can't give you your change, I gave it to Hector as a tip. I thought you weren't coming back." I shifted nervously as I delivered the news a few minutes after Hector left out of the kitchen door, happily clutching the autograph he'd promised not to show for at least three weeks.

Jack watched me through hooded eyes as he ate the last few French fries on his plate. He hadn't said anything yet about the fact I was a lousy secret keeper.

I tried to put a positive spin on it. "Thank you for doing that for Hector. His granddaughter, Maria, is a fan of yours. But you can trust him."

"He had a good night, huh? A hefty tip *and* an autograph." Jack's tone was teasing. Thank God. "What about you?" His eyes searched mine.

"What about me? Why didn't I take the tip?"

"No, not that. But why didn't you?"

"We both do the work around here."

Jack nodded, tapping his fingers thoughtfully on the side of his plate. "So, do *you* need an autograph?"

"No!" I blurted, my face flushing warm. "I mean, no, that's okay. But thank you for asking." I swallowed. Could I sound any more petulant?

Jack laughed.

It was a mesmerizing sound. Coupled with the way his gray-green eyes twinkled when he did so, and the dimple in his left cheek . . . it was no surprise half the world was in love with him. This was bad. I did *not* want to be a Jack Eversea groupie. But I was beginning to realize what charisma really meant. He certainly knew how to use it.

"Why?" he asked.

"*Why?* I don't know why! Maybe because you sound full of yourself for just asking." I huffed at him. "God, I'm sorry, I act bitchy when I'm nervous."

He pursed his lips and nodded sagely. "I wouldn't call it bitchy. God knows, I'd know the difference." He thought for a moment. "Let's call it . . . well, bitchy works."

"Hey!" *Great*.

"Yeah, bitchy . . . and disapproving . . . like unimpressed."

"I am unimpressed," I snapped.

"I can tell."

My face flamed again. "Sorry. I mean . . . obviously, I'm impressed."

That sounded wrong. Groupie-ish, not bitchy. Oh man, which was better? "With your work, I mean." I went on awkwardly, "You are very . . . talented."

He rolled his eyes. "Stop. Stop. Kill me now." He held his hand dramatically to his heart.

I stared at him.

"I'm teasing you, Keri Ann."

"Oh." I took a deep breath.

He looked at me, unblinking for a few moments.

"What?"

"What do you drive?"

"A red truck, why?"

"Figures." He smirked, but didn't elaborate. "And given your . . . bitchiness, I'm obviously making you nervous, so it's my fault I guess. I'm sorry."

Jack laughed again, a slow, easy sound that ran over my skin like too many soft caresses. It must be the humidity. That, or I had managed to avoid having an unrealistic crush on this heart-throb through all of his many movies designed to make girls swoon, including playing my favorite fictional hero, only to have him walk into my place of employment, in the flesh, and deploy the swoon-bomb that was rapidly detonating over all my good senses. Had I been singled out? Did the devil look up and see one sensible girl left and decide on tactical warfare to bring me into line?

Jack was asking me a question.

"What? Sorry."

"I said, can I stay a bit longer? I'm still on California time, and well . . . as you heard," he winced, "I have a lot going on in my personal life right now, and I don't want to think about it tonight."

No, no, no. This was a bad idea. I found myself shaking my head. I needed this bizarre incident to be over. On the other hand, I was developing a crush on someone I didn't know, not really. All I needed was some more time in his self-absorbed sphere to come to my senses. If he really *was* self-absorbed. Maybe he was just used to getting his own way. Why was I making excuses for him? I mentally kicked myself.

"I'll just stay 'til you finish up and walk you to your truck or whatever. It's late . . . and dark."

He noticed my almost imperceptible negative head shake. "Please?"

Damn. The same 'please' that had gotten to me earlier. The one asking for me to keep his secret.

I sighed and nodded. "Okay."

He looked relieved. "Oh and also, may I have another drink?"

"Bar's closed," I tried, predicting his cheeky smirk.

"I know."

I rolled my eyes, and smiling, grabbed his glass to fill with ice. This was going to be the longest closedown ever.

CHAPTER THREE

"How old are you?" Jack was sweeping. *Sweeping!* Sometime during the last ten minutes of conversation while he asked me questions about Butler Cove, he must have started feeling guilty while I was sweeping around his feet. Tomorrow, I would wake up and this would all be a bizarre dream. I was sure he was thinking the same thing. Hoping more like.

"I'm turning twenty-two next month."

He looked up, surprised. "You seem older."

I narrowed my eyes at him. "Thanks? I think . . . Why?"

He shrugged. "You don't *look* old." He stopped and perused me from head to toe. He was taking in my brown hair, my black regulation t-shirt tucked into jean shorts and my bare legs, which were thankfully nice and tan, and my white Keds. Fashion parade I was not. Harried and tired waitress, yes.

My cheeks burned under his scrutiny. "Are you done?"

Jack cleared his throat, cutting his eyes away and resumed his sweeping. "You just act . . . I don't know, older than you are."

"How old are *you*?" I asked, deflecting back to him after the self-conscious moment he'd given me.

"Don't you know that already?"

I paused in the middle of lowering the blinds and crossed my arms at him. He really was annoyingly full of himself. "Contrary to what you may have seen earlier this evening with my friend Jazz and her tabloid magazine, I don't follow gossip all that much. I've got too much to do, and I prefer reading books to magazines. Not that I begrudge Jazz her favorite pastime."

Jack had the sense to look slightly conciliatory. "Sorry. I'm twenty-six."

"What? Are you kidding? You look . . . younger." I walked back over to the bar and grabbed the beer he'd persuaded me to have. I took a gulp. "And you act younger, too," I couldn't help adding.

I saw his grin as he bent down to finish up with the dustpan. God, that dimple was going to be the death of me.

"Touché."

Everything was done. The restaurant was as clean and put away as it could possibly get. I had zero excuses to continue hanging out with Jack Eversea. I had to head home. I also had to figure out how to stop referring to him by his full name in my head.

After putting away all the cleaning stuff, I grabbed my purse from behind the bar and the set of keys to lock up behind us. "You ready?"

"Yeah." He put his cap back on, curling his one hand around the peak and mashing the back of it up and down on his head a few times with his other the way guys do. I have never understood that—like it has to be just perfectly molded to their heads or something. Joey did exactly the same thing. Jack pushed his arms through his hoodie and popped the hood up over the cap.

"It's, like, eighty degrees still outside. I should have seen through your disguise sooner. You're going to have to think of a better way to blend in or you're gonna die from the heat." I shook my head, amused. Then a thought occurred to me.

"Are you staying here? I mean, in Butler Cove?" I was treating this encounter as a one-time deal. Which, of course, it was. Even if he was staying close by, there was no way I would be seeing him again. I'd been awkward enough already to last me a lifetime of horror and humiliation.

I locked up the restaurant behind us.

"Yeah, I'm borrowing a friend's beach house for a while," he responded. "How long depends on if I can stay here without being found out. You have no idea what the paparazzi are capable of. I didn't think a lot of stuff through before I got here, I just drove. I was pretty upset." He scowled off into the distance.

It was the second time he had made mention of his current issues. It must be weird to meet a person for the first time and have them know all this stuff about you already. I really wanted to ask him about it, but with my track record, I was as likely to make him feel worse. Anyway, what was there to say? He was broken hearted over his girlfriend cheating on him. He was hardly going to tell me, a complete stranger, the lurid details.

It was time for me to get out of here. I may have been getting over my initial star-struck moment, but he was still absolutely and sinfully gorgeous. Hanging out with him wasn't going to get me over that. And the last thing I needed was to get pie-eyed over him when he was going to vanish about as quickly as he'd arrived.

"Okay, well . . . thanks for helping me close up and . . . good luck."

"Wait. Keri Ann?" For a moment he looked unsure, with his hands deep in his pockets and his toe absently kicking a pebble. "I really hate to ask this. It's just I don't know anyone else here and I trust you. For whatever reason."

"Thanks," I said, surprised. "You should." Even though it was going to kill me not to tell Jazz about tonight. "Soooo, walk me to my door—it's only about a hundred yards—and you can ask me whatever you like." I couldn't believe the words coming out of my mouth. But regardless of this being my hometown and it not being a far walk—it was eleven thirty and dark as Hades, even with the moon. I turned toward home, not waiting for an answer. Immediately I regretted it, wondering what this hotshot Hollywood type would think about my run down, falling apart southern home. It was built of plaster and wood in the 1800s. In the hot and humid south. Need I say more?

Jack's tall frame fell in beside me. "Jeez, it gets dark here," he said, echoing my thoughts of a few moments ago.

"It's the sea turtles."

When I didn't elaborate, Jack scratched his head. "Sea turtles?"

"Hmm? Oh, they nest on the beaches and when the babies hatch they follow the moonlight to the water. Too many house and streetlights can confuse them, so we keep it pretty low key around here. Prepare to get lost a few times if you're driving at night."

"Huh. Who knew?"

"I'm pretty sure they have sea turtles on the west coast." I looked over at him.

He furrowed his brow. "Yeah, I guess I haven't paid attention. That must seem pretty dumb to you, huh?"

I shook my head as I directed us left to a narrow path.

Our feet crunched on crushed oyster shells as we made our way under a huge magnolia dripping with Spanish moss. "No. Sea turtles are important in a small town that's big on eco-tourism. You kind of pick it up by osmosis living here. You've had more going on with your life than I am sure I could possibly fathom, so it doesn't seem dumb."

"Just shallow. Right," he added, as if he was filling in a blank I'd not said.

"No! Not at all."

"It's fine, I'm not offended. I've been living a pretty shallow existence lately which isn't really . . ." He trailed off.

We had stopped at my back deck. He looked around and I tried to see the place through his eyes. Bringing him to the backyard wasn't the best idea. I quickly kept walking and he followed me around to the front. I jogged up the front stairs onto the porch and fished around in my purse for the key.

Jack sighed. "Shit. I dunno, I'm not in the best mood these days." Running a hand over his hooded head, a silver ring he wore on his middle finger glinted. He looked around. "Hey, this place is awesome." Reaching out, he ran his hand along the porch railing and stepped back to see the whole house.

"It's the Butler family home. It's been in our family for generations." I couldn't hide the touch of pride that came out in my tone. "It's seen better days." An understatement, but it was still beautiful. To me anyway, and any historical architecture buff. "There were some . . . mishaps . . . of the family money kind." If that's what you called them. "Anyway, Joey and I are trying to fix it up."

He cocked his head to the side. "Joey?"

"My brother. He's at med school right now . . . so I guess it's just me trying to fix it up at the moment." I realized I better head him off at the pass if I didn't want to get into my life story. It wasn't something you just blurted out to someone you'd never see again. "Thanks for walking me. What was the favor you wanted to ask? I'm not going to tell anyone, so you don't have to worry about that."

I finally found the key and stepped forward to press it into the lock while I waited. Wow, I was avoiding spending more time with Jack Eversea.

"I'm embarrassed to ask, but I'm starting to feel like I don't have a choice. If you can't . . . or won't, I totally understand." Oh God, did he want to come in? Was *that* what this was about? When he said he wanted to forget his troubles for a night, did he mean . . . with *me*?

What was even more disconcerting was my reaction to that thought literally caused my insides to flip over and strength to leach from my legs. I held onto the doorframe and was suddenly short of breath. This was . . . *not* a comfortable feeling. He seemed to be still deliberating. What? I wasn't hot enough? Too bitchy? Too plain Jane? Who was I kidding? My hair wasn't brown, it was . . . mousy. Even the highlights Jazz had persuaded me to put in were dull.

I gritted my teeth. Wait, I didn't want to do anything with him anyway. I had gone from semi-calm to nerves stretched taut over a razor's edge in the blink of an eye. Ugh. This was *exactly* why I didn't do this type of thing. Crushes, guys, whatever.

"Out with it," I finally said with exasperation.

He grinned at my tone, seemingly oblivious to the internal meltdown I'd just had. "You are so . . ." He shook his head and closed his eyes. "Never mind. Okay, look. Here's the thing. I'm scared someone's going to recognize me. I have no food in the house, that's why I came out for a burger tonight.

But I don't think I should go to the grocery store. So . . . I was wondering . . . hoping . . . I could pay you to do that for me?"

I couldn't work out if that was actual buzzing in my ears or if it was so damned quiet it was deafening. He didn't want to come in, he wanted to pay me to shop for him?

He waited patiently, a hopeful, if slightly worried expression on his gorgeous face. Thank God I'd always been a good poker player. Of course he didn't want to come in. What on God's green earth had even given me that idea? He had been nothing more than friendly since I'd first allowed him back in to eat his dinner.

I looked around at the worn house I was struggling to fix up. I should say yes, but in reality there was no way I was taking money from him for going to the grocery store where I went anyway.

I shook my head. "You don't have to pay me. I go anyway, I don't mind getting a few things for you."

"Thank you for agreeing," he said, letting out a long breath. "I will pay you though, the same that I pay my assistant in Cali." He looked at me carefully, "Just so there's no . . . confusion."

"Confusion? Oh!" Mortification found me again for the umpteenth time that night. This time with an ounce of extra humiliation just for kicks. Aaargh! I hated this guy! What did Jazz see in him anyway? I drew myself up to my full five-foot-six frame and squinted at him. "Let me reiterate what I said earlier tonight." I wasn't sure, but I might have stomped my foot. Sometimes I couldn't control it. "I think fame may have gone *a little bit* to your head."

He shrugged and pursed his lips. "Well, in the same sentence you also said I looked like God's gift to humanity."

"Aargh, that doesn't mean I lust after you." My cheeks throbbed with heat.

"Yes, you have made that patently clear," Jack argued back, his voice rising and his body leaning dangerously close to mine as he suddenly seemed to tower over me. His green eyes were even more mesmerizing up close.

"Keep your voice down," I hissed at him, furtively glancing over to Mrs. Weaton's house. She rented the small cottage in front that was part of the Butler estate. Another one who had too much to say about my business, although I loved her dearly. Jack rocked back on his heels, his hands still in his pockets, and took a deep breath.

"I guess I'm just making sure by asking you to help me, I'm not taking advantage of you. I've been burned, okay? Try not to take it as an insult, but as more of a show of respect for you and your time." He pursed his lips, and then let out a puff of air, like he was about to say more. "Look, forget it. Forget I asked." He turned to go.

I leaped forward and grabbed his arm, turning him back to face me. "Okay. I'll do it."

"Don't worry about it." I couldn't tell whether he looked disappointed or regretted asking me in the first place.

"No, seriously, I'll do it. I want to do it. I think you're entitled to some time away like a normal person to figure your . . . stuff out." Or whatever it was he needed to do.

He looked away at that.

"I know what it's like to need that time," I went on. "You can pay me if it makes you feel better." I let go where I'd been clutching his strong arm so hard I had to flex my fingers. "Sorry."

"Shit, you're strong. I may bruise tomorrow." He rubbed his arm in a mock show of discomfort, then added more seriously, "I actually think I might. Bruise, I mean."

I rolled my eyes. "No you won't. I guess I got strong hands from fixing up the house. It takes some muscle to wield those power tools, you know." And his arm had felt pretty muscly to me. That thought made me swallow hard. What the hell was I doing?

Jack arched an eyebrow. "You and power tools? That I have to see." Then he stepped back and appraised the house once more. Taking in the white expanse of the front and the large Lowcountry-style rocking chair front porch, I knew he could see past the peeling paint and broken shutters. His gaze took in the careful way I had planted pots on either side of the door and how clean and swept I kept the place. This house had pride.

"Do you happen to know what I did before I got famous?" he asked.

I shook my head. "I told you. I'm not your groupie."

He pursed his lips. "I know, I know. Sorry. Well, let's just say I have an idea."

CHAPTER FOUR

"I'm coming. Ouch!" I yelped as I stubbed my pinky toe on the hall table on my way to the front door. Grabbing my foot, I hopped the last few steps.

For obvious reasons, I'd lain awake for several hours the night before reliving every single nuance of my bizarre encounter with Jack Eversea. My dreams, when sleep blessedly arrived, hadn't given me much reprieve. So the pounding on the door at nine in the morning had caught me in a full-on coma.

Opening the door, I squinted into the bright day just in time to see a tall, bare-chested mess of sweat and exertion in dark glasses pushing past me into my house. *What the—?*

Jack.

I lost my balance and went flying backwards. The next few seconds were a ridiculous cacophony of squeals, grunts, and flailing limbs as Jack tried to reach for me and kick the door closed behind him at the same time.

"What the hell?" my winded voice finally managed just as we hit the floor, Jack sprawled completely on top of me. He scrambled up quickly like he'd been stung.

"Shit. Sorry. I just . . . people were walking past and they were looking at me. I panicked." He glanced back at the door to make sure it was closed and took his sunglasses off.

I still lay sprawled like a starfish on my hall floor, dressed in the small Hello Kitty sleep shorts and spaghetti strap tank I'd slept in. Not enough clothes to be meeting male visitors. Certainly not how I envisioned seeing Jack Eversea this morning. I could almost hear Nana sniff disapprovingly from wherever she was haunting the house at this precise moment. Thank God I hadn't removed the old floral carpet yet or I'd have a butt full of splinters to round out the moment.

"So you thought accosting me half-naked as I opened the door would arouse less suspicion?" I narrowed my eyes, making a colossal effort to keep them on his face and not stray down his glistening . . . I slipped just once . . . yes, glistening chest. *Seriously?* I groaned and closed my eyes, letting my head fall back hard on the floor, ignoring his outstretched hand. Maybe I could knock myself out and I wouldn't remember this. And my God, up close, he smelled like sand and sea and the ocean breeze . . . and . . . like . . . man. I'd always thought my avoidance of all things male would keep me out of trouble long enough to see my dreams of leaving town through, but I was beginning to sense my mistake. A little prior romantic experience with men would have really helped about now.

"Sorry. I ran straight here from my jog. Are you hurt? Let me help you up." Jack's worried tone made me pull myself together.

I grabbed his hand and got to my feet. My tank was damp from his sweat. I wanted to be disgusted, I really did. I thought back to my brother Joey and the way he'd be all like "let me give you a hug, sis" right after coming back from working out. "Gross!" I'd yell. But, now? Now, I wanted to lick the sweat off this guy's six-pack. And that tattoo on his shoulder . . . surprisingly, it was real, not painted on for a movie. I sighed. This was so not good. There was only one way this was going to end. Me: ruined for all men, sitting on my own, or maybe with Jazz, in the back of dark theatres shoveling popcorn into my mouth for the rest of my life. Watching him on celluloid.

"So . . . what's the deal here, you said you and your brother were fixing the house up, where are your parents?" Jack was standing, still shirtless with just a pair of longish black gym shorts on, in my kitchen finishing up the coffee I had made us. "Sorry. I'm not prying, just curious."

"It's okay. Sorry if I seem tense, it's not you. Some people in this town are always breathing down our necks because this is the Butler House. My brother and I inherited it. It was my grandmother's and should have gone to my parents, but they died about six years ago in a car wreck driving back from Savannah."

I was proud of my ability to rattle off these facts with zero emotion. "My grandmother passed a few years later of heart failure, so it falls to us. It's an historic monument of sorts, being that we are the Butlers of Butler Cove, so everyone in town is always complaining that it needs to be fixed up, but they won't allocate funds to help unless we sell it to the town. Or at least agree to set it up as a museum or something that will help tourism. They know our parents had life insurance money, so they think we should have used that. Except, we needed it for Joey's college. We still work on the house when we can. Or I do. As I said before, Joey's at med school."

"That's tough." Jack looked like he wanted to say something more. "I'm sorry about your parents."

"Yeah, well. It's life, huh?" I smiled to show I wasn't expecting pity. "So this deal of yours may work for me after all. It will be good to make some headway on the interior stuff. I keep focusing on the outside because that's what everyone sees. Are you sure it's still okay?"

"It's fine. Sorry I can't help with the outside, I'd be too conspicuous. I told you I miss the days when I worked construction while juggling auditions. It was good, busy, creative work. A different sense of accomplishment. It's good exercise, too." He flexed his biceps jokingly, all his upper body muscles tensing. I found myself scowling at him.

"Well, I seem to be getting the better end of the deal," I managed. "Or maybe I'm not, I haven't seen your work yet."

He laughed and ran his fingers through his unruly dark hair. "Let's just say, I had a 'day job' to go back to, if the acting thing didn't work out."

"Okay, well, I'll quickly go and change and get to the store." I headed for the kitchen doorway. "There's a toolbox in the attic. Text me if you think I need to pick up anything for the house. Help yourself to cereal or whatever. Oh, and . . . borrow a t-shirt from Joey. Please. Second door on the left upstairs." And on that note, I bolted up the stairs before I said anything else.

I locked myself in the bathroom and climbed into a cold shower. Maybe I could shock some sense into my system. Pointing out his shirtless state bothered me was not a smart move, but there was no way I could go another second with him parading around in front of me like that and pretend not to ogle him. He really was just the most arresting specimen of man I had ever seen. Ugh, I was so shallow. I should just tell him right away I didn't want the help. But it was too . . . tempting.

I had wanted to pull the carpet and re-finish the floors forever. And he could build bookshelves, he said. I was dying to make that parlor into a gorgeous library: a place to curl up and lose myself for a while. Getting a head start on the interior stuff, and free labor to boot, was too much to resist.

I climbed out of the shower, having scrubbed and washed every inch of myself repeatedly and absently, because apparently my mind was nowhere to be found. I wrapped my wet hair up, pulled my robe on, and scrambled, lest I bump into Jack again, back to my room to get dressed.

I looked around at the sage green walls and white linen bedclothes. They were supposed to be soothing colors, even though I could barely take it in with my books piled over every available surface.

I was anything but soothed. I was extremely uncomfortable, both with my shallow, lustful reaction to Jack, and the fact that Jack, a relative stranger, was in my house at all, especially while I had been in the shower naked. I knew I had been raised better than this, I just couldn't for the life of me figure out how I was supposed to deal with this situation.

I pulled on jean shorts and a t-shirt, my staple wardrobe. I combed and pulled my wet hair up in a bun, shoved my feet back into my Keds, and headed back down toward my new bizarre reality.

The Piggly Wiggly grocery store was blessedly quiet. Schools had started back up and the summer crowds had gone home. Most back to Ohio. For some reason people from Ohio loved this part of the country. One would think the drive would be a little much, but apparently someone from Ohio must have had an amazing vacation down here once many years ago and bought some billboards or something when he got home.

I consulted the list Jack had scrawled out for me. His handwriting was atrocious.

Milk
Capn Crunch
Bananas
Cheese sticks
Sandwich bread
Peanut butter
Jelly
O.J.
Pasta
Pasta sauce
Eggs
Bottled water

I couldn't help rolling my eyes. It was like shopping for a toddler. Without thinking, I fished out my phone and pulled up where he had saved his number under the name of *Late Night Visitor. That* wouldn't arouse curiosity if Jazz ever saw my phone. I made a quick mental note to change it, and then tapped out a text.

Me: Cheese sticks? What r u? Like 5?

I moved on down the aisles collecting his and my purchases. A few minutes later my phone chirped back.

Late Night Visitor: You were rushing me, I couldn't think. You don't like cheese sticks?

Me: I love cheese sticks. In my lunch box. You eat any vegetables?

Late Night Visitor: I'll have you know my body is my temple ;-) I'm on vacation from California crunchy. Yes, I eat vegetables. Grab some carrots, too.

I huffed just as my phone chirped again.

Late Night Visitor: Please.

I grinned and ignored the slow fizz in my belly that jumped every time my phone dinged with his response.

Me: Baby carrots and ranch dippies. Got it.

He just begged to be given a hard time.

Suddenly, my heart started going a mile a minute and I was breathing hard. *Jack Eversea was in my house!* I willed myself to calm down and catch my breath. He was just a person. A human being. Right? I bent down for a moment and stuck my head between my knees, hoping my blood would circulate normally again. Standing up a few moments later, I pulled myself together, looked around, and straightened my shirt.

I got what Jack needed, then added organic salad leaves, balsamic dressing, fresh salmon, wine, granola, yoghurt, and artisan bread to his pile in my cart. He'd given me enough money after all. At least he could eat a little better.

"Hey, Keri Ann!" I looked up to see my friend Liz from high school waving to me from the checkout as I approached. That was the thing about a small town, you pretty much knew someone everywhere you went. No wonder Jack Eversea was nervous about going out. I sincerely hoped my idiotic little display over in produce hadn't been witnessed.

"Hey, Lizzie, how are you?"

"I'm good, glad the rush is over. How've you been and how's Joey?"

My brother had been most girls' crush at some point, I was sure. After our parents died, he added tortured soul to his list of assets.

"Good. He's good. Just a year more before he starts his residency, so he's pretty busy."

Liz nodded. "Good, well he was always so smart. Destined to do great things," she added with a smile.

She was a kind-hearted girl. Unfortunately, her kind heart and trusting nature had gotten her into early single parenthood and a job at the grocery store rather than the career she had planned on. She never spoke about who the father was, although the town had been rife with gossip touching on most of the senior class that year. Liz had stayed tight-lipped, even when urged to confess for the sake of child support from the father. As she scanned my items, we chatted about some online college classes in education Liz was taking, and how her son Brady was doing. I was glad she was getting her life back on track.

Out of the corner of my eye, I saw Jack's face peering at me from the checkout tabloids. One had the headline, "Hit the road, Jack!" Another read, "Where in the World is Jack?" I had to physically restrain myself from reaching for them.

Chances were if anyone had seen an unknown male on my doorstep this morning, Liz would have asked about it.

Knowing Liz and I were friends meant that the curtain twitchers of Butler Cove were bound to dig for clues at The Pig while they shopped. The town's obsession with Joey and me and what we were doing was extremely tiring. If I didn't feel obligated to the Butler home, I would've been gone ages ago.

Not for the first time, I longingly thought of Joey and his Butler Cove-free life at college. Living here gave me a small idea of what it must be like to be Jack Eversea living his life in a Hollywood fishbowl. But seeing his face all over these magazines reminded me he had it far worse than I could imagine.

"Planning a nice dinner with someone?"

"What?" I looked down to the salmon steaks and wine that Liz was indicating and felt myself flush red again.

"Um, no. I mean yes, it's just for . . . I'm trying to eat more healthy." I swallowed. Well, *that* wasn't awkward.

Liz looked at me with a funny expression and then shrugged. "With wine . . . okay. I heard Jasper is in town again before he heads up to Charleston for school, you seen much of him?"

I had never noticed before, but suddenly it seemed very obvious from the slightly wistful expression on Liz's face that Jasper McDaniel featured in some of her daydreams. It was no secret he had asked me out way back when. Not that I'd accepted, of course, not on a date anyway. But we were friends, we all were. Maybe Liz thought the dinner was for him. Not ideal, but better than suspecting anyone else. Luckily, she didn't ask more questions. I quickly paid in cash, noticing belatedly I hadn't separated out Jack's and my purchases, then realizing that would have been more obvious anyway. God, I really wasn't good at this cloak and dagger stuff.

"Bye, Liz!" I tinkled breezily, hightailing it out of The Pig.

"Bye, Keri Ann."

I could feel Liz watching me curiously as I left the store and put the groceries carefully in the back of my truck. I climbed in and just sat for a few minutes in the baking cab, my forehead resting on the hot steering wheel. Then, taking a deep breath, I gunned the engine and headed home. Home to a girl's most secret fantasy. I just hoped said fantasy had managed to find a t-shirt.

CHAPTER FIVE

"Andy. Jack. What's up?" Jack was on the phone as I came in through the back door, into the blessed air conditioning. I guessed he was talking to the agent he had told me about earlier.

He'd found a plain black t-shirt in Joey's room. It molded to his muscled frame a little snugger than when on my brother. It was devastating.

I sighed.

"What's up?" Jack's agent howled through the phone, causing Jack to pull it away from his head. He caught my eyes and mouthed "*sorry*".

I busied myself unpacking the groceries and separating out his money.

"What's *up*?" Andy yelled again; clearly there was no need for speakerphone with this dude. "I'll tell you what's up. This is the most viral news story since Britney shaved her head, and you are nowhere. To. Be. Found."

"Yeah, look, sorry about that, it's just—"

"Sorry! Sorry?" Andy cut right over Jack's words. "Don't be sorry, Ace. It's fucking fantastic. Are you kidding me? My

God, you should see it here, it's like the fucking eight days of Hanukkah and Christmas all rolled into one. The phone hasn't stopped. You are the number one search term on Google. *Number One!*"

I winced at his volume even from where I stood.

It seemed like Jack knew from prior experience not to interrupt Andy when he was on a roll.

Jack looked at me apologetically again.

I shrugged and went into the hall to see about eavesdropping out of sight. Andy's caustic personality continued to emanate from my kitchen. "It's fucking genius. Everyone's all like, where in the world is Jack Eversea? There's a bounty on your head, my man! It's like the celebrity version of *Where's Waldo*. We couldn't have planned this better, I'm telling you. So, where the fuck are you? Wait, I'm gonna drop pin you."

I heard a muffled "Oh shit" from Jack and peeked around the corner to see him fumbling hastily with his phone. Presumably, to disable the locator app Andy was referring to. Milliseconds later, his shoulders sagged in relief.

Andy grunted as Jack brought the phone back to his ear. "Shit, I don't see you on my map. Okay, where are you?"

"Andy, don't freak out, okay? I'm not telling you or anyone where I am right now." Jack held his breath.

"Oh, don't tell me, you're with a chick. You sly fox." Andy's lascivious chuckle made my hair stand on end and I ducked back as Jack glanced over in my direction. "I hope she's trustworthy 'cos right now the whole world is on your side. The poor, betrayed hero. Don't fuck that up for me, okay?

"Okay?" he yelled again when Jack didn't answer. "And you have until next Friday, then I want you in my office so we can go over your statement and calm the boys from Peak

Entertainment the fuck down. You have a publicity contract to fulfill for them. With Audrey."

Jack took a deep breath, and I imagined him wincing as he delivered his next words. "Actually, Andy, I'll be gone for three weeks. I'll see you in time for the first event in that contract. Bye." He hung up on what sounded like Andy having a stroke, then clenched his fist hard and pounded on the kitchen counter.

I jumped.

He caught the movement and turned my way.

"Sorry. I'm so fucking—" he cleared his throat, "freaking frustrated. Since when did my life get so freaking out of control? It seems I have other people running every single aspect of it. Andy, Sheila; my publicist, the entertainment company that pretty much owns my soul right now with the third movie coming out, and Audrey, my *supposed* girlfriend, who even now is probably bribing my assistant Katie for my whereabouts. I didn't even tell Katie where I was going, and I probably trust her more than my own mother."

He ran both hands through his hair. He seemed unaware he was sharing all this stuff with me. "Katie has my credit card log in, I just pray she won't share it with Auds to figure out where I am." He quickly pounded out a text on his phone, speaking the words aloud as he typed:

"Do, not, try, and, find, out, or, tell, anyone, where, I, am, under, pain, of, being, fired, dash, will, be, back, in, three, weeks. There." Presumably that text was to Katie.

He looked like he wanted to throw the phone across the room.

I stood uncertainly, not really sure what to say. I noticed he had found some tools upstairs; there was a pry bar, a hammer, some gloves and a box cutter sitting on the counter. He saw where I was looking.

"Yeah, thought I'd start on the carpet," he said, his shoulders slumping a bit as he calmed down.

"Okay," I squeaked. "I'm painting the porch, see you in a bit."

If Jack was surprised at my sudden departure, I didn't see it, because I hightailed it out the front. The door banged shut behind me. If I were a different girl, I would have hung out and been a shoulder to cry on; teased out his problems, taken advantage of the situation to help him over his broken heart. No strings attached, of course.

Jazz's favorite advice for getting over someone was to get under someone else as soon as possible. Obviously, she wasn't doling out that advice to me, and hardly used it herself, but it sounded fun. And it may work for Jack. But I wasn't a different girl. I was Keri Ann Butler and I was only passably pretty. While I was hardly insecure, I also knew that even if Jack Eversea was single and not a mega star, he was *way* out of my league. Then again, if he wasn't having relationship issues, he wouldn't have had to borrow a friend's beach house on the other side of the country to get away, and I would have never met him.

And who was I to pass judgment on Audrey Lane? It hadn't escaped my attention he had referred to her as his 'supposed girlfriend' earlier, but that sounded like they were more on a break than broken up. For all I knew, he was a ghastly boyfriend, and she had gone running and screaming into another man's arms. I shook my head and got to work on the porch.

Jack worked for hours.

I peeked in on him every now and again through the windows and he caught me spying twice. But much to my gratification, I did look up one time to catch him looking at me. Okay, maybe he was just looking out the window, I couldn't really tell.

He did the hall and the parlor, cutting the carpet into strips. He hauled and rolled each strip as he went, coming back for the underlay. There was dust everywhere. Years of it. Then he moved into the living room. At some point after he had most of the furniture in the living room moved into the parlor and the carpet had almost fully been removed, I came in and handed him a plate. PB&J with the crusts cut off, baby carrots and a bottle of water.

He stood up and smiled. I was sure I'd been about to say something but couldn't for the life of me remember what it was. He was sweating again so he rubbed his hands down his t-shirt, and then lifted it from his abdomen to use on his face.

I closed my eyes tight against the view and counted to three before I opened them.

He let the shirt fall back and gave me a funny look. He clearly knew I thought he was attractive and was obviously used to it, although I'd bet few tried to ignore it as much as I did.

My cheeks were hot again. Great.

"Thanks," he said, taking my offering.

"No problem." I backed toward the door, tripping on a tack strip still left behind on the floor. Klutz did not begin to describe me right now.

I cleared my throat, trying for nonchalance. "It's pretty dusty. I am eating on the porch." I nodded toward the window behind him that looked out the front of the house.

"I'll stay in, thanks."

He looked down at the plate, finally noticing my attempt at treating him like a toddler and burst out laughing.

CHAPTER SIX

The floors in my house looked amazing. It was old pine that was soft and showed its age and character. They would have to be re-sanded and refinished, of course, and looked like they needed to be replaced in a few parts but Jack had been around every edge pulling or hammering down every single nail. I all but moaned in happiness imagining them with a gorgeous walnut stain.

I had agreed to give Jack a ride home and before we left I ducked into the hall bathroom. It would have been nice to say I was glowing, but anyone could see that was a crock. I smelled of mosquito-repellent, my face was bright red and shiny, and there were humid frizzies sticking up all over my head. That's what I got for avoiding Jack by staying outside all day. There was not a whole lot to be done. Running upstairs to shower would take too long and felt too vain. I was just going to pretend he was like Jazz or Jasper or Liz or any other of my other friends. I wouldn't make a special case for them, and Jack was just a friend. A friend who was rich, famous and so attractive he was actually hard to look at, but a friend nonetheless. I splashed cold water on my face and ran my fingers through my unruly hair, scraping it back and off my neck into a knot on my head.

"Thank you so much for the floors. They look amazing," I told Jack as we grabbed his groceries out of the fridge. He stopped and looked at me a moment, and taking in my frazzled appearance, grinned.

"What?" I asked, defensively.

He shook his head. "No problem. They're in great shape, just a few places to replace, but they look good." He mashed his cap on his head again and picked up the bags. "Tomorrow, I'll tackle wallpaper. I'll go put these in the truck, see you out there."

I grabbed my keys and purse and followed him out while he apologized for "smelling rank." I kept my reaction to myself.

He glanced furtively around in his cap and dark glasses before sliding into the front seat and hunching down. I rolled my eyes.

I was hyper aware of him sitting next to me inside the cab as we drove, and pointedly stared ahead not wanting to catch his eye. I could have sworn he was looking at me, but I'd die before looking over. It was almost like any eye contact right now would suddenly make the moment way too intimate. There was just this current and energy around him all the time. It was like swimming endlessly, trying to keep my head above water.

I saw him swing his face forward again out of the corner of my eye, and he directed me down toward the beach plaza, and then down Magnolia Road.

I nonchalantly followed directions down the millionaires' row like I did it every day in my old jalopy. The good thing about being down here was that most of the houses sat empty except for the weekly renters at high season, so there was less chance of being noticed by nosey neighbors.

There were some stunning homes, all first row ocean. Some had seen better days, the land being worth more than anything that had been built prior to the real estate boom, and some were big, brassy monstrosities. But there were also a few low-key and truly elegant homes that had tried, with some success, to emulate the southern style. We passed a tall hedge and turned into a small driveway that led to a house mostly hidden from the road. It was gorgeous; a simple but contemporary beach cottage raised off the ground, as most were, for flood codes, painted white with periwinkle blue shutters and huge baskets of pink hibiscus under each window. It was a slice of California right here in the Lowcountry.

"Wow, it's gorgeous," I said, hopping out. "So this friend of yours who owns the house is also an actor?"

I went around to open the tailgate for him and spotted a motorcycle, the same motorcycle with California plates from the day before, parked under a palmetto tree to the side of the house. Great, so I had also almost killed him. I paused a moment and looked up into the bright blue sky. If it wasn't so at odds with the reality of my everyday life, I'd say fate was literally throwing us together. Though I preferred the outcome of me being his grocery shopper to me side swiping him off his motorcycle. Either way, there were definitely some celestial hijinks being played.

"Yeah. Wait 'til you see the inside. Completely different." I followed him up the stairs and waited while he unlocked the door.

He stood aside to let me into the cool interior, a relief from the hot day.

"Wow!" It was like walking into a photographer's lightbox

with a postcard of the ocean at one end. Squinting against the glare, my eyes were immediately drawn to the view outside the glass windows and doors that perfectly framed the bright blue sea beyond. Inside was an exercise in Zen minimalism gone awry. It was all bright white, sparse and modern with light from outside bouncing off every available surface. Although not my style, it was arresting and beautiful in its own way. I liked things more comfy and distressed so I could imagine a whole history by just looking at them.

"You can see why I woke up at the crack of dawn, despite being on Pacific Time, right?"

I nodded. The sun rose on this side of the island. It must have been bright.

"I hope you have some blinds in your room."

"I do, but I stupidly didn't close them last night. You get sunsets, not sunrises in L.A.—it didn't occur to me. But it was pretty awesome to wake up to the sunrise and the beach and go running."

"It's low tide in the mornings this week so you must have had some good hard packed sand to run on. Awesome." I made a mental note to pick him up a tide chart next time I was out.

"You run?"

"A couple of times a week. I do some kayaking and paddle-boarding in the marshes too, that's pretty big down here."

"Never tried it." Jack made his way over to the sleek modern kitchen with its stainless steel and miles of white marble surfaces.

"You should. When in Rome." I turned back to the living area and took in the white tiled floor and low-slung couches.

"You come running with me one morning, and I'll go

kayaking with you. You can give me an eco-tourism lesson on sea turtles."

His suggestion surprised me. I didn't imagine him choosing to spend more time with me than was necessary. I turned to look at him as he unpacked the grocery bags. There was nothing behind the tone of that suggestion at all. It was so bland and innocuous, like just one of those things people say. Maybe it was his version of the Hollywood classic "let's do lunch."

"Sure." What else did one say? Ask me again when you're serious?

"So you're working tonight again?" he asked, unpacking the groceries. He held up the salmon. "I think I accidentally got some of your stuff."

"No, that's for you. It's easy, just salt and pepper and bake at three-fifty for seventeen minutes. Simple, but delicious. And yeah, I start at five, so I need to get home and get showered."

I was starting to get uncomfortable again. Being in Jack's space just did weird things to me.

"Easy for you to say. You lost me at salt." He smiled at my raised eyebrows. "I'm kidding." He paused a moment looking at me. "You want a quick tour before you go?"

"Uh. Sure."

He came around the counter, and I followed as he pointed out the various rooms and headed for the staircase.

"You know Devon Brown and Monica Black?" he asked. *Did I know them?* They were only a Hollywood power couple who'd been together since I was a kid. I nodded. I'd heard a rumor they were buying a place here, but thought nothing ever came of it.

"This is theirs. Their production company owns a piece of

the *Erath* franchise, so I got to know them pretty well. Devon's a good guy and a good friend, he called me up after the Audrey stuff broke and offered me a place to get away. Thank God."

I nodded again, like we were just talking about regular people and he was a regular guy.

It was like walking around in a magazine spread, nothing out of place and not a knick-knack or personal picture to be found. But it was beautifully built, I could see that.

"Why didn't you go home? Like to wherever your family is?" As I asked, I realized I knew absolutely nothing about where Jack was from. I wished I had Jazz's fan-based insight, so I wouldn't put my foot in my mouth or ask the wrong thing.

"Well, I don't have family here really. It was just my mother and me, anyway. I grew up in the UK until I was nine. Then moved to New York until I was done with school and moved out to L.A. to try my hand at movies. My mother moved back to England. She would kill me if I brought a trail of paparazzi to her door."

"You don't have an accent." I decided to avoid asking about his mom.

"Not any more, but I can do one if I need to."

We got to the bedroom where Jack was clearly staying. There were huge French doors onto a Juliet balcony over-looking the view. I walked over to them, studiously avoiding the unmade king-sized bed with its white covers still pulled back and tried very hard not to think of him lying there sleeping. I wasn't very successful and felt my cheeks flush with warmth. It was becoming a hazard. The room smelled of him already. Something indefinably male and all Jack.

I pulled my attention back outside and looked down to

see the sparkling blue of a lap pool set into a stone patio below us. It wouldn't be visible from the beach as the dunes would shield it from prying eyes. In fact, with the foliage on either side of the property lines, it was extremely private. Perfect for famous occupants. It was funny how you could live in a town like Butler Cove for years and never see these places. I heard Jack clearing his throat behind me.

"Check out this bathroom, it's incredible." He made for the doorway in the side wall.

"It's the size of the bedroom!" There was a huge picture window capturing the same view and the white tub was in the middle of the room set in a sea of tumbled travertine. I looked up and saw that water fell from a faucet in the ceiling. *Wow!*

Suddenly, an unexpected image of Jack and I in the tub with water cascading over us flashed in my head. A bolt of pure heat lanced through me, robbing me of breath. *Where had that come from?* My cheeks were still burning with my reaction to his bedroom, and now this. This was way beyond feeling like a giddy groupie, and I was totally out of my depth. I had to pull myself together. I clamped my lips together and screwed my eyes closed for a moment.

"Are you okay?" I opened them at Jack's voice and saw in the mirror he was watching my reflection with what looked like a smug grin on his face. God, he must be so over this stupid reaction from hormone-fueled teenage fans. I turned away from him without comment and didn't realize how close he was. My arms had swung out a little away from my body and . . . *oh the shame!* I brushed against his groin. We both started.

"Shit, sorry," I mumbled, my face puce in the reflection of the mirror. Gah.

Jack laughed. "Hey, no big deal. Although, I'm used to people buying me dinner before they cop a feel."

"Well, technically, I did," I shot back with a haughty tone that made Jack's smirk break free into a bellow of laughter that had me grinning like an idiot. It was a moment of complete abandon and watching him in it was breathtaking.

His eyes opened and I dropped mine, hastily.

"Should I expect you to be doing that again, then?" he asked, still amused.

"Ha, ha," I managed, pretending like I wasn't moved by the situation at all.

"I mean, a guy can hope, right?" He winked.

I rolled my eyes at him. "Yeah, you can hope." God, I was embarrassed. "So the wall color in here is nice." *What?*

I continued making bland statements about the house as I anxiously made my way back to the safety of anywhere but his bedroom. I basically bolted. I had almost made it down the short flight of stairs to the front door before Jack caught up with me.

"Hey, careful!" Jack's voice reached me as I slipped on the last step in my haste and barely caught myself. "Keri Ann?" His voice morphed from amused to concerned. He quickly hopped down the last few steps to catch up with me and put a warm hand on my arm.

"Sorry," I managed. "Just felt light-headed for a second."

Jack chuckled. "Okay?" He didn't sound convinced, and he sucked his lips between his teeth to keep from smiling again. "Do you want to sit down?"

I smiled, ruefully. "No, I'm fine. Look, uh, thanks for the tour . . . I'm, uh, I have to get going. To work," I finished lamely and pulled my arm free.

By some miracle, he decided to follow my lead and move on from our embarrassing groin brush. "Okay. No problem. Thanks for the ride. And the groceries." He held the door open for me, a small furrow between his eyes. "See you tomorrow, Keri Ann."

The way he said my name was soft, and altogether too appealing. He said the words deliberately and separately, very unlike the way it had been said to me my whole life . . . which was more like Kerianne. I turned and hopped down the steps outside and got into my truck.

I was going to try and recreate the way he said my name in my head for the rest the evening, I just knew it.

CHAPTER SEVEN

The Snapper Grill was busy. It was Friday night. The weekends, now that the tourists had mostly gone home, always drew the locals out. For me, it meant I hardly had a moment to think about my strange day with the runaway Hollywood hottie. *Yeah right.* In less than twenty-four hours, he had taken up residence in my life and mind. If I was honest with myself, it was all I could think about. I just couldn't work out whether my feelings were about Jack the man or Jack the hot Hollywood actor or more specifically his character Max. I knew in part it wasn't about Jack the man because, and I couldn't kid myself about this, I hardly knew him. Part of me had to be projecting my feelings for a nonexistent perfect hero onto him.

I thought about what I did know. He was gorgeous, that was a given. But he was also talented, hardworking, funny, and from what little I had gleaned from his conversation with his agent and things he'd said, he was at odds with his life right now. And he was also potentially heartbroken over his ex. That had to point to some kind of depth in him, unless it was just a bruised ego.

Unfortunately, what I kept having to remind myself was that it didn't matter either way. In fact, it would be better for me if he was just a smug celebrity. I needed grounding, badly, and I didn't know who I could talk to about it without revealing who he was. I tried to call Joey right before leaving for work but ended up just leaving a message. It wasn't like I was going to tell him, I just needed to remind myself I wasn't in the midst of a very long and amazing dream.

The busy sounds of the restaurant drew me out of my head. The talk was all about the potential path of the hurricane that formed in the Atlantic a few days ago and headed our way. Butler Cove hadn't had a direct hit in a hundred and sixteen years. People surmised it was something about the way we were kind of tucked in a bit above Savannah before the land curved out seaward again as it went on up to Charleston and Myrtle Beach. I knew it meant our insurance was a bit lower than other seaside towns, and for that I was grateful.

It sounded like the hurricane might be downgraded to a tropical storm, but it reminded me that Mrs. Weaton's cottage needed a new roof. As her landlord, it was my, and Joey's, responsibility. Luckily, I had managed to save up most of her rent money for the last year knowing it was imminent. I needed to see about getting it done though.

"Hey, Hector," I said, swinging through to the kitchen with some dishes. "Is your nephew still on that roofing crew down in Savannah?"

"*Chiquita!* How is Meester Mystery?" He waggled his eyebrows at me. So much for being surreptitious. Luckily, Brenda, one of the other waitresses who worked with me on our busy weekend shifts, had been on her way out as I entered.

I hissed at him anyway. "Hector!"

"*Lo siento! Lo siento!* But it is love, yes? You can fix hees broken heart?" I knew Hector wasn't that naïve. He was waggling his eyebrows again.

"Stop that. And the only thing that's getting fixed is Mrs. Weaton's roof. Your nephew, can he do it? He'll need to quote me a price first, okay?"

Hector looked totally disappointed I wouldn't play his game. "*Si, si.* I call José tomorrow, give him your number."

"Thanks, Hector." I smiled prettily and thumped his shoulder. "*Graçias.*"

Jazz popped in around ten o'clock, along with Jasper, Cooper, and Vern and a couple of other regulars from our extended circle. There was a small crew of us left in Butler Cove either by choice or circumstance, and we'd all gotten pretty close. Liz never made it out to the grill unless her mom agreed to watch her son, and pretty much everyone else from our graduating class had moved away for college or greener pastures. Lucky them. It was another busy evening, but as it wound down and got near closing, I found myself looking up every time someone walked through the front door. At close to eleven, I looked up just as Jasper headed over to talk to me. He was looking sleek and put together in his polo shirt and chinos, croakies around his neck like he'd just had lunch at a country club or played a round.

"Hey, Keri Ann," he greeted me. His blond hair was brushed sideways across his forehead, just so. I thought of Jack with his dark, mussed hair and wondered how long it took Jasper in front of the mirror to make his look perfect. I felt mean for thinking that. He had been the golden boy of our class and finished college in three years. I wondered idly why I had never been interested in him romantically. He had certainly had his fair share of the high school girls. He'd never let his popularity go to his head though and always chose to stay friendly with everyone.

"Hey, Jasper. What's up?"

"Nothing." He slung a leg over a bar stool across from me, his eyes earnest. "So my dad says you need some help with the house Sunday. I was going to come over after church, about twelve thirty. I'll bring some lunch."

I had completely forgotten about Pastor McDaniel sending Jasper over on Sunday. So much had happened between then and now. I had no idea how I was going to get out of it without arousing some major suspicion, and I didn't want to cancel Jack coming over. I tried not to analyze that too much.

"Oh. Um." I had to do some quick thinking. "That's okay. I actually don't even need help at the moment." Okay, maybe that was a dumb thing to say. All my friends knew I always needed help.

Jasper quirked an eyebrow at me with a puzzled look. "Yeah, okay," he said, his tone implying anything but. "I'll see you at twelve thirty."

"No, really. It's just that I was going to take a break from the house on Sunday. I'm really tired. It's been a long week."

"Keri Ann, it's okay, you know. I know you don't like to ask for help, but I don't mind helping you. Besides, even if you want to take a break from the house, you've still got to eat. Like I said, I'll bring lunch. Anyway, I won't be able to stay long, I have to head back up to Charleston."

I nodded. There wasn't really much else I could say. Jasper was a good friend, but I was careful not to take advantage of him. Sometimes, not accepting help was more hurtful to the person offering. I grabbed at the topic change.

"Your parents must be happy you are closer." Jasper had been looking at going further away, but I sensed things at home, namely his father, had caused him to make the last-minute decision to stay near Butler Cove.

"They are." There was something amiss with Jasper though. He seemed more introspective and thoughtful than usual. "So, how's Liz doing? I haven't seen her lately."

I smiled. "She's good, still working at The Pig. Brady keeps her busy, but he's doing great, getting big. Apparently he's super smart and way ahead of the curve."

He nodded. "That's great. It must be tough doing that all on her own."

Thinking back to Liz asking after Jasper at the store, I looked at him carefully. We were all friends, it was natural for us to inquire after each other, and I was pretty sure Jasper was not the father of Liz's baby. I'd never noticed any awkwardness between them that would signify something that big, but stranger things had happened.

We chatted some more before he headed out. I should talk it over with Jazz and see if she had any vibes about what was going on with him. I also needed to tell Jack not to come over on Sunday, a thought that was ridiculously depressing since I had the day off.

I knew I couldn't tell Jazz about Jack, but I really needed to talk to someone. She offered to stay and help me close up, so I waited until we were alone and almost done before bringing it up.

"Hey, sooo remember Hoodie Guy from last night, who left right after ordering a burger?"

"Yeah?" Jazz was straightening up the piles of coasters, the one job we really didn't need to do, but it was good to have company.

"So he came back for his burger after you left." I grant you, that sentence, in and of itself didn't say much, but this was me and she was Jazz. Her head whipped around, her eyes suddenly laser sharp and focused on me.

"And?"

"And . . . he came in, he ate, we talked. I saw him today—"

"You saw him today? Oh my God. Is he nice? Was he hot? This is fantastic, so was it like a date? Did he ask you to meet him today?"

This was so not going according to plan. "No, Jazz. Slow down with the questions already. It wasn't like that."

"Sorry, I was just excited that you might actually be interested in someone. Are you?"

I stayed her with my hand. "I mean he's nice and not from here, but he's going through a break-up. Well, it may not be a break-up, just a break, but basically he's not free."

"What do you mean he's not free? If he's here and going through a break-up, he's totally up for grabs. I mean, he wouldn't have seen you today if he wasn't interested, right?"

"It wasn't *like* that. It was just friendly. Look never—"

"Well, wait. Did he say the words break-up? Because if he did, that means it's a break-up, not a break."

"He didn't use either." I sighed. This wasn't going well. "Look, it was just friendly."

"If it was just friendly, why are you telling me like that and looking like that?"

"Like what?" Now I was confused.

She rolled her eyes. "You are bright red and flustered. The only other time I saw you like that was when Colton Graves asked you to dance in front of the entire senior class at prom. You liked him and you like this guy." Trust Jazz to bring that up.

When I was fifteen, Joey invited Jazz and me to his senior prom. It was just after our parents had died and he thought it would be a fun thing for us to do to take our minds off stuff. Colton Graves was on the football team with Joey and he was, without a doubt, the hottest boy there, with Joey supposedly being a near second. Colton and Joey floated down school hallways on a waft of sighs and dreamy eyes. It wasn't that I 'liked' Colton Graves as much as I'd probably needed to let off some teenage emotional steam and he happened to be the target. I was so embarrassed and flustered while we danced I hardly remember the experience. I did a lot of staring at his bowtie. That part I do remember. It was red. Okay, so I had 'liked' him a bit. And remembering the experience definitely put my feelings for Jack in perspective.

I was in serious trouble.

"Okay, look. I do like him. But the problem is he's really attractive, and I guess I am not sure if I like him for him or just because he's hot."

Jazz looked exasperated at my lame explanation, but I pressed on. "Also, he's only been friendly to me, no come-ons at all."

"Can I meet him? Maybe I'll be able to tell if he's interested or not."

No.

"Well, he says he's hiding out here, in case his girlfriend finds him, so he doesn't want to be seen out and about." Even to my ears that sounded weird.

Jazz narrowed her eyes. "Do you think he might be married and is worried someone will think he's cheating? Where's he live?"

"California." It was out of my mouth before I could think.

"Okaaaaay." Jazz looked at me with concern.

I didn't say anything. How could I respond? *No it's okay,
Jazz. It's just that he's super famous and despite the fact you
and I tell each other everything, and I am forever in your
debt for helping me through all the deaths in my family, I
am going to keep this huge whopper of a secret from you,
even though he's actually someone you've had a crush on for,
like, five years.*

I wished I had never brought it up.

I knew part of me looked at Jack and saw Max. The situation was a little surreal. Big time Hollywood actor at the mercy
of small town girl. I mean technically he needed me, he'd either
starve or blow his cover. It was probably pretty natural to
project a sappy 'romcom' outcome of that particular scenario.
I wasn't letting myself go there though. The fact of the matter
was, whatever I thought of Jack or why, it was on my side
entirely and it would be me who dealt with it when he left, as
he surely would in exactly three weeks' time. In the meantime,
I would have to steel myself against his obvious charm.

I was just so inexperienced with men.

I had been kissed approximately once, two years ago by
Jasper. It was fine. A bit awkward, but over quickly and had
not, thank the stars, ever happened again after I told him I
didn't feel that way about him. I understood this was a little
unusual for a girl my age in this century—to have only kissed
one boy. The truth of the matter was no boy I knew lived
up to the fantasy I'd created from the many books I'd read,
and I wasn't going to settle. And I for sure wasn't going to
have sex with any of them.

I was inexperienced, but I wasn't naïve.

"What's his name?" Her question caught me completely
unaware. I hadn't really thought anything through about what
to call him.

"Um . . ." I wondered if I should make one up but what if I forgot it? "Jack?"

It couldn't hurt to be truthful about this one thing. There were plenty of Jacks in the world.

"Jack. Okay, you don't seem sure. Keri Ann, are you okay? You are acting really odd, it's wigging me out."

"I'm fine. Totally fine. Just tired."

She seemed to buy that. "Okay, let's get done here and I'll drop you home."

After she pulled up at my house, she made me promise to be careful of Jack and call her in the morning. I was already trying to be careful. It was a confusing situation, made more so by the fact I couldn't tell if my feelings were based on anything real.

I'd felt my phone buzz with a text while Jazz and I were finishing up at the grill, but had forgotten to check it. Pulling it out, I went inside and closed the door. The text on the screen made my stomach dip.

Late Night Visitor: Walk you home?

Shit. I checked the time, fifteen minutes ago. Had he been waiting outside for me? I quickly texted back.

Me: Sorry, got a ride with Jazz, didn't see this.

My phone buzzed back immediately, searing my palm, or perhaps my nerves. I pressed my lips tightly together, keeping my breath tightly inside me a moment.

Late Night Visitor: Noticed. No problem, have a good night.

So he *had* been outside. I was surprised, warmed, and regretful all at once that I hadn't checked my phone right away. I bit my lip and tapped out a reply.

Me: Thank you. You, too.

I waited, staring at my phone. Would he text back again?

CHAPTER EIGHT

I woke up at eight, right on the tail end of a dream that was ending way too soon. I was out on the marsh, my bright orange kayak stark against the glittering water as I glided my paddle in and out of the water in perfect rhythm with my breathing.

The sudden sound of ripples and a puff of air had me looking to my right to catch the sight of a dolphin as it dove back under. In its wake, my eyes were drawn to the paddler in the kayak next to me.

Jack was there, his chest bare and tan, smiling at the dolphin. He looked up too, catching my eye. Slowly his smile faded, and his gaze became intent. "I want to kiss you," he breathed quietly across the water.

His words and the intense way he said them, pounded into me, each one a fist that slowly took ahold of something deep inside. My breath caught. I stared back at him. I think I tried to form some words after a few moments but couldn't, and then he faded away. The glittering of the sun on the water grew brighter. I blinked a few times and opened my eyes as the morning light in my bedroom crossed my face.

It was another warm fall day. I shifted my gaze out the

windows where the light filtered through the branches of the huge Live Oak in the front yard. The draped Spanish moss slowly swayed in the breeze. At least the air was moving more today, maybe it wouldn't be so hot.

I thought about Jack in his bed and whether he had remembered to close the blinds. If he had, he may not wake up and get over here before I had to leave for work.

We hadn't really worked out a plan of how and when he would come over today. Riding his motorcycle might draw too much attention. I guessed he would jog over again, but maybe I should go and get him. I dropped that idea as soon as it crossed my mind. If he showed up, that was great. If not, then I guess that meant he was getting his shopping done elsewhere. That thought filled me with the appropriate dread expected of a miserable groupie.

I hadn't heard back from him after my last text.

I sat up abruptly, mentally pulling myself together. I had made it through some pretty traumatic experiences in my life. I was definitely beyond being a sappy little mess who was grateful for a scrap of time and attention from a divine being like Jack Eversea.

I would reap the benefits of our little arrangement as long as it lasted. I would be thoughtful and courteous of Jack's time, and I definitely would not expect us to form any deep or emotional bond of friendship when our time was up. The fact that electric heat tended to zap through my veins at the sight or thought of him, something I liked to think of as the 'swoon-effect', was just a hazard I would have to weather.

I needed a run. I threw on a sports bra and my running shorts, grabbed my iPod and earphones, and jogged out to the truck.

Normally, I would go straight down Palmetto to the public beach access and start my run by turning right. But I didn't want to run past Jack's house, so I went further down to the Islanders' Beach and after parking and jogging down the boardwalk, I turned left. It would be a short run that would end at the inlet, but at least I was getting some exercise and clearing my head.

The sea was getting cooler even though our days were still warm. There was a haze over the water. One or two people were out with their dogs, but the beach was mainly empty.

I got into a great rhythm, my strides long and sure, my breathing even and deep. I made it about half a mile before an approaching figure in black shorts and a white t-shirt with familiar aviators came into view ahead. I slowed a tiny bit, wondering if it was Jack. Shit, I knew it was. Should I acknowledge him or stop and talk to him? Damn it. This was supposed to be a Jack-free run. I should have gone kayaking instead.

I could tell when he noticed me, as he did the same thing where he slowed slightly, and then picked his pace back up. When he was about fifteen yards away, I gave up my internal battle about what to do and smiled politely at him. He didn't slow like he was going to stop. So I didn't either. *Seriously?* Were we really just going to run right past each other without saying hello?

My spirits sank with disappointment when he passed me, much as I hated myself for it. But then a few seconds later he appeared up alongside me. I snuck a sidelong glance at his profile, trying to form a question with my eyebrows. His dimple quirked but he didn't say anything. Okay then. I affected a nonchalant shrug, turned my music up and picked up the pace.

He'd obviously already run to the inlet and was headed home, and he was going to have to double his run to keep me company. I wasn't sure what to make of it, but I wasn't going to try and talk and break my running mojo. When he was around I didn't think I could walk and chew gum at the same time, let alone run, talk, breathe, and try not to trip over my own feet.

Jack kept pace with me, our footfalls finding a rhythm. We got to the inlet and I turned quickly and headed back. I was sure that had probably been a natural place to stop and rest and I don't know . . . say hi, like a normal person. But I didn't act normal around him. Following my lead, he smiled at me. As we headed back, I cursed the fact he had his sunglasses and I didn't. And of course, because of his glasses, when I repeatedly glanced at him, my eyes were drawn straight to his mouth. Ugh. I squinted inelegantly back into the sun.

As we approached my exit, I was heaving with exertion, and probably looked my best again. I slowed and got ready to peel off with a wave, but Jack slowed too and before I could react he reached toward me. I paused, surprised, as he lifted my earbud out of my ear and held it up to his, listening to my music.

"The Cult? I seriously don't think I'll ever figure you out," he said, laughing and gently placing the bud back in my ear. Then he jogged backward for a few steps and gave me a two-fingered salute like he had from his motorcycle that first day, before he turned away and ran off.

All day Saturday at the grill I was mentally at home and bodily at work. I guess I was technically 'mooning', despite giving myself a mental kick in the ass earlier. Having never gone through 'mooning' over someone before, I wasn't quite sure if that's what I was doing. Whatever it was, it was embarrassing.

I kept thinking of our run and how hardly a word had been exchanged and how it still felt like an important moment. I was totally reading into it, I knew.

Hector kept catching my eye and winking. I'd told him what the arrangement was between Jack and me, swearing if I heard even one rumor, I would know it was him and tell Paulie I saw him stealing silverware. He had clutched his chest in outrage. "*Tienes mi palabra*," he muttered, which I believe, from what I remembered of high school Spanish, meant something along the lines of *I had his word*. At least I hoped it did.

I had texted Jack right after I showered from my run, letting him know the back door was unlocked. He never responded. In the quiet moments between the lunch and dinner rush, I had almost given in to the temptation to pop home and see if he was there. It was like some kind of bizarre reality home-makeover show, or worse, I was being punked. I expected a camera crew to jump me at any moment.

On Sunday morning, the only evidence I had that Jack had been in my house was half missing wallpaper, and a grocery list on the counter along with a request for spackling and sandpaper. His handwriting looked like he'd missed his calling to be a doctor.

We hadn't talked about whether he'd continue working on the house Sunday and I hadn't had a chance to tell him about Jasper coming by.

I decided to run over to The Pig to get his groceries while most people were in church. Driving straight to his place afterward, I piled the bags outside his door. I rang the bell, and without waiting for a response, maturely hopped down the stairs and back into my truck. It was only when I pulled out of the driveway and noticed his bike wasn't there that I realized what an ass I was being. I quickly grabbed my phone and texted him.

Me: Your groceries are outside your front door. Sorry I had to run, a friend coming over for lunch today.

My phone chirped back by the time I got to the end of the street.

Late Night Visitor: Thank you.

I hated the prick of disappointment I experienced at his simple text.

When Jasper arrived at lunchtime armed with my favorite chicken salad and 'everything' on nine grain, I thought I might finally have reached a calm and stoic state of mind.

"Wow, you've gotten so much done," Jasper said as he walked around the house.

"Yep, been working hard," I said from the kitchen where I busied myself getting plates so I didn't have to meet his eye. "Grab some waters, would ya? Let's sit on the porch swing, it's a stunning day."

We headed outside and chatted comfortably on the swing as we ate, although he did look at me curiously while I picked out the onions on my sandwich. I loved onions. I noticed what I was doing and resolutely stuffed one of them back into what was left.

"So there's a guy?"

"What? No!" Jeez, I'd have expected that kind of pointed observation from Jazz. The fact that Jasper noticed meant I was definitely not fooling anyone, or maybe Jazz had told him about Hoodie Guy.

"Right. Do I know him?"

I sighed. "No, you don't. And it's not like that anyway."

"You mean for you or for him?"

"For either of us. He's the one who's helping with the inside of the house." At least I could come clean about that.

"Keri Ann, I know I'm not your best friend, but you know you can talk to me, right? I wish I could take back that kiss two years ago. I totally made it awkward between us, which I regret. You should know there's someone else I like, a lot, so if you need to talk to me about anything, you don't need to worry about hurting my feelings."

I looked at him, surprised. Liz?

"Don't ask me who it is, Keri Ann, I'm not ready to even talk about it."

I grinned. "Well, I'm not ready to talk about this guy either."

"Okay, then, so we agree not to talk. Awesome. We're so healthy." He laughed.

"Is she the reason you decided to go to law school so nearby?" I asked.

He looked off into the front yard, and sighed. "Yeah, partly. But also, I need to keep an eye on Dad. I'm sure you've noticed he has a slight weakness of the alcohol variety."

I nodded. "What does your mom say?"

"Well, apparently it's not the first time. Now that I know that, I have vague recollections as a kid before he got some help. Let's just say, I'd like to stick around."

I'd had a feeling that was why.

Part of the reason I stopped going to church, aside from

how angry I was at God for letting Mom and Dad die, was that Nana didn't go.

One summer when we were visiting, I may have only been eight or so, I overheard Nana and my mother arguing quietly. Nana said something that, at the time I didn't understand, about Mrs. McDaniel not doing a good enough job of hiding the marks if she expected Nana not to get involved. She had never elaborated, but it stuck in my mind, especially when I went to Church every Sunday with my parents after we moved to Butler Cove permanently.

I felt bad for Jasper and laid my hand on his arm just as I heard the rumble of a motorcycle in the street. Jack, with his helmet on, wearing a pair of faded jeans and a white t-shirt, slowed to a stop beyond the front picket fence. Before I could react or even let out the breath I'd sucked in, he kicked the bike into a roar and headed off. Hot blood rushed to my cheeks as I realized I'd snatched my hand off Jasper's arm.

Jasper laughed. "It's not like *that*, my ass."

Oh shit. I had it bad. It would be obvious to anyone who knew me.

"Shut it, Jasper. Otherwise, I'll tell Liz how you feel." The look on his face was priceless. "Relax, I won't," I added. "But *you* should."

He swallowed. I had never seen him look so nervous and unsure of himself, yet so hopeful. It was kind of adorable.

"Really?"

"Yes, really. You keep my secret, I'll keep yours. Deal? Now, let's get some work done."

It was the last thing I wanted to do. My pounding heart was telling me to jump in my truck and go after Jack. I couldn't believe he had come by. Surely he wasn't checking up on me? Why would he do that?

CHAPTER NINE

$\mathcal{J}$ got a text just after the lunch rush on Monday.

Late Night Visitor: Hi

The flutter in my belly made me grit my teeth.

Me: Hi

Late Night Visitor: Are you planning on getting a dumpster for the carrot I left outside?

Huh?

Late Night Visitor: Carpet! Autocorrect. Sorry.

I couldn't help it, but getting a text from Jack made me ridiculously and annoyingly giddy.

Me: Oh, thought you'd gone off your vegetables again. I've got roofers coming for the cottage this week, so I can use theirs.

Hector's nephew had called the night before and given me a price I could live with and would start the next day. The hurricane had weakened back to a tropical storm, but it was still on a projected path in our direction by later in the week. At the very least it was sure to bring heavy rain. I was relieved to be getting the roof done.

Late Night Visitor: You're funny. Mrs. Weaton's place?

Me: How do you know?

Late Night Visitor: She came by. Nosey lady, but nice. Don't worry she didn't recognize me. She seems to care for you a lot.

Me: Sorry, should have warned you she'd probably come by. She and Nana were close. Who did you say you were?

Late Night Visitor: That I was a friend doing you

My eyes widened.

Late Night Visitor: A favor! A friend doing you a favor! Sorry. Damn phone. Banging head on wall . . .

I bit my lip, trying hard not to laugh out loud. A warm buzz ran through me. I bit my lip even harder to pull myself back in line while thumbing the keys, wondering how to respond. A few seconds later another text chimed on my phone.

Late Night Visitor: If only we had a wheelbarrow, that would be one thing . . .

What on earth?

And then I got it and grinned. It was a quote from *The Princess Bride*. It just happened to be one of my favorite movies. I used to watch it with Nana all the time. I racked my brain to come up with an appropriate quote back.

Me: Go away, or I'll call the brute squad!

Late Night Visitor: I am the brute squad!

I giggled and put my phone away just in time to see Hector smiling at me.

"What?" I asked.

"*Nada.*" He shrugged his shoulders.

It was almost midnight Monday by the time I jogged up my back steps. I was a little disappointed Jack hadn't offered to walk me home again since Friday night, and then mad at myself for being so.

The moon was full, so although I couldn't see stars clearly, it cast such a strong white glow I could make out every bush and tree and person sitting with his back against my door. I jumped and did a double take. Yep, there was definitely a person sitting there, head down, cradling a six-pack of beer. I'd know that glossy dark hair anywhere. Jack. My heart sped up in spite of myself.

"Jack?"

He started, sending the bottles clattering off his lap. "Shit!"

I stuck a foot out to stop the bottle nearest me and bent to help as he picked them up.

"Sorry," he said. He sounded tired. He looked tired too from what little I could see. Like he had fallen asleep.

"It's fine. What are you doing out here?"

"I, uh," he looked around. "I guess I just got bored and was going to see what you thought of the walls." He got to his feet, brushing off his dark jeans.

"The walls," I repeated. I had spent every second of the day thinking of him alone in my house supposedly working on stripping the wallpaper. However, it wouldn't hurt to at least pretend he wasn't the first thing on my mind. And having him right here when I got home did strange little jiggy things low in my belly.

"Right. Well, let me have a look." I stepped past him, breathing in his showered scent surreptitiously. Something fresh and outdoorsy I couldn't quite put my finger on. My light-headed reaction to the scent was annoying.

I walked in the back door ahead of him, turned on the lights, and put my purse down on the counter.

"You want a beer?" he asked. "I found some at the beach house. They're cold."

I turned and looked at him. He was a little flushed from sleep, making his green eyes all the more startling. He must have been out there a while. "A beer?"

He nodded, putting the box on the counter.

"Are you okay?" I asked him, even though I was the one who kept repeating words back to him.

"Yeah, I'm good." He ran both hands through his hair, leaving it standing up. How did he do that? "I just, I can't be with myself at the moment."

I turned to the counter and grabbed two bottles, unsure of what he meant. I handed him one and twisted my cap off. We raised our bottles and clinked necks.

He smiled and took a sip.

I wondered if, in his Hollywood life, Jack Eversea had ever had to really just enjoy his own company. I didn't want to become his therapist, but if we were going to have this sort of strange trade-for-services friendship, I guessed I could be a shoulder to lean on. Of course, that would make me the sad lovelorn 'good friend' at the end of this, but I could hardly see it ending any differently at this point. I might as well discover a little more about Jack in the process.

"I'm guessing you don't have to be on your own a lot?" I tried.

"I'm sure that's pretty obvious, but what no one tells you is how isolating it can be to be surrounded with people all the time." He took another sip. "I know that sounds weird, but it's like, when you are surrounded by things and people and requirements all day long, you stop thinking for yourself. You become automated. Just doing what's required, when it's required. And you forget who you are inside all that and how *you* feel and what *you* like to do and how *you* would react."

He leaned back against the counter, crossing his feet at the ankles. "And then, suddenly, when you get away from it for just a moment, it's like you are in this big drowning vacuum of nothingness. There's no you. There's no one telling you how to be you or what to do, it's just you, except there's no you any more."

I wasn't sure what he wanted me to say. "So you don't trust who *you* are inside any more?" I surmised.

"Exactly," he said.

I felt stupidly pleased I'd said the right thing.

He went on, "You can't see what you want, what you feel, whether you're any good at what you are doing. You suddenly feel like you need the fame, the attention, because it's the only thing that's telling you that you are any good. But then you wonder, it's all just bullshit anyway, right? It's not you and your talent, it's your luck. It's the fans and their whims. It's the money on the deals, the franchise. They spin the story, create your life, and if they take it away then you're nothing. You don't exist."

Whoa.

He stalked across the room and grabbed a kitchen chair, straddling it backward. His forearms rested over the top, the bottle dangling from his fingertips. Forearms were a really big turn on for me, apparently.

I hadn't moved while he talked. In all honesty, I had no response. I could see what he was saying. The emptiness was written all over his face, the void dark in his eyes. I saw parts of him in our few brief encounters, like now, that were incongruous with famous Jack. I wondered for a moment if he had any vices he used to deal with that void and emptiness he could feel inside him.

"God, listen to me. Don't I sound like the pathetic schmuck? Spoiled movie-star complaining about his life, to you, a waitress, who's still waiting around for her life to start."

I flinched slightly, taken aback.

He didn't notice.

"Well, then fuck you, Jack."

His head snapped up.

I said it nicely, but I was irritated. "You think you don't know yourself? Well, you sure as shit don't know me, or anything about me, so if you could keep me out of your pity party I'd appreciate it." I folded my arms over my chest, projecting a defiant and offended look I had perfected over the years.

How could this guy be so attractive and get on my last nerve at the same time? Wasn't lust as blind as love? I guessed not.

Jack's eyes narrowed a moment, then his shoulders sagged. "Oh God, I'm so sorry."

"Yeah, right. Well, it's late." I shrugged like I was over the conversation. I felt bad in a way. I wanted him to be able to talk to me, but for some reason I always found myself wanting to shut it down and get him out of my space. It just felt too crowded all the time, like I couldn't keep a sense of *my*self with him there.

"Look, I'm sorry," he backtracked. "I didn't mean anything by that. I'm not myself." He sighed and ran his hand through his hair again. "You're right. I don't know you, and you don't know me. Everyone always thinks they do. But for some reason, I want to be able to talk to you. I want to know you. You seem . . . grounded I guess. And you look at me like . . ."

Great. I was normal and grounding. I truly would have preferred to be magnetic or enigmatic, but I wasn't sure what either would accomplish for me. "Like?"

"Like you don't see me as a famous person, but just as a person."

Surprised, I said quietly, "You *are* just a person."

I stared at him and his gaze snagged my own. He seemed to be looking right into me, like he was sifting over who I was inside. I was pinned for a moment, unable to drop my eyes from his, and after a few beats his gaze wandered over my face. The air seemed to swell up around me. I bit my lip, whether in nerves or a sharp reminder of reality, I couldn't say.

The small movement hooked his gaze and his green eyes zeroed in on my mouth.

It was too much for me. I cleared my throat, breaking the spell I was under, and taking a sip of my drink, turned away.

What kind of game was Jack playing with me? Obviously, he knew the effect he had on girls. On me. If he thought coming here tonight would help fill some of that void he was feeling, I was going to have to be seriously careful. The plain truth was, part of me wanted to be that for Jack. There was no question of how he had gotten to where he had today. Yes, he was talented. I had seen his work. I knew the nuances and depth he brought into his roles. But I was also, now, a firsthand witness to his gravitational pull. He was like a bright and beautiful rogue planet. He pulled the entire galaxy into a gravitational wobble until he got close enough to suck you in and tilt your axis head over heels.

"If you say you can talk to me, talk to me." I congratulated myself on the right amount of polite interest and concern. The fact that I was keenly *over*-interested in everything to do with him, didn't escape my attention. I truly wanted to know what this guy who had everything going for him was doing in my kitchen at . . . I looked at the microwave clock . . . *midnight*. "I mean, you keep saying you're not yourself, so speak. I'm listening."

CHAPTER TEN

Jack finally dropped his eyes away from me and drained the rest of his beer.

I watched his throat work down the last sip. "Sorry," I said, suddenly wanting to take back my unburdening his soul challenge. It was way too intimate between us already. "I didn't mean to snap at you. I just don't get it. You're right. I mean, I get what you're feeling, I just . . . surely you must have friends you can talk to, people who are in the same boat as you?"

He shrugged. "Well, perhaps if I had felt like anyone would understand, I wouldn't have had to go to the other side of the country to figure my shit out. Look, forget about it." He sighed and smiled. "So, what's the latest news from Butler Cove?"

"Hmmm. Let me see." I laughed, relieved, and ran through some of the conversations I'd overheard this evening at work. "An alligator got stuck in a storm drain, and Sheriff Graves and the fire chief had to work together to get him loose. It drew a big crowd, not because of the alligator, but because the sheriff hasn't spoken to the chief in seven years since the chief had an affair with the sheriff's wife. That makes for some interesting town council meetings when decisions have to be made, I can tell you."

Jack laughed. "So are they still together? The sheriff and his wife?"

"Oh, yes!" I said in mock outrage, hand to my heart. "She still attends church with her head held high every Sunday and refuses to admit she did it. But you can't get away with much in a town this size."

"You go to church?"

"Actually, no. I just hear *she* does. Anyway, what else? Oh, the hurricane ended up being a tropical storm, but let's hope it stays that way so they don't issue us an evac order. It looks like it may head past us up to Charleston, anyway."

"I guess if they evacuate, I'll head back to California," he said.

The thought of him potentially leaving by the end of the week made me ridiculously depressed.

"But in the meantime, I've clued my assistant in about where I am so she is sending me more clothes and scripts and stuff."

"I thought you didn't want anyone to know where you are?"

"I didn't, I don't, but that's not really realistic, and I can trust her. I traveled with what I was wearing and what I could fit in the bike bags. And I have a mountain of scripts waiting for me."

I could already see that Jack was not dealing with his self-imposed isolation well. He was either going to give this 'getting away' idea up and go back, or he was going to try and find some way to distract himself. Either way spelled devastation for me if we continued to spend time together.

I fleetingly wondered about his relationship with Audrey Lane. Was he truly heartbroken, or was it all just an ill-thought-out excuse to explain his obviously out of the norm behavior? If he was going to stay and try to distract himself, I wouldn't be doing either of us any favors by letting on that I was crushing on him, especially if I was not only just a distraction, but also playing seconds to his girlfriend. I liked to think I thought a little more of myself, but I hated that, for a moment, I wondered what it would be like.

The thought of the rejection when it came, as it inevitably would, whether by him politely ignoring my desperate crush or by him leaving, was a cold shower on my thoughts.

The truth was, I was lonely, too. I was still a young teenager at heart who had had to grow up way too fast. There'd been no time for whispering and giggling over boys and having my mom do my hair for the prom or to ask about dating. That had all been lost to me too early. I had loved Nana so much, but in the end it was me taking care of her and not the other way around. I hadn't had my giddy, angsty, hormone-filled teenage-hood that I always seemed to read so much about, despite Jazz's efforts to get me out of my shell. Perhaps if I had, I would be better equipped to deal with all the tangled emotions I felt in this situation with Jack.

I couldn't even look at it objectively, because he wasn't just a boy. He was a dazzling, heart-stopping aura of a man who in just five days had me feeling like I was perched on the edge of a precipice and seriously contemplating throwing myself over the edge. The idea was terrifying in its finality and in its inevitability.

He broke the silence.

"So, go check out the walls, let me know what you think."

Ah yes. The walls.

Leaving my beer behind, I stepped into the hall.

I looked around me. It was amazing. The plain pine floors and bare walls were suddenly swollen with the promise of what the house could become. I could see it so clearly. Dark wood floors with wide white moldings and high ceilings against pale dusty blue walls.

"I saw the chandelier project you're working on." Jack's voice came from behind me. "I thought it would be amazing in here." He was referring to my hobby of collecting old wrought iron, driftwood and sea glass. I had, indeed, been working on fashioning one into a chandelier of sorts thinking to put it in my room or a library room, if I ever converted the parlor. I thought of him seeing all my stuff and unfinished projects in the attic that I had left neglected for too long and felt a moment of embarrassment. Jazz was forever nagging me about it, telling me to bring my pieces to the store. I didn't know what held me back.

I was hyper-aware of Jack standing behind me, but I had to be imagining he was so close. I swore I felt a zap of energy from his body along the length of mine. Closing my eyes instead of answering him, I wondered if I turned around right now, whether his proximity would be all in my head. And then I felt it, his breath against the back of my neck. I swallowed hard. He slowly inhaled the air around my nape, and the fine hairs stirred to stand on end.

"What is it about you, Keri Ann?" The words were thick and quiet. Lacking the lightness of a whisper, they plummeted down through my body like an anchor. I shivered and willed myself to know what to do. Yes, what was it about *me*? This normal girl from a normal place, having this extraordinary moment with no hope or means of navigating this unchartered water.

I realized in that moment it didn't matter. I'd never had a choice. The circumstances of my life meant nothing could have prepared me for the entrance of Jack Eversea into my world. This was his show to run. His moment to live or leave, and he had chosen to be in my house and my life for this brief span of time. He could have gone anywhere. Perhaps, he would have been better off bumping into a person more sure of herself, or more jaded. Maybe another girl, a girl with a tiny bit more experience than I had would have thrown herself into his arms hoping to make him forget his troubles or hers for a little while, taking what she could get and having light-hearted fun while she was at it. But I was just me. I was also, at this particular moment, incapable of moving or responding. Or breathing for that matter.

"Turn around, Keri Ann," Jack said, softly.

I finally let my breath go and turned. My eyes collided with the place where his neck met his dark sage green t-shirt. His skin was beautiful. Flawless even, save for the smattering of dark stubble shadowing his jaw. His Adam's apple bobbed as he swallowed, and he smelled . . . amazing. Like pine and waterfalls.

The walls were too close in the hall. There was little room to step back. Even though my reflex was to create space between us, he stepped in time with me and my back instantly pressed against the wall.

Was this really happening?

How had we gone from light-hearted banter in the kitchen to this? I was confused and light-headed all at once. My God, was there enough space in the universe to breathe?

I was aware of his one hand caging me in as his other came up to my face. His skin was warm and slightly rough, his palms callused in a way that belied a life of script reading and spoke more of his true nature. *Jack was touching my face.* I closed my eyes like if I didn't look up at him, didn't make eye contact, this wouldn't be really happening.

"Please." My voice sounded strange. I didn't know what I was asking for. A reprieve maybe, time to process what I was feeling. I had never in my life felt the currents that were coiling up inside me, gathering into ever sharpening spears. I had never *expected* to feel this way either and certainly had no idea it could feel so amazing and so terrifying all at once.

He slowly tilted my chin up.

"Please what?" he asked as I opened my eyes to his intense stare. His gaze was earnest and questioning and held none of the arrogance I was expecting to glimpse.

My tongue snuck out to moisten my lips just as his thumb slid gently across them. The contact was electrifying.

I froze.

Jack groaned. "Christ," he managed, his eyes squeezing shut and his forehead creasing, as if in pain.

"I . . ." I cleared my throat. "I . . . please don't. Please don't kiss me."

CHAPTER ELEVEN

Please don't kiss me?

Jack's eyes snapped open. I glimpsed confusion for a split second as the words, my ridiculously uttered words, rang out in the silence around us. I wanted to pull them back in so badly. I wanted him to kiss me, I wanted his lips on mine, I wanted to know what he tasted like, what his tongue felt like, what his mouth would do when fused with mine. Whether he kissed fast or slow, hard or soft. If he was hot or cool. It suddenly became imperative to know that beyond anything else. I gritted my teeth, wishing back the words of my rejection just as he pushed abruptly away from me.

I gasped.

"Shit, I'm sorry." He blew out a breath and raked his hand, that same hand that had been cradling my face moments before, through his hair. "I thought . . . shit, I don't know what I thought. Sorry, okay? I just seem to be fucking up with you all around, don't I?" He fell back against the opposite wall, putting some distance between us, his face tilted up to the ceiling.

I lifted a shaky hand to my mouth that was aching over a loss it didn't even know.

"I'm sorry," I said.

"Don't apologize."

"But I am," I insisted. I took a deep breath and came clean. What the hell, right? I was already a goner, at least he didn't have to feel like a heel about it just because I was an inexperienced prude. "I wanted you to kiss me."

He looked back at me. "So why did you stop me? Apart from the obvious, that you were smart to do so."

What?

"What do you mean?" I wasn't going to try to play some sophisticated guessing game with him. I wanted the bare and ugly truth.

He bobbed his head at me. "You first. Why did you stop me?"

Because I might melt. Literally. And because I may never survive it? "A few reasons, you want the main one or the list?"

"A list again? Is one of them that I should have brushed my teeth before coming over?"

I laughed. I couldn't help it, it was such an unexpected question, delivered so teasingly it relieved my nervous tension. I was grateful.

"No!" I shook my head with a smile.

"Good." He raised his eyebrows, expectantly. "Go on."

"Well, I haven't . . ." I twisted my fingers as I tried to decide how much to tell him. That I was inexperienced except for one awkward kiss, or that the feelings he made me feel were scaring the crap out of me, and I wasn't ready for what that could do to me if we were to continue. Maybe I should just tell him I didn't like him like that. *Liar, liar, pants on fire*. Anyway, I had just admitted I wanted him to kiss me, so that was a lame one.

"Please don't tell me you have never been kissed," he said with a laugh. I looked at him, surprised at his tone. Would he ridicule me if I hadn't? I was aware I was taking a little too long to answer.

His light tone faded. "Oh my God, seriously?" His body pitched forward slightly off the wall.

"What? No! I mean yes, I have been kissed, once, I mean it wasn't really . . ." I took an awkward breath. "I mean, it was okay, not a *kiss* kiss . . ." Why was I babbling and why couldn't I stop? "I mean, it was, but . . ."

"What's not a *kiss* kiss?"

"It was a kiss that shouldn't have happened."

"Like ours shouldn't happen?" He eyed me speculatively, his hands interlacing behind his neck.

It shouldn't?

"No, because we were two friends who shouldn't have kissed, and I didn't like him . . . like that." I swallowed. I sounded so young.

"But you like *me* like that? Or is it just because of who I am?"

"No! I don't know," I said, honestly. *Oops.* I looked down, avoiding his eyes.

"Well." Out of the corner of my eye I saw him drop back against the wall, and his hands came up and grabbed two tufts of his unruly hair. "At least you're honest." He sounded flat.

"Look, I don't mean that. I just mean . . ." How did I explain this without making it seem like I had no self-esteem? He was so Goddamn beautiful, and I was just me. I couldn't, so why worry about it. I opened my mouth to say just that but he cut me off.

"Who was it?"

"Who was what?"

"Your first and only kiss?"

"Oh, um, Jasper McDaniel. He's just—"

"The Pastor's son."

"How do you know that?" I looked at him, curiously.

"I overheard the Pastor and your friend at the Grill the other night." He scowled. "Was he the one who was here on Sunday?"

"Yes, and he's just a friend. Which reminds me of the rest of my list. You aren't available, so whether or not I want to kiss you is a moot point. We are just friends."

Jack snorted.

"What?" I asked.

"Nothing." He shook his head. "So, stop me if I am being too personal but—"

"You're being too personal." I smirked. Oh yes, thank God. Feisty Keri Ann was back.

"So you had one kiss. I'm presuming you haven't ever . . ." He caught my eyes and held them. My face flamed. "Made love?"

Oh, God. Why did he say it like that? Like he was thinking it, imagining it, right as he was saying it.

Liquid heat pooled low in my belly.

"Didn't I say you were being too personal?" I croaked.

"Yeah, but you didn't stop me. I said, 'Stop me.'" He looked altogether too smug and something else I couldn't quite put my finger on.

I had to gain the upper hand here, even though my heart was pounding in my throat. "So what did you mean when you said there was an obvious and smart reason to stop you?"

"How did I know you weren't going to let that go?"

I shrugged.

"Well," he went on, "why don't you finish your list first."

"You have a girlfriend—"

"Had."

Okaaaay. *Had*. That was interesting. "Until you forgive her and get back together?"

He nodded.

I just stared at him.

"Did you just nod?" I asked, incredulously. The guy had almost kissed me and was now admitting he was planning on getting back together with his ex. My stomach rolled. Poor dumb southern hick girl falls for self-proclaimed asshole, willingly. It wasn't like I didn't already have an inkling he could be that shallow, I mean the guy was an actor. He *pretended* to feel things for a living. God, I was so out of my depth.

"Yeah, but that's because it's in my contract. We *have* to stay together. I don't expect you to understand that."

If it was possible, I felt sicker. "You're right, I don't. I mean I do understand the concept, I just don't understand anyone agreeing to something like that." This was good. He was an empty vessel—a shallow, self-absorbed actor who would prostitute his love life for the sake of being famous. I could definitely get over someone like this. Wow, his relationship with Audrey Lane was based on a contract? Millions of fans had been duped.

"You look pretty disgusted right now."

"I am a bit." Not *enough*. *Ugh*.

"You don't pull any punches, huh?" His fingers slid into his pockets.

"Not really."

He crossed his ankles, like he was settling in for a while. "Any more reasons?"

"Do we need them now? I mean it's purely theoretical at this point. It's *never* going to happen."

He sighed, let his head fall back again, and closed his eyes.

"So . . . what did you mean it was smart?" I asked, since we were being so honest and all.

"That was it. I'm in a contract. At least until after the movie finishes its run in theaters. Globally. Or Peak Entertainment stops caring so much about it. Us. Me."

We both stood in silence a few minutes, each with our backs against opposite walls. I catalogued his face. His hair was a little shaggy like he was overdue for a cut, his long black eyelashes rested on his cheeks as he closed his eyes again. His beautiful mouth, the one I had missed my chance at tasting, pursed slightly as he worried his lips between his teeth.

"Did I mess this up?" he asked eventually, looking back at me.

"Which part?"

He nodded. "Good point. I meant the part where we happily coexist in a mutually beneficial grocery-buying for handy-man services relationship, as bizarre as that is."

"It is bizarre, isn't it?" I grinned. And for some reason I just started giggling and then couldn't stop. I laughed so hard my eyes welled up and my sides hurt. Call it a release of tension or a complete free-fall into dorkdom. I probably snorted at some point. I'm sure it was a highlight. Either way, it ended up with Jack chuckling along at my laughter and shaking his head in bewilderment.

"Jeez, Keri Ann. I don't think I have ever met anyone with a range of emotions like yours. And I'm an actor, so that's saying something."

Feeling suddenly awkward, my laugh trailed off. I knew what I looked like in the midst of a giggle-fest—there was a picture Nana had taken of Jazz and me, the summer right before my parents died. I don't even remember what we were laughing at, but I remember my nostrils flared and my cheeks were splotchy. I always thought I looked like a horse in that picture. Wiping at my eyes self-consciously, I attempted to pull myself together.

"It's amazing," said Jack, shaking his head and looking at me.

"What's amazing?"

"It's amazing," he repeated, "that you seem to have no idea how fucking beautiful you are."

Instantly sober from my laughing episode, I stood dead still staring at Jack.

He just looked right back at me, arms folded, as if challenging me to contradict him.

I was speechless, otherwise I would have. Man, this guy was good.

"It's late. I should get going," he finally said.

I nodded dumbly.

"You working tomorrow?"

I shook my head.

He pushed forward off his side of the hallway and stepped toward me. If it was possible, he suddenly looked predatory.

Pressing my back further against the cool wall at his approach, I held my breath as he planted his palms flat against the wall behind me, his body hovering a scant inch from mine and his head ducking straight down to my neck.

"I'm glad we have our reasons laid out, Keri Ann," he said quietly, breathing his words into my ear in a torrent of snapping electricity. "But that doesn't mean it's *never* going to happen."

My stomach flipped over, and my breath whooshed out into a deep and embarrassing pant. Placing my hands against his hard chest, I pushed him away to arm's length. "Wow, did anyone ever tell you how arrogant you are?"

"Not arrogant. Confident. There's a difference."

"Well, you can stop being confident about kissing me." I hardened my eyes. I felt like some kind of plaything, a yo-yo he kept rolling out and back. Every time I thought I caught a glimpse of who the real Jack might be, he presented *this* side of himself to make me think I had imagined it.

"This isn't a movie! You just told me you were getting back together with your *girlfriend*, and agreed that it was a smart idea not to kiss me, and now you're acting like you've had a temporary setback." I was mad and humiliated. "Forget it, Jack. I may be inexperienced, and I may think you are gorgeous, but I don't think so little of myself I'd let you use me for a little distraction to get you through your boring three weeks in Butler Cove."

If eyes could flash, his were doing it. Damn, but his angry eyes were even more attractive. He leaned forward again, too close. "That is *not* how I think of you." His voice was a low growl.

I tilted my jaw up at him defiantly.

His eyes dropped to my mouth again, both of us breathing hard in our frustration. He acted like he was about to say something more, but stopped, and his face came even closer.

"Just . . . just leave, Jack." Part of me couldn't believe I was turning him down. I mean, if I was honest with myself it was going to kill me when he left regardless of whether we kissed or not. I was inexplicably drawn to him, to something inside him I had glimpsed at fleeting moments. Something vulnerable. Something similar to me.

God, I wished I could ask Jazz for advice. But I knew she would say kiss him—I mean it wasn't every day you got to kiss a Hollywood superstar.

He looked at me a few more moments, an unreadable expression on his face, and then he pulled away, turned, and walked back to the kitchen.

I heard the screen door bang shut a few seconds after that. Sliding down the wall, I buried my face in my hands. Oh my God! What was I going to do? How did I get here? I was just minding my own business and someone lobbed a grenade into my life—in the form of Jack Eversea.

CHAPTER TWELVE

$\mathcal{J}$ was up at the crack of dawn despite how late I had finally gone to sleep. I was tired, but wired. I grabbed my rubber-soled water shoes and dragged my beat-up kayak and life-vest into the back of the truck and headed over to Broad Landing on the mainland side of the island.

The marsh grasses were getting a little browner as fall went on, and low tide saw the craggy brown and gray oyster beds poking out of the soupy water. To some, whose idea of seaside towns included the blue water of the Caribbean or the clear emerald green of the Florida Panhandle, the colors of the Lowcountry could be a little dull. But to me, they were beautiful. Soothing. It was real. The murky water meant an abundance of marine life from crabs, shrimp, and oysters to bottlenose dolphins, stingrays, and visiting Atlantic whales.

Out on the water, I could breathe and think. There were huge rains forecasted for the next few days from the tropical storm, so this was the last time I could kayak for a while.

I plugged my earbuds into my phone and put Keane on shuffle. Those boys always knew how to speak to my mood. I paddled out toward the sound against the tide that had just started its six hour journey back in. It was hard on my arms and back. Panting with the exertion, I reveled in the fact my mind stayed clear and focused.

Music belted through me, spurring me on. There were a couple of shrimpers out, hauling their large nets into boats. They were surrounded by a flurry of swooping gulls, pelicans, and the churning waters of dolphins all trying to get a free breakfast. It was a sight I loved.

On a whim, I fished my phone out of my life vest and snapped a picture. My mouth made a grim line as I remembered the dream of Jack and I kayaking. Even more annoying, I wanted to send him the picture. It was so quintessentially Lowcountry. I knew he would enjoy it. Instead, I sent it to Joey with a caption: *When are you coming home?*

The music was instantly replaced with the shrill beep of an incoming call.

"That was fast." I smiled.

"You're up." Joey's voice was a welcome balm. "I was going to wait and call you in an hour or so, but then your text came in. Didn't you work last night?"

It was good to hear his voice. "Yeah, I did, but I couldn't sleep. Thought I'd take advantage of the time out here."

"It's always the best time on the water." Joey was an avid paddler, like me, and coupled with being an early riser, I knew he missed it. "Why couldn't you sleep? Is everything okay?"

"What? Oh, yeah, I just have a lot on my mind." I wondered if I should tell Joey. I knew he was trustworthy, but I had no idea if he would freak out. I tucked the phone back into the top of my life-vest and clicked on the hands-free microphone. Sticking the paddle in the water, I steered back toward the creek.

"About the house? Are they giving you a hard time again?

I swear to God, they have no fucking right." Joey always got heated about the town's meddling and the way they tried to 'citation' us into doing something. Actually, it wasn't really the whole town, just some—in particular, Pastor McDaniel, who persuaded Sheriff Graves to do it. Against the sheriff's better judgment, thank goodness. It was finally dropped, and no more citations had been issued.

"No, calm down, nothing like that. McDaniel's still annoying, but he hasn't done anything recently. Maybe because he knows Jasper and I are friends and he doesn't want to cause problems." I thought back to Sunday. "Actually, I think his latest angle is to push us together which is actually kind of funny."

"You and Jasper? Hmmm. Is that what's getting you all twisted up so you can't sleep?"

"Jeez! I'm not twisted up. Okay, maybe I am, a little, but not about Jasper, and I'm dealing with it just fine."

"But about another guy? Seriously? You *never* date. At least to my knowledge. Which I prefer by the way, since I ain't there to keep their asses in line. Well, who is it then, and should I be worried?"

I found myself jamming the paddle harder and harder, so I pulled it out of the water to slow myself down.

"No, I'm fine. If I could talk to Jazz about it, I'd be fine. I think. God, I dunno." I sighed. I had said too much, I knew it. I was going to have to come up with something to appease my overbearing and over-protective brother. I'd texted Jazz last night to let her know there was an almost kiss and that I needed to talk to her today. She would find me or text me as soon as she woke up, I was sure. In the meantime . . .

"What the hell is going on, Keri Ann?" His tone told me I was going to have to think fast. Or tell the truth.

"God, I don't know, Joey. You know Jazz and I tell each other everything—"

"Yeah, y'all are a nightmare like that."

I grinned as I remembered Joey being completely embarrassed and pissed off when he realized Jazz had shared all the details of their first kiss. Not that I had wanted all those details mind you, it being my brother and all. Ack.

The kayak rocked on an undulating wave and a breeze ruffled my hair. I made a decision. "Joey, this is big, way too big, and even though I made a promise not to talk about it, I have to tell you."

I debated exactly what to say. Joey and I were pretty close, and one thing I did know was he was trustworthy. Jazz would be told. I needed her. But it would be good to tell Joey, too. He wasn't here, so there wasn't a chance Jack would find out.

"You're freaking me out. Do I need to come back there? You're okay, right?" he asked.

Was I okay? I didn't know. I was going to break Jack's secret twice today and hope for the best.

"Are you pregnant? I swear to God—"

"No! Jeez! How did you think I went from not dating to that?"

Joey blew a breath down the line. "Thank God. Wow, that scared the shit outta me."

"Calm down, it's not that."

"Okay then, it can't be that bad. Hit me."

"I want to tell you, Joey, but you are going to have to swear to me, and I mean *swear*, like on Mom and Dad." I paused letting that sink in. We had always said we would never use them like that unless it was something super serious.

"Shit, Keri Ann, I'm freaking again. Tell me. Now."

Good. He got it.

"Okay, well, I haven't told anyone about him because first of all, there's *nothing* going on apart from us spending some time together." If you didn't count our almost kiss last night. "And second of all, he's famous, and I swore to keep his identity a secret."

It sounded really dumb to my own ears, but I knew that since I had just invoked Mom and Dad, Joey was listening. The tide was slowly pulling my kayak back into the Intracoastal Waterway, so I rested my paddle across my lap and settled back.

"Okaaaay." I could almost hear Joey's mind whirring a mile a minute trying to figure out what to ask me. "So *he* thinks he's famous, or he actually *is* famous? I mean The Situation from *Jersey Shore* thinks he's famous, but I doubt ninety-nine percent of the population would recognize him walking down the street . . . or care." He snorted.

I should've known Joey wouldn't believe me.

"Wait, it's not him is it?" he asked.

"Shut it, Joey. God, never mind, Okay? Forget I ever mentioned it." Ugh. Sometimes big brothers were a pain in the ass.

He laughed. "I'm kidding, sweetheart. Look, I don't want you mixed up with some arrogant jerk. He'd eat you for breakfast. Who is this guy?"

I could tell from his tone Joey had already stopped taking me seriously despite my having invoked our parents. How had I never noticed how condescending he could be? "I'm not a kid any more, Joey. I don't think you get to decide who I date." I was getting pissed off.

"So you are dating him, then?"

"No, I didn't say that!" I snapped. "We just hung out. I'm getting some stuff for him, and he's helping me out with the house. He helped me strip the wallpaper and . . ." I trailed off, it sounded ridiculous, even to me.

"So this big famous guy is stripping wallpaper in our house? *That* sounds normal, and what exactly is he expecting from you in return, huh?" He sounded like a father, or maybe like a vague memory I had of my dad. "Wait, how old is he?"

"Not what you're thinking." I huffed. "And he's twenty-six." I needed to end this call soon.

"So, why are you freaking out, kiddo? I mean, you say you guys are just hanging out, right? Is he making you feel unsafe? Who is this guy? I think you better tell me in case I need to whoop his ass . . . Do I need to come home?"

I sighed and rolled my eyes, thankful he couldn't see me. "No, Joey, don't be an idiot. I'm fine, I'm a big girl. And no, I'm freaking out because I do actually like him, I think, and he is waaaaay out of my league." I laughed.

Making my way across to the approaching dock, before the tide floated me right past, I grabbed on. I was careful not to dislodge my earbuds as Joey's voice boomed out of them.

"What the hell, Keri Ann? Who told you that? Did he tell you that? I *will* come and kick his ass. You're gorgeous. I always had to threaten the guys at Butler Cove High with bodily harm if they ever so much as looked at you wrong. They all thought you were hot as hell."

"What?" I got onto the dock and jerked the kayak up with more force than necessary. "You kept boys away from me?"

"Yes. You're my kid sister. Who else was going to look out for you?"

I was a little dumbfounded. I'd always thought I just wasn't that attractive to guys. Not ugly, just a bit girl-next-door plain. In the years after Mom and Dad died, I was way too in my shell to even consider dating, and after Nana died and

Joey was studying, my feelings of claustrophobia about Butler Cove precluded me from even wanting to. Being hit on by drunk tourists didn't qualify as an indicator.

I should have been annoyed. "Did you just tell me I'm gorgeous? Seriously?" It was just so surprising, I wanted to hear it again, even though I knew he was biased.

"Yes, you idiot. So don't give me that BS about this douche being out of your league."

I didn't respond as I looked out over the water. So maybe Jack was truly serious last night when he told me I was beautiful. Maybe he wasn't just putting the slick moves on me. Either way, it didn't negate the fact he had a girlfriend, contractually or not, and that any kind of relationship with him would end in tears.

"Keri Ann?"

"Yeah, I'm here."

"Who is it, then?"

I sighed. I was tired of over-thinking this, I really was.

"You swear you won't say anything? To anyone?"

"Yes."

"Okay, it's Jack Eversea." I cringed a bit as I said his name. There was a long pause.

"Jack Eversea? *The* Jack Eversea? As in the actor?"

"Yeah."

"Oh," Joey said. "Holy shit."

"Understatement," I muttered.

"Holy shit," he said again. "What the hell is he doing in Butler Cove? And how did you meet? Wait, isn't he dating someone?"

"Yes." I sounded about as thrilled as I felt about that. "Audrey Lane. That's why he's here staying at a friend's beach house and basically hiding."

"Holy shit."

"You said that already."

"Yeah, I know. Jeez. Jack Eversea." Joey's voice was awestruck. "And he's doing work in our house? What the hell? Why? Are you joking?"

"Nope, apparently he used to work construction." I laughed nervously. Hearing a movement on the gravel parking pad behind me, I turned around. Jazz was standing there, her mouth hanging open wide enough to catch a Frisbee. Shit.

"Joey, I gotta go, Jazz just found me." I tried to gauge her reaction.

"Wait!" Joey called out just as I went to hit 'end'. "Just be careful. Okay, kiddo?"

"Yeah, I'm trying. Bye." I hit the button, pulled the earbuds out of my ears, and walked toward Jazz.

CHAPTER THIRTEEN

"I'm guessing you heard that. I was going to tell you who he was, Jazz, I swear."

Jazz ripped her sunglasses off her face and looked at me like I was a rare species.

I went on, "I didn't want to keep it from you at all, and then he swore me to secrecy. But I decided I couldn't keep it to myself any more. You can't tell anyone, Jazz. You have to promise." The words tumbled out and I sounded so lame, even to my own ears. I wouldn't blame Jazz if she never spoke to me again.

"K!" She held up a hand. "I need time to process." She then proceeded to pace the parking lot with her hands on her hips.

I stopped and waited for her to *process*, at least until I thought I'd explode. "I—" I tried.

"Uh-uh," she cut me off, shaking her head and quickening her stride.

I closed my mouth. Thinking it might take her a while, I walked over to my truck and perched against the open tail-gate. I tried to look a little contrite, but man, I wanted to get over this part where she was mad at me.

"How—" She stopped and flung her arms up, letting them fall and slap her thighs as she glared at me. "I don't even know where to start. Jack Eversea is Hoodie Guy?" Her voice pitched up. "Seriously?"

I nodded.

She slowly shook her head side to side. "As in: my all time favorite actor, number one on my top ten *laminated* list. Max from *Erath*? *That* Jack Eversea?" she squeaked.

I winced and nodded sheepishly. I really was a bitch of a best friend to have kept it to myself. And yes, she had a laminated list of her top ten sexiest men who she apparently would always be allowed to sleep with even if she was married.

"Sooo," her squinted hazel eyes bore into mine, "were you worried he might prefer me over you, so you kept him to yourself?"

"God, no!" I snapped, my eyes wide. Here I was worried she would be upset I was keeping such a big secret from her, and she thought I did it deliberately to keep *him* away from her?

"No, Jazz. I don't . . . didn't—" I corrected, "like him like that."

She snorted. "I'll come back to that, and I was joking." She flipped a hand out. "Kind of. So first of all, I was worried about you. Worried." She pointed at me in emphasis. "About *you*. And you didn't confide in me. And now that I know, I'm not worried any more," she threw her arms up dramatically, "I'm completely freaked-the-fuck out!"

"Me too?" I offered tentatively. My toe was absently kicking a pebble like a naughty school kid. I willed my foot to keep still.

"You should be. Oh God, Keri Ann, why didn't you tell

me? This is huge. Are you okay? Wait, don't tell me. You're not. I can tell you're not. Because you're—"

"Naïve?" I supplied.

"No, you're Keri Ann. The *nicest* person I know. And he's—"

"Jack Eversea. I know. Joey already informed me someone like Jack would 'eat me for breakfast.'" I made the air quotes. "Why does everyone think I can't handle myself?"

Jazz looked surprised. "That's not what we think. I know you can handle yourself. I just also know you have a heart bigger than the state of Texas. If any of us could pick someone for you he would be someone solid, strong, dependable—"

"Boring?" I interjected, my eyebrow raised.

"No. Just someone who would hold your heart, or your virtue, as if it was the most precious gift he had ever been given. I might think Jack Eversea is one of the hottest men alive, but a famous Hollywood actor with women screaming for him on every street corner is not who I'd pick for you to get some experience with. Not that I have any say in the matter. Clearly." She mashed her sunglasses back on her face, and pursing her lips, put her hands back on her hips. "And," she huffed, her voice a little shaky, "you told Joey before me. *And* . . . I'm so flippin' jealous everything looks green."

"That'd be your sunglasses." I grinned, and then with a grimace, set her straight. "Well, you can relax. My virtue is safe. He is going back to Audrey Lane, so nothing is going to happen between us."

"Puh-lease. You told me you almost kissed last night, that doesn't sound like 'nothing is going to happen' to me. You better tell me the whole story."

We hauled my kayak up to the truck while I tried my best to answer her barrage of questions about what he was even doing in Butler Cove. Then we climbed into Jazz's car since her air-conditioning was a tad better than mine—as in, it actually worked. I proceeded to tell her, in minute detail, about everything that had occurred since Jack walked into the grill last week.

"Holy hell," she said when I was done. "You are in so much trouble."

"I know," I groaned, letting my head fall back against the seat.

She shook her head slowly back and forth still trying to get her mind around it. Her expression was a cross between awe and completely freaked out. I could relate. I'd seen the same look in the mirror the last few days.

"Soooo . . .?" She prompted, looking at her watch. I knew she had class this morning.

"So? I don't know. I guess we'll continue as friends, if he even shows up today. I mean it may be way too awkward, and I won't see him again."

"Let me ask you something, K—if there was no Audrey Lane in the picture would you have let him kiss you?"

"I'd like to say that was why I stopped him, but to be honest, I only found out about his weird contract with her after we almost kissed. I think I stopped him because I was scared. You know what I'm like, I tend to run when things get intense. And being with him is . . . *intense*. I've never felt anything like it. It's like I have to consciously remember to *breathe* around him."

"I get that, but scared of what?" she probed. "Is it because he's famous, or are you scared to get close to someone? I mean I know you were scared of getting tied to Butler Cove, not that I understand you wanting to leave a place where everyone cares about you, but this is not one of the local boys who you think would keep you here, as if you would let that happen anyway."

"Did you switch your major to psych?"

"Ha ha. Seriously, Keri Ann. I want to help you with this. I mean it's Jack Eversea. Most girls would kiss him just to say they had. I'm not saying I want you to be shallow, but I want you to *live* a little. Realistically, regardless of whether he has a girlfriend, he's still going to disappear back to Hollywood."

My stomach churned at that obvious truth.

Jazz continued, "And you are going to stay here not doing anything with your life until God knows when. So in the meantime, if life comes to *you*, to give *you* some amazing memories I think you should go for it. Maybe not sex, but why can't you have some fun? God knows you deserve to have a little."

I couldn't help the butterflies fizzing through my belly at the thought of giving myself permission to let something happen with Jack. I also couldn't help the dread of dealing with my poor, pathetic heartbreak when it was done.

"I'm scared of how I feel about him, Jazz. I am so attracted to him, it's scary."

"Well, duh, he's only like, the most attractive man in the universe, and coupled with the fact that we are all in love with Max from *Erath*, I can hardly blame you."

"I know, Jazz. You know how I felt about those books, I was obsessed with Max. I even dreamed about him." I'd be embarrassed to admit this if Jazz didn't already know and feel the same way.

"I know, but we've all had fantasies about Max visiting us in our sleep like that. And yes, those scenes were hot. But you are way too sensible to let that make you crazy over the actor who played him. It seems like you've spent time with him and like Jack *the person*, not the part he played."

That's what I was afraid of. And the penny dropped for Jazz too as soon as the words were out of her mouth.

"Well, shit," she said. "I guess I'll be back to the job of helping you pick up the pieces of your broken heart when he leaves. I take it back—don't let anything happen between you guys. Stay sweet and virtuous and 'un-Jacked'."

I punched her in the arm. "I'll do my best."

"Yeah, right." She sighed, and then she leaned over and gave me a quick hug, and I gave a small smile.

Her eyes twinkled. "Sooo, can I meet him?"

I laughed. "Yeah, I guess I need to tell him I broke his secret. Twice. Assuming he isn't mad about that, swing by the house on your way back from school. I have no idea if he'll even be there after our awkward encounter last night though."

"He'll be there," she said confidently as I climbed out of the car into the warm humidity. "Oh, and don't forget, on the subject of hot guys from books, it's book club this week, and we've volunteered you to host this time. Expect everyone at four tomorrow." She winked and drove off.

I'd totally forgotten about book club. Jazz had been going on and on about getting one set up and finally started one last month with Liz, Brenda from the Grill, Faith who owned the boutique where she worked, her mom, and I think she even invited Mrs. Weaton. It was a strange grouping of ages, but surprisingly, our book tastes were rather similar.

As I climbed into my truck, my phone beeped with a text. My heart sped up a moment, but it was just Jazz—texting and driving, as usual.

Jazz: I just squealed out loud at the traffic light. Ppl looking at me weird. OMG—can't believe convo we just had! But seriously, if he breaks your heart, I'll break his beautiful face—See you this PM. Xoxoxox

I smiled. She may be ditzy at times, but there was no one who looked out for me more than Jazz. She was like a sister, a crazy lovable aunt, and a best friend rolled into one. She was an old soul—that much was certain. Not for the first time, I hoped things would eventually work out for her and Joey.

CHAPTER FOURTEEN

$\mathcal{I}$ pulled into the driveway at the back of my house behind Mrs. Weaton's cottage and peeled my bare legs, like a Band-Aid, off the hot vinyl seat. I felt like every day was getting unseasonably hotter, not cooler, as we moved away from summer.

Hearing the whine and screech of a large truck, I realized they must be delivering the dumpster around the front of the house, so I jogged up the back stairs, through the blessed cool of the house, and back into the hot wet air on the front porch, trying not to look around for Jack as I did so.

Mrs. Weaton's cottage was off to the side. It used to be the old kitchen block, back from the days when kitchens were built outside to avoid the heat of the cooking in the summer months or the whole house burning down in the case of a fire. It had been remodeled into servants' quarters after the end of slavery, and then into a rent-producing cottage once the land started being sold off after the depression.

José was out front speaking in Spanish to the two guys who were with him unloading packs of roofing shingles. I made sure everyone knew what they were doing and directed the guy with the dumpster to drive around to the back of the property before the town council had a kitten about it being parked askew on my front lawn. Then I went to knock on Mrs. Weaton's door. I waited a few minutes and after getting no answer, headed back to my place.

Upon re-entering my house through the front door, I heard a cackle and a deep chuckle coming from the kitchen. Lo and behold, there sat Jack and Mrs. Weaton hamming it up over coffee at the table. She was giggling like a schoolgirl, her bony hand on his arm, and he had his head bent toward hers conspiratorially.

They both turned and looked at me guiltily as I walked in. I tried not to look at Jack and instead focused on my elderly neighbor as she greeted me.

"Hi, dear! Jack was just keeping me entertained with secrets of Hollywood while that awful racket was going on outside the house. But I must be off!"

Wow, he was really getting comfortable trusting people.

Mrs. Weaton patted his shoulder, and I noticed his nonplussed expression.

She grabbed me for a quick squeeze, enveloping me in a waft of lavender and cinnamon. "See you tomorrow at book club. I'll bring lemon squares." She pulled back and held me at arm's length, a big grin on her friendly, lined face. Then pulling me in for another quick hug, she whispered, "Nana works in mysterious ways." And with that she shuffled out to the hall.

I turned back to Jack whose jaw was slack.

"Oh my God, she knows who I am. Did you tell her?"

"No. I thought *you* must have. I haven't spoken to her since I told her about the roofers. What were you talking about then, if you weren't filling her in on star gossip?"

"You. Funny childhood stories about you."

"Oh." How horrifying. "Like what?"

He grinned and winked. "Well, I quite like knowing something about you that you don't know I know. It's a novel feeling for me to be on the other side of that."

"Okaaaay." I decided to let that go. For now. "Any more of that coffee?"

"Sure." He looked me up and down as he stood and walked round to the coffee maker. It was amazing how comfortable he looked in my house. "Where've you been?"

I was instantly self-conscious of my barely there Lycra athletic shorts and tank. "Uh, kayaking."

"Did you manage not to side swipe any bikers on your way home?" He handed me a cup of coffee with cream.

Self-conscious turned into unbelievably embarrassed at his mention of our near miss. I was kind of hoping he hadn't put the whole thing together. "Um . . ." I managed, flustered.

He winked. "Kidding. So was it fun?"

I exhaled and tried to smile. "Yeah. It wasn't long though, I ended up chatting with Joey and also Jazz came and found me." I realized I should tell him sooner rather than later. "Mrs. Weaton isn't the only Butler Cove resident who knows of your existence, I told Joey and Jazz," I admitted, wincing.

He stilled in the act of pouring himself another cup. Then he put it down and braced his forearms against the counter, his back to me and his head hanging down. The action brought his shoulder blades into sharp focus beneath the same dark green tee he'd been wearing last night.

He sighed. "Then it's just a matter of time, isn't it?" He went back to pouring his coffee.

"Until what?"

"Until someone calls in the story for a small fortune."

"They wouldn't do that."

"People will do anything for money, Keri Ann." He turned to me with an expression that said I should have known better.

"These people won't."

"Why don't *you* do it?" he asked, pushing off the counter and coming toward me.

"Do what?"

"Call it in. You could renovate this kitchen with the money. Heck, probably the whole house." He raised his eyebrows.

"I wouldn't ever do that!" I was outraged. How could he say he trusted me one day, although I'd obviously broken that trust by telling two, no, make that three people, including Hector, and then ask me if I'd sell him out the next?

He stopped in front of me but looked into the distance. "I know you wouldn't."

"How?" I asked.

"How do I know you wouldn't sell me out?"

"Yeah. Especially since I admitted to outing you to two people just this morning."

He lifted a hand and ran it through his unruly hair. It caused my eyes to drop to his broad chest. "Well, here's the thing, it seems to me you have a lot of people around here who care very deeply for you, and I doubt they would jeopardize you by selling *me* out, so I guess that makes me lucky to know you."

I shrugged, warmed by his observation, and took a sip of coffee to cover my nerves at his nearness. I was relieved neither of us felt we had to mention our awkward almost kiss the night before. We could just move on as friends, as if the moment never occurred. As if just remembering my tongue touching his thumb by accident, and the sound he made when it happened, didn't have my insides flipping over again. But sure, if he could forget so could I.

Yeah, right.

"Do you need to stay at the house today?" he asked.

I looked around. The walls were bare and washed and ready for paint. The floors needed to be sanded, cleaned, and stained, but that would require renting equipment, and I needed funds for that. The roofers would be busy all day, and I didn't have to work until tomorrow. But there were always things I could be doing like cleaning, finishing the front porch, picking a paint color, working on some of my sea-glass and driftwood projects.

"I guess not, but—"

"Great," Jack interjected. "Grab your swimsuit and whatever else you need for a day on the water. You are going to teach me to paddleboard. There's some equipment under the beach house and we may as well take advantage of this good weather before the storm gets any closer."

Swimsuit? My only swimsuit was a white string bikini Jazz had persuaded me to buy two summers ago. My black one piece had recently given up the ghost, and by that I meant it had become almost completely see-through. I could probably swim in the lycra shorts and tank I was wearing or I could just bite the bullet and try and be normal and unselfconscious.

"Uh . . . sure. Let me just run upstairs and grab some stuff."

The water was a little choppier than it had been that morning, but still calm enough to learn to paddleboard. We dragged the oversized surf-looking board out from under the beach house and over the small dune path. I was still wearing what I had kayaked in, but Jack had changed into the black board shorts I had seen him in the first morning he ran over to my house. I tried to watch where I was putting my feet rather than his muscly back carrying half the board right in front of me. It was mighty hard though, so I gave in and did an inventory of his body while he couldn't see me.

His right arm with the medallion tattoo, signifying he was a Warrior of Erath, was flexed with the weight of the board, and his tan shoulder blades were dusted with the odd mole and freckle from time in the sun. On his left hip I could see a tendril of black ink from some hidden tattoo peeking out from his shorts.

I inhaled over the lump that seemed to be permanently lodged in my chest. His long legs had a sprinkling of dark hair over his calves and a chain of ink around his right ankle. God, even his feet were beautiful. And I kind of hated feet. How did people get made like this? We made it to the beach without me tripping.

Luckily, the tidal gullies that formed like long rivers in the low parts of the beach were still there and stretched out parallel to the ocean for several hundred yards in either direction. We wouldn't have long until the tide was in. I directed him to the gully and we lowered the board in.

"This is a great way to learn, because you won't be as afraid of your balance in twelve inches of water as you will out there with the swell of waves."

There wasn't anyone on the beach in our area as far as I could see. It was the middle of the week and we were in a section of seasonal rentals. "I'll show you first."

I grabbed the paddle and showed him how to straddle the board a bit further forward from where you wanted to end up and work your knees onto it. Then I tucked my toes under and with a hand bracing and balancing me, I used my bent knees to slowly raise myself into a standing position with my feet on the outer edges of the board rather than one in front of the other as one would on a surfboard. Using the paddle, I stuck it in the water to my side and used it to propel myself forward. Then I changed sides.

"See? Easy as pie. Just make sure and use your body, not your arms to paddle." I grinned at him walking along beside me on the sand. "And to keep your legs slightly bent with your weight centered. Your turn," I said, hopping off and using a foot to stop the board continuing away from us. We switched places. He was a fast learner.

We went back and forth along the gully until it almost disappeared with the incoming tide.

He nodded out at the water. "Time for the deep blue sea?"

"Yeah, you think you can keep your balance with me sitting on the end?" I challenged him.

"Is that even possible?"

"Well, I weigh a little more than a Golden Retriever, but I've seen it done with them, so let's give it a shot." I grinned.

I directed him to move his feet back a little, carefully climbed onto the board facing him, and crossed my legs. He was bracing all his muscles tight to keep the board from tipping, and I swore I could see every single muscle he had. We got to a balance point and he paddled toward the end of the gully that naturally curved toward the open sea.

"Wow, this is a workout." He laughed as he turned the board and slowly slid over the small lapping waves out toward the ocean.

"Yeah, people actually do yoga on paddleboards if you can believe that."

"I'll be doing that in no time," he joked. "My abs are steel fortresses that can handle anything."

"I noticed," I said, and then looked away quickly as I felt my cheeks heat. He cleared his throat but didn't say anything, and I mentally kicked myself for creating an awkward moment just when we had gotten past our almost kiss. I didn't notice we had gone a little too far out and suddenly a wave came on at an angle to the board. I braced to hang on, but we tipped and both of us splashed sideways into the water. I came up sputtering and lunged onto the board as he treaded water next to me, laughing a big throaty chuckle.

"You did that on purpose!" I yelped.

He tipped his head back and laughed again.

"Seriously, I am terrified of sharks, get me back on the fucking board." I tried unsuccessfully and ungracefully to kick my upper body onto the board amid the undulating waves as Jack tried to get his laughter under control.

I glared at him. "Could you help me at least?"

"Can't you stand?"

At that point I realized Jack had the upper part of his chest out of the water. Mortified, I lowered my tiptoes to the invisible sandy bottom, but I could only reach it between each wave.

"There are still sharks out here, you know," I said petulantly. I wasn't kidding. I was also a complete coward when it came to swimming in 'dark water' as I called it. I really couldn't even get in a lake without shuddering. Call it an overactive imagination, but I would rather be 'on' the water than 'in' it. Jack must have seen something on my face because he instantly stopped laughing and came close. He laid the paddle on the board and came next to me.

"Hold onto the board and lift a leg up," he said, reaching down into the water.

All thoughts of sharks fled as I felt his hands make contact with the bare skin of my thigh and his fingers run down behind my knee. A shark could have nose-butted me right then, and I would have only swatted it away. Flicking my eyes down nervously, and trying to keep my breathing even, I lifted my leg and his hand continued down to my foot where he cupped it into a stirrup.

"Thanks," I mumbled, glancing at him.

"No sweat." He nodded tightly.

Completely embarrassed by my idiotic outburst and reeling from his touch, I went to climb onto the board, but all of a sudden Jack let go of my foot and pulled me against him. I gasped and instinctively grabbed hold of his hard shoulders.

The contact of my sliding skin against his in the water made my heart pound in my throat and something uncomfortable happen deep in my belly. His arm at my waist gripped me hard as each new swell of water gently rocked us. I looked up at him.

A bead of salt water trickled from his water-darkened hair down the side of his face to his full mouth. I braced myself to look into his eyes, but before I could, he tucked his face in close to my jaw, his stubble setting my nerves on fire.

Breathe, Keri Ann, breathe. So much for us ignoring the almost kiss and being just friends. Clearly, he was having a hard time with that. I gritted my teeth. So was I.

He suddenly pulled away, and his arm shot out to grab the paddleboard before it got out of reach. "We almost lost that." He grinned.

I blinked, confused, as he resumed helping me up onto the board.

"You paddle, I better swim back," he said, then turned and cut through the swells with strong strokes.

What on earth had that been about? I took a deep breath and paddled slowly back to shallower water on my knees before standing up.

He'd almost kissed me again. Actually, I had almost kissed *him*. One more second and I would have. All the reasons I had last night for not doing it just didn't seem to matter any more.

CHAPTER FIFTEEN

Jack and I didn't say much on our way back to the beach house until he handed me a beach towel and suggested I change so he could throw my wet stuff in the laundry.

Grabbing my backpack, I stepped into a downstairs bathroom.

We'd talked earlier about hanging out by the pool after we paddleboarded and eating some sandwiches for lunch, so I figured it was time to break out the bikini.

Drawing my confidence together, I pulled it out of my bag along with the matching and way too gauzy white cover-up. I put the bikini on and adjusted the ties, making sure there wouldn't be a wardrobe malfunction displaying my assets. My breasts weren't overly large, but looking in the mirror and taking in the white triangles on my top half, I felt like an awkward offering. Quickly, I pulled the cover-up on too, noting it had been severely misnamed. Since I had nothing else to wear, there was nothing to do but be confident in myself.

My hair was wet and full of salt and sand, which I would have to deal with later after the pool. I let it out of its hair tie and used my hands to shake it loose so it could dry faster.

At least the salt water helped it dry with a little wave and body. I grabbed up my bundle of wet clothes and headed for the laundry room.

Still in his swimsuit, he must have only brought the one, Jack was throwing a bunch of his clothes in the dryer. Barely turning around, he grabbed my sodden stuff.

"Thanks," I said.

He shrugged. "Sure, no problem."

He still hadn't turned around, and his shoulders looked tense.

"Are you okay? Do you want me to go?" I didn't want to hang around if I was only pissing him off. Besides, it was no picnic for me either. If being around Jack was fraught with tension on a normal day, this moment was totally throwing me off-kilter.

"No. It's okay."

He glanced over his shoulder at me, and then at my outfit and shook his head.

"What?" I asked, self-consciously.

"Nothing. You hungry?" he said, still shaking his head with what looked like a rueful smile.

I nodded.

He made no move to go anywhere though; he just turned and leaned back against the machine, his arms folded across his chest. His eyes slid slowly down my entire body.

My belly flip-flopped with enough waves to make a sailor sick. If he could just stop looking at me like that.

"It's not fair," I whispered, deciding it was time to address the issue.

"What's not fair?"

"What you're asking of me." Wow. I had really just said that, I was going to take this bull by the horns.

"Do you want to spell it out for me? What is it you think I'm asking of you?"

I stared at him, incredulous.

"Are you serious? You can't be that obtuse. Look at you. I was already half in love with you before I even met you because of the character you played, and you are totally taking advantage of that right now. I guess that makes me an easy target, but I'm out of my depth, Jack." I steeled my nerves, my voice shaking slightly. But I was right to do this. I couldn't be on tenterhooks the whole time with these almost kissing moments. It might kill me.

"I'm just a normal girl, and I'm definitely not sophisticated enough to deal with you wandering off back to your girlfriend and your Hollywood life when you are done here."

"So you *are* only attracted to me because of Max? I mean, you mentioned it last night, and I kind of hoped you were joking."

"It's not because of Max." I owed him the truth, and in that moment I knew even if it had been the initial reason—it wasn't any more.

He nodded, a cynical look in his eyes. "Yeah, right."

"Well, it's the truth. Not that it changes anything." I thought I sounded bitter. Well, so what if I did? I was basically admitting I was attracted to him, and he was asking for permission to break my heart. Way to go, Keri Ann.

"Of course it does. It changes everything." He pushed away and stood right in front of me, too close but not close enough. He seemed to struggle a moment, as if he couldn't articulate what he was thinking.

"God," he finally said, his tone exasperated. "Do you think it's normal for people to feel this," he motioned between us, "whatever this is that happens when we are in the same room with each other? Maybe *you* have no idea, but I do. It. Doesn't. Happen. At least not to me." He stopped, seemingly surprised by his admission.

I was too. I held my breath, my heart thudding.

He sighed and went on, "I can't make you the promises you probably want, Keri Ann, I'll only break them. But I can promise you I'll always tell you the truth."

Great. How could the perfect man come along and tell you he was feeling all the same feelings you were, but you couldn't keep him?

"The truth? And what is that exactly?"

He was quiet so long, I thought he wasn't going to answer. Then he raised his eyes to mine. "The truth is . . . you're right. It's not fair what I am asking of you. I want you."

Time slowed down as his words floated around me. He wanted me. I didn't know people said that to each other in real life. Now, Jack Eversea 'wanted' *me*. My pulse ticked in my clogged throat.

He went on, his eyes never leaving me. "I have never wanted to kiss someone as badly as I want to kiss you right now. Ever. But I *am* going to leave here. I have to. I have to go back to Audrey. It's a pretty messed-up situation, but I'm not going to lie to you and say my relationship with her wasn't real because it was, for a long time. But it has also been over for a very long time." He took a breath and ran a hand through his hair. "Or should have been. Shit, I shouldn't even be having this conversation with you. You are absolutely right to tell me no."

But God, I wanted to say yes. I wanted to make a move, badly. It was like being strung out over an abyss. Whether I made a move or not wouldn't make a difference in whether I would make it across, but only how fast I would hit the bottom. And hit the bottom I would, as soon as he left, but I would be okay. I would survive it. He was just a boy, at the end of the day.

If I couldn't handle these *almost* moments, then I decided I should just turn them into moments. If I was going down, I might as well go down hard. I stepped a little closer.

Our bodies skimmed against each other, and the light contact created arcs of snapping current. I felt it from my head to my toes and everywhere between. Jack's breathing turned irregular at my boldness, his expression unreadable, like he was trying hard not to react.

My breasts, which now felt full and achy and unfamiliar, pressed against his chest, and I raised my face to his. "I don't want to tell you no." My admission hung in the air, accompanied by the steady thunk, thunk, thunk of my wet clothes tossing in the drum behind him, lending a throbbing cadence to the already heavy atmosphere between us.

His green eyes turned dark and hooded as he lowered his head. There was that smell of pine and waterfalls again, now mixed with salty southern sea air.

His face was inches from mine, and a flush crossed his cheekbones. "So tell me yes," he whispered, his warm breath fanning across my mouth. Then his hands were at my sides, his searing fingers curling into my hips and pressing me hard against his body. As I felt how turned on he was, arousal flared through me, making me feel light-headed. I gulped nervously, but steeled my resolve.

It was just a kiss. That was all I wanted. I don't know how I knew Jack would never push me beyond what I was ready for, but I did. And what I was ready for was his mouth on mine.

"Yes," I said, simply.

I could almost see his pupils dilate. One of his hands came up and curled into my hair at my nape, tugging my head back. He hesitated just once, and then his mouth—his warm, delicious mouth—covered mine.

His lips were amazing—hard and soft at the same time. They coaxed and moved over mine until I let out a small sigh—relief at finally having his lips on me. It was like finding water at the end of a long, hot trek. His unshaven jaw was rough and exquisite on my skin and all I could think, as I clutched his shoulders and wound a hand up into his soft, damp hair, our lips moving together, was that I wanted more. I wanted to taste more. I needed more of him. More. More.

Tendrils of warmth ignited through me. We both moved at the same time, and my hand tightened on his neck as he pulled me harder against him. And then his tongue slid into my mouth. I whimpered as the soft warmth burst into a flare of searing heat deep inside me.

He tasted of salt and coffee and mint.

He tasted of Jack.

My tongue returned his thrust as I became parched and desperate for him. My reaction caused a low rumble through Jack's chest. I had no idea it could feel this way. Even my skin was on fire, like every nerve in my body could feel what he was doing to me with his mouth. I wanted to do this forever.

Suddenly, I found myself turned and pressed back against the dryer, and then Jack was lifting me and stepping between my legs.

"Cold!" I gasped against his mouth as the icy metal of the appliance met the heat of my thighs.

Jack chuckled. "Sorry." And then the heat of his kiss took over again.

After a few drugging and decadent moments, his mouth moved away from mine and slid to my throat and up to my ear, his hot breath and moist lips causing me to shudder.

My hands roamed over the smooth skin of his back. I was completely lost. His mouth came back and captured mine again. In my new position, I pressed myself even more firmly against his body, straining to ease the aching void that had somehow sprung up inside me, causing him to make a small sound in the back of his throat.

All I wanted was Jack.

He must have had a moment of rational thought, because he gave me one last drugging kiss and pulled his mouth from mine, putting a small piece of space between our bodies. His ragged breathing mingled with my own, and he dropped his forehead against mine.

My mouth reached for his again of its own volition.

He nipped at my lips and backed away again, his face flushed, his eyes dark and glazed.

"God," he said, between breaths. "If that's what you kiss like with no experience . . ."

I smiled and threaded one hand through his gorgeous soft hair. He pressed his mouth into the crook of my neck as I tipped my head back, and I couldn't help moan as his teeth nipped and sucked at my skin. I rocked against him again. His erection, rather than making me nervous, ignited some primal part of my womanhood. Could it really be *me* that made him feel this way?

His voice breathed into my neck. "You have to stop, *we* have to stop . . . or I won't be able to."

What was I doing? I couldn't believe I could lose complete control this fast. I didn't want to stop. It was *wanton*, as my Nana would say. My God, he was right. We had to stop. I couldn't believe I had let a simple kiss get so out of hand. I was terrified to realize that if Jack hadn't stopped, I would have let him take my virginity right there in the laundry room. In fact, I'd never wanted anything more. He stepped back, and we both struggled to get our breathing under control. The more we settled back to earth, the more horrified I was at my behavior.

"I'm sorry," I muttered, a little mortified by the way I had thrown myself at him.

He smiled, but his brow furrowed. "What for?"

"I can't believe I just did that, and that I . . . let it . . . get so . . . um . . ."

"Out of control? Well, there were two of us there, sweetheart."

"Don't call me that. It makes me feel young . . . and naïve."

"Well, you *are* young. But after that kiss, I wouldn't call you naïve." He chuckled.

I pressed my lips together in indignation and punched him right on his tattoo.

He laughed louder. "You're cute."

"Stop it. I'm not cute."

"Okay." He reached out and brushed a piece of hair off my cheek. Even that sweet simple gesture had me sizzling.

"I've just . . . uh . . . I've never felt anything like that before," I offered, honestly.

He sighed. "Me either, Keri Ann. So I guess that makes two of us."

CHAPTER SIXTEEN

$\mathcal{I}$ couldn't remember the last time I had spent a day not working on something to do with the house. At about two o'clock— exactly two hours and fifteen minutes after Jack and I had kissed in the laundry room—I was clutching my sides with laughter at stories he was telling me about some of his first auditions. He had almost landed on the proverbial 'casting couch' and also once mistakenly ended up at a porn movie audition.

We were lying on the sun loungers by the pool, and periodically we would trade quotes from *The Princess Bride* trying to one up each other. I was taking my cover-up off when he quoted that there was "a shortage of perfect breasts in the world". That shut me up. I wasn't going to win that one.

I was getting a very tanned front because I was too nervous to ask Jack to put sunscreen on my back. Despite that, I couldn't believe how comfortable I suddenly was with him. I still felt like I was plugged into an electrical outlet in the sense that my nerves were aware of him at any given moment, but somehow having kissed him, and even though I wanted to do it again, as soon as possible, I felt like a small pressure valve had been tapped. Slightly.

"So why doesn't Keri Ann Butler have a boyfriend?" Jack's sudden question caught me by surprise. I looked over at him. He looked genuinely interested.

"Who's to say she doesn't?" I threw back at him, to cover my nerves.

"Your history of kissing, or lack thereof, for one."

"Maybe I just have a hand-holding boyfriend." I smirked.

"Sweetheart, I'm not sure what kind of men they make around here, but they'd have to be made of stone to settle for just holding your hand." My insides flipped. He continued, "So do you?"

"Do I what?"

"Have a hand-holding boyfriend?"

"No." I sighed. "I haven't been that interested in anyone. Plus no one's really asked, but that could also be because I have a protective older brother who I recently found out threatened anyone who might."

"Seriously? Wow, what did he say when you told him about me?"

"He said, 'Be careful.' He could have been referring to me, or in fact, you." I grinned.

Jack laughed, and then reached out and took my hand. It shocked me into silence. I looked at him.

He just closed his eyes, a dimple still showing, and turned his face back up to the sun.

I swallowed the large lump in my throat. What was he doing?

"So why did you want to act?" I asked to cover my reaction to his gesture. I was sure this was a classic interview question, but I was curious, and the silence was way too heavy with my hand in his.

He looked at me like it was the first time it had been asked.

"What?" I said, defensively. "And no, I don't already know the answer to that question either."

"It's not that." He shook his head. "I've never answered it honestly."

"Really? Why?"

Jack let go of my hand abruptly, got up from the lounger, and stepped off the edge of the pool into the deep end. I flexed my hand, missing him terribly already. He propped himself up on his elbows at the side of the pool as he seemed to consider my question.

"It's just that I don't want other people to be bothered. It's the same reason I keep my mum out of the spotlight. They—other people in my life—didn't make a decision to become a public figure like I did. Not that I really thought about becoming this famous when I started out. I just wanted to act. I loved it. I love it," he corrected.

I nodded. It made sense to me. I actually found it kind of honorable that he would try to keep the insanity of his life away from others he cared about.

"So who are the others, apart from your mom?"

"Well, to answer your first question, the person who totally inspired me to pursue this, probably more than I realized at the time, was the headmaster at the school I was at in England. I guess you call them principals here." He ran a hand idly across the surface of the water. "But Mr. Chaplin was the headmaster at the boarding school I was at. He taught math—or 'maths' as we called it—and he also put on these elaborate productions at school that people had to audition for and rehearse for months. We would perform six or seven times for all the parents who wanted to see it at the end of the year. It was usually sold out. They were musicals, mostly." He grinned at my raised eyebrows. "Yeah, I can sing."

"Wait, you used to sing in musicals? How come the tabloids haven't tracked down any of *those* pictures? Or maybe they have . . . Jazz would know."

"Why would Jazz know?"

"Oh yeah, I forgot to tell you. She is your *biggest* fan. She almost fainted when she found out about you this morning."

A shadow passed over his face again.

I rolled my eyes. "Seriously, you don't know her, but trust me, she's been my best friend since almost the first day I moved here, she'll keep it to herself. Besides," I added, "if she tells anyone, she'll have to share you." I suddenly remembered Jazz was going to come looking for me at my place that afternoon. "On that note, I told her she could meet you, is that okay?"

He slunk down and dunked his head under the surface. When he popped back up, with water streaming down his face and body, I had to quickly look away before I embarrassed myself by drooling or something. He flicked the water from his dark, glossy hair with a quick shake of his head and leaned forward on his forearms again.

"Uh, yeah, I guess so." He fixed me with a dark look. "But that means I have to share *you*. That's not fair."

Wow. I gulped.

"Do you know how many times a day you blush?" His dimple made an appearance.

I ducked my head in mock chagrin. "Yes," I mumbled, but I couldn't help returning his smile. "I can feel it."

"It's sexy as hell."

"Uh . . . um," I stuttered, my cheeks even warmer. "Thank you? I think?"

He shrugged, like it was no big deal. Inside, I was dancing.

"Sooo, back to the topic at hand," I said, when my voice was steady. "You . . . you sang in musicals? I'm not sure I can picture that."

"Yeah, well, I wasn't some flamboyant Broadway wannabe. I was shy and young. Mr. Chaplin was always trying to build confidence in kids, not that I recognized that at the time. He was so passionate about getting the kids you least expected and putting them in these parts that built character and confidence and respect from our classmates. I look back on that and realize what he did for me. In fact, what that school in general did for me."

"Wait," I said, doing the math and watching Jack carefully. "You said you left England when you were nine, so how come you were in boarding school at such a young age? How long were you there?"

Who put their kids in a boarding school in second or third grade . . . or younger? My heart squeezed. There was such a slight tightening of his jaw I almost missed it.

He left the wall and stretched his body back doing a couple of strokes into the middle of the pool. "Oh well, it was just what some people did in England back then, and I wanted to go. We had some family friends whose son was there and loved it. He raved about it one summer, and I begged to go." He shrugged as if that's all there was to it and slipped under the water again. Something didn't ring true about that last part, but I decided to let it go.

I waited until he emerged and circled back away from that line of questioning. "So, this principal of yours, Mr. Chaplin, must be proud of you. Does he know how much he inspired you?"

What an amazing gift to give a teacher, to know how you changed a kid's life, and even more that the child had grown up to become world famous. I shook my head with wonder. I couldn't remember any teacher having such an impact on me, although I'd liked my English and art teacher in high school. But it was mostly Nana who had inspired my love for the written word and allowed my creativity to flourish. She and I, with all of the art projects we would work on all summer long, and look what I'd done with it . . . a big fat nothing. Yet. My heart squeezed as I thought of Nana. I missed her so much. I wondered what she would think of Jack. If she would approve.

"Mr. Chaplin, as far as I know, has no idea."

"He *must* know, I mean surely you are as famous over there as you are here." In fact, the Erath saga was a global phenomenon. There was no way he wasn't recognized the world over.

I was obviously straying into dangerous territory again. I hadn't meant to. Jack turned without answering and broke into a powerful stroke. Though we'd only known each other a few days, I was already picking up cues for when he was uncomfortable. When he turned at the other end, I quickly moved to the edge of the pool where he was headed and slipped my feet into the water.

"I'm sorry," I said as he came up in front of me. "It's none of my business. I'm not trying to pry, I was just curious about you. What makes you . . . you. But, as I said, it's none of my business. I'll stop." I smiled. "Sooo, how about this fall weather we're having? Hmm?" I waggled my eyebrows trying to lighten the mood.

"Yeah," he said, going along with it for a moment. "Gorgeous."

I waited. He seemed like he might say more.

He did. "My life in England is not something I talk about. Ever. I'm sorry. I will tell you, though," he took a deep breath and looked up at me, "that the reason Mr. Chaplin doesn't know who I am is because I wasn't Jack Eversea back then. My mother and I changed our names when we came here. In fact, she doesn't go by Eversea any more either since she remarried. So, for the most part, no one bothers her, which is how we both like it."

My vivid imagination could only grapple with the kind of reasons a mother would first put her young child in a boarding school, and then flee to another country and change their names. My stomach churned at his words, and my heart hurt. He must have seen my reaction, because he came forward and put a hand on each knee. My pulse sped up.

"Don't, Keri Ann. Don't feel sorry for me. It's not something I want to talk about, but suffice it to say that for some reason, you know more than anyone. It's not that bad. If it was, I would never have put myself in such a public position." I wanted to feel warm and fuzzy that he had confided in me just a little, but knowing the little bit was torture. "Okay?" he asked.

"I wish you hadn't told me anything," I said quietly. I saw a flash of something in his eyes, and just as quickly, it was gone. I realized my words could have sounded callous, I hadn't meant them that way.

"Me too." He made to move away, but I grabbed his arm.

"Wait," I said, in case he had been about to shut me out, or swim away. "That didn't come out right. I didn't mean you couldn't tell me, or that I . . . well . . ."

He shook his head. "It's fine, Keri Ann."

"It's not fine. I just want you to know, I wished you hadn't told me because . . . I care about you. I'm not pitying you, I care about you." I paused. I really did care about him—as crazy as that could be after only knowing someone a few days. And I didn't mean in the way you care about another human, just because you're human. But I'd keep *that* tidbit to myself until my grave.

I decided to forge ahead. "When you care about someone, you don't like to think of them hurting whether now or way in the past. Especially when you can't fix it. That's all I meant by saying that. In reality, I want to know everything about you, but I understand your boundaries." I took a deep breath and shrugged. "I have them, too."

He didn't say anything for a moment, and then suddenly I was squealing as he grabbed my waist and pulled me down into the water with a huge ungraceful splash. As soon as I surfaced, I smacked a wave of water at his face. This was a skill I had perfected defending myself from an older brother.

"Hey," he yelled and returned the gesture. I quickly slid down under the water and swam away.

When I popped up at the other end of the pool laughing, Jack was still where I'd left him leaning against the wall watching me. Even without the safety of my sunglasses on, I was unable to hide the fact my eyes wanted to take in every mound, curve, and ridge of his muscled body. It was truly a work of art. It wasn't that steroid-fueled over-worked body-builder type, but he was tall and obviously packed with strength. I swallowed my nerves as I let my eyes slide down his abs to the vee his hips made as they disappeared into his shorts.

"You'd better stop that," he said, his voice husky.

I didn't want to stop. I wanted to kiss him again, but I didn't want to be so forward. So I shook my head.

"No?" he asked.

"No."

I leaned back and rested my elbows behind me on the ledge, mimicking his stance. A challenge. I almost didn't recognize this new me.

His eyes narrowed as if he was trying to suss me out. I realized my position had thrust my bikini-clad chest forward, but it was too late to suddenly get shy.

"Come here," he commanded, quietly.

I held his eyes. "You come here," I countered.

His dimple reappeared as he shook his head slightly with a small lopsided and bemused smile, and then he swam four strong freestyle strokes to stand in front of me.

Breathe, Keri Ann, breathe, I reminded myself for the second time that day. I stayed perfectly still as he held my eyes. His wet skin and hair made his eyes startling. Then he stepped forward between my legs, pushing my feet apart. My pulse tripped over itself.

"This is a good spot," he murmured, echoing my unformed thoughts exactly. His hands came to my bare waist, the water allowing his skin to slide across mine. It was exquisite, and despite the warmth of the sun, goose bumps formed all over me as the fine hairs of my body reacted to the sensation. I wondered briefly what it would feel like to be fully naked and pressed against his skin.

"What was that?" Jack asked with a grin.

"What?"

"That thing you do when you suddenly bite your lip and you blush furiously."

"Um . . ."

"You did it when I was giving you a tour of the house the other day and a few other times."

There was no way I was telling him the truth. "Uh . . . it's just when I'm feeling nervous," I offered, staring at his mouth. I sounded way too breathy. Ugh, it was like some bad movie. Except Jack was starring in it, so I was riveted to the spot.

"I thought you became bitchy when you were nervous," he answered, his face inching closer to mine. "I think you were thinking about something . . ." his lips came closer still ". . . else."

I shook my head slightly.

"Liar," he whispered.

"Arrogant ass," I whispered back.

"Ahhh, there she is." He chuckled slightly, his eyes never leaving my mouth. Then one hand left my waist and trailed down my hip and thigh just as warm fingers from his other hand drifted to my belly and trailed up between my breasts to splay on my chest.

My breathing hitched as it got shallower and more rapid. I was sure he could probably feel my heart about to pound out of my chest.

His hand continued its journey up to my throat and around to cup the back of my neck at the same time as he pulled my thigh up against his body and pressed against me.

I let out a whimper as sensation jolted through me, leaving a hot, molten and needy ache at my center. *Holy shit,* I thought. And then any coherent follow up was lost as his lips crashed into mine.

If I had thought the fire he had ignited in me during our first kiss had been intense, it was nothing compared to the inferno now billowing through me.

It was like all of me, all of my childish yearning and wanting, all the emotional trauma and denying myself feelings like this, every single moment of every single book and movie that had made me quietly wish for more, while studiously avoiding anything that would bring it to me, was swept up and out of me in a tidal wave of longing. And *yes*, I thought, *yes to it all*.

Jack's hands roamed along my skin leaving a scorching trail before his fingers worked the knot at my nape. His hot mouth left mine and trailed kisses down under my ear. A really sensitive spot, I'd discovered.

I moaned and rocked against him without thinking and heard his sharp intake of breath as his fingers fumbled and he cursed. I wanted to do it again, to relieve some of what I was feeling. But I wasn't so innocent I didn't know what that might entail.

"God, Keri Ann," he rasped, and his mouth claimed mine again, his tongue sliding against my own. I kissed him back with everything I was feeling, wrapping myself around him.

He pulled his mouth from mine a few moments later as my bikini straps came loose in his hand and slid down my chest. We were both breathing hard. His eyes looked glazed, I'm sure mine must have too.

I was solely and completely aware of him and of every single part of my body that was in contact with his.

"We have to slow down," he whispered roughly, as his gaze involuntarily dropped to where the small white triangles covering my breasts were a second away from revealing me to him.

"I *have* to slow down," he said again but instead kissed my lips slowly, his tongue sliding along my lower lip in a way that did nothing to make me want to stop. In fact, I swear I thought I felt it in other parts of my body. I wanted his hands on me. But he took my bikini straps and pulled them back behind my neck fastening them as he pressed small chaste kisses along my face and cheeks.

Oh no. Don't stop.

He was right, of course. Twice in the same day and the first time I had ever kissed anyone like this, and I was ready to throw caution to the wind. Strangely enough, I wasn't as horrified with myself as I had been this morning, but I also knew I wasn't ready. I already knew, despite my inexperience, that anything more happening with Jack would push my precarious heart over the edge. And he still had unfinished business with his ex. That should be a deal breaker—but at that moment, with every part of my body throbbing, I had trouble remembering why it should be so important.

The distant chime of the doorbell broke through our haze.

Jack tensed and, pulling away from me, turned to the edge of the pool. After several moments of mumbling something that sounded suspiciously like "dead puppies, dead puppies, dead puppies", he lifted himself out.

I raised my eyebrows, and he winked at me with a grin before reaching for his shirt.

CHAPTER SEVENTEEN

$\mathcal{J}$ack pulled his shirt on and went to check if it was his anticipated delivery from his assistant in California.

I offered to sign for it, but he said he'd arranged for deliveries to be dropped at his door.

After he left, I toweled off and lay back on the lounger to catch my breath. Checking my phone, I found a text from Jazz.

> *Jazz: Leaving campus now, back in 30. Headed to you. So excited . . . SQUEEE!*

I checked the time and quickly tapped a text back to her before she got to my place.

> *Me: not home, at his, come here . . .*

I wondered if I should ask Jack first, then I decided if Jazz knew about Jack, she may as well know where I was, too. I sent her the address just as another phone beeped from the other chair. Jack's phone.

Instinctively, I reached for it, then froze. I wanted to look at it so badly. At the very least I thought I should probably take it to him . . . and if I happened to see his text on the way? What if it was from Audrey? It was none of my business, except that the Audrey angle really affected me . . . I struggled with the temptation to grab his phone and realized I was staring at it like it was a coiled-up Copperhead snake.

I needed to talk to Jack about what his plans were with Audrey. I knew he had contractual appearances with her and stuff, but surely the rest of their relationship was over. Jack had intimated as much, and surely now . . . I banged my head back on my lounger as I realized how naïve that last thought was. A few kisses and handholding did not a boyfriend make.

I wondered if Jack had even spoken to Audrey since he'd gotten here. Probably. And here I was acting like we were 'going steady' just because we'd both acknowledged our mutual attraction and shared a couple of kisses. God, I really was acting young.

I needed to remind myself that whatever this was with Jack, it was temporary, it had to be. Firstly, he would be leaving, and secondly, I had no business opening my heart up to any more agony. It was going to be hard enough to say goodbye when the time came. Throw in a few more kisses and *feelings*, or worse . . . ending up in his bed, and I may never get out of *my* bed again.

Just then I heard voices. The sound of Jack's deep and amused voice as well as the lilt of my best friend's laugh.

Damn, but I really should have been there to witness Jazz meeting Jack Eversea for the first time.

I couldn't help grinning as I stood and threw on my cover-up. Grabbing our towels and seeing Jack's phone again, I finally gave in and picked it up, careful not to look at the screen. My eyes caught Audrey's name though, and I glanced down again despite myself. I literally couldn't help it; it was like a magnet. Words like "fix this" and . . . "thank you" and . . . "I love you, too" swam in front of me not making sense. *Too?*

Either I was having a head rush from standing too quickly, or it was the words I was reading, but suddenly my vision blurred around the edges and I felt sharply nauseous.

The issue wasn't helped by the fact that Jack chose that exact moment to come out of the patio door above me. He was in mid-sentence when he saw me with his phone.

I quickly held it out, swallowing the bile that threatened to come up.

His face, that had initially flashed with concern, probably due to the fact I looked like I'd seen a ghost, went carefully and swiftly blank. He came down the stairs and slowly took the phone from my hand.

I needed to leave and think about what I'd just read. Glancing at Jazz, I saw her smile fade, her eyes snapping back and forth between Jack and me in confusion.

"Uh, Jazz. I was just getting ready to go." I looked at her pointedly, hoping she would go along with this and not point out I had literally *just* told her to come over. "And . . . uh . . ." I searched blindly for something that was important enough, when Jack stepped in.

"Yeah, I got a bunch of scripts I need to read through," he said, his tone polite, but agonizingly cool. "It was nice to meet you, Jazz. I'll walk you guys out."

I tried to catch his eyes, but they skated over mine as he headed back the way they had come. Oh my God, he totally thought I'd been looking through his phone on purpose. I guess he interpreted my reaction as getting caught with my hand in the cookie jar.

Well, I hadn't meant to snoop. I wasn't going to feel guilty about that. I thought maybe I should apologize anyway, but the other part of me was rationally saying he wouldn't be mad if he had nothing to hide. Then again, this was Jack Eversea, who had to keep everything in his life hidden and private due to the nature of his work. I had a small twinge of understanding for him before my thoughts landed back on the text. *He* should be feeling guilty right now, and I had every right to feel the way I did.

We got inside and I headed straight for the front door, pausing only to grab my backpack and shove my feet into my sneakers. My clothes in the laundry room would have to stay. I definitely wasn't coming back for them. My hands shook. This needed to be over.

I shouldn't have been so surprised, but it turned out I had fallen hard and fast for Jack, and that one text had totally punched me in the gut. I was definitely not cut out for this. It would be tough, but I had to end this now. Regardless of Audrey Lane, I would never fit into his life so there was just no point in trying to save this situation. I shouldn't have let it get this far. It was my own fault. It had been me who closed the distance and crossed the line.

As I grabbed the bag and swung it onto my shoulder, I turned to him, and my stomach dipped. "I wasn't snooping, Jack. I was bringing you your phone, but I couldn't help read the text since it was *right in front of my face*. I apologize for whatever breach of privacy you think that violates. Clearly, I wasn't aware of my boundaries as they pertain to you and your girlfriend while you're trying to patch things up." My heart squeezed as I made it over those last words. I went on, "So, I apologize for this morning."

Jack cocked his head to the side.

"In the laundry room," I clarified, in case he didn't get exactly what I meant. "And in the pool," I added, and saw his eyes narrow and his jaw tighten.

Jazz cleared her throat. "I . . . uh . . . um, Keri Ann, I'll wait for you outside. Nice to meet you again, Jack," she said to him and turned for the door.

"No, it's okay, Jazz, I'm on my way out, too." And I swung around to follow her. I half expected or hoped Jack would argue with me, but he didn't.

Then I remembered something and stopped. After digging around in my backpack, I pulled out the flyer I'd found at The Pig about their new online ordering and home delivery service. I held it out to him.

Jack glanced at it, enough to read it, and didn't move. He just stared at me, his face expressionless, a muscle ticking in his cheek.

I set it down on the small glass coffee table and headed out the front door, stepping over the mound of boxes that had arrived.

CHAPTER EIGHTEEN

"*W*hat the hell was *that* about?" Jazz hissed at me as we reached the bottom of the stairs.

I did the thing where I just look at her and hope to heck she gets it. She had seen a look of emotional pain on my face enough times to recognize the signs. I'm sure I probably resembled a kicked dog, but hey, I needed to lick my wounds.

"Oh," she said. Thank God, she was giving me a temporary pass on an explanation. "Hop in my car. I'll borrow your bike to come back and get your truck . . . because I freaking love exercising in eighty-five degree weather."

I stomped around to the passenger side of her yellow car and sank inside. Flinging the door closed, I dropped my head between my knees.

"Thanks," I mumbled toward the floor before I flopped my head back against the seat and buckled in.

As we made our way the whole long three minutes to my house, Jazz glanced at me repeatedly.

"Soooo . . . awkward," she sang. "You wanna tell me what just went down, 'cos for the love of roast fish and corn bread, I swear you just broke up with Jack-freakin-Eversea back there." She paused, and then when I didn't answer, slapped my knee. Hard.

"Ow! Jeez! What was that for?"

"Well, you weren't talking so I was just checking. Oh, and also . . . for ruining my first ever celebrity meeting. *With Jack Eversea!*" she yelled and then grinned. "I'm just kidding. Kind of. No, seriously I am," she added at my raised eyebrows.

I smiled in spite of myself. "Yeah, right."

"I know, I know. I still can't believe he's here in Butler Cove, first of all. And then that you met him, had an almost thing with him, and then dumped him before I even got a chance to ask him what he had tattooed on his glute." She huffed. I knew she was trying to calm me down and cheer me up while still staying on the topic of Jack.

"How do you know he has a tattoo on his glute?" I asked. I thought of the ink I had seen peeking out of his shorts when we were carrying the paddleboard down to the beach. Well, I wouldn't be finding out either. I felt sick and a little bit empty, like I'd just lost my mother's wedding band. And I knew *that* feeling because I did misplace it once. Now I wore it most days on a chain around my neck.

"Apparently, he had it done during the filming of the first *Erath* movie, someone got a pic of him at the inkshop. But no one's talking about what it is, not even the guy who did it. It's a mystery. Although, obviously, Audrey Lane knows what it is. Shoot, sorry," she added, at my slight wince.

"It's fine, I'm just annoyed you know so damned much about him. Ugh."

We were at the stop light by the Snapper Grill. There was no way I could sit around at home tonight. I needed to stay busy. I craned my neck to see down the side of the grill through the bushes to where the courtyard was and saw Brenda outside bussing a table.

"Nuh-uh!" said Jazz. "You are *not* working. We're putting the lime in the coconut tonight and watching sappy movies."

Making margaritas and watching movies sounded like heaven and totally what I needed. Nothing with Jack Eversea in it, obviously.

"Nothing with Jack Eversea in it. I know," Jazz muttered like an echo. I turned to her and slapped her hard on the knee.

"Ow! What was that for?"

"For knowing *me* too damned well, too." I grinned at her to show her I was okay. At least until we broke out the margaritas.

She huffed dramatically and pulled onto the gravel of my driveway behind a van with a big flooring sign on it.

That was odd, I thought I was doing roofs today. I looked over to Mrs. Weaton's and saw a brand spanking new roof. Man, those guys worked fast. Not a moment too soon either, I thought, seeing the ominous clouds gathering overhead. I guess it was time for some tropical rain. I climbed out and went to investigate why there was a flooring company here.

With the day I'd just had, nothing would surprise me. Or so I believed until I saw two men hauling a large piece of equipment out of my front door.

"Um . . . hi . . . who are you?" I asked the big one closest to me.

"I'm Chuck, this is Andy," he responded with a jerk of a fat thumb behind him, as he informed me they had just finished sanding my floors.

"Excuse me," I managed. "I live here, and I didn't hire anyone to sand the floors."

"Oh," said the smaller one, I assumed this was Andy or whatever his name was. "Well, we got a prepaid order to do it, and that nice lady who lives in the cottage was expecting us. Anyway, we're almost done, and we'll be back to finish up and start the staining tomorrow. You just have to approve the color. Do you have somewhere you can stay during that time? You won't be able to walk on the floors for about three days."

"What?" I was totally confused.

Jazz came up and stood next to me. Apparently, she was the only one thinking clearly because she asked to see the invoice.

They maneuvered the machinery down the stairs to their van, with Andy trying valiantly to ignore my sheer outfit. I imagined they weren't greeted by a girl in a bikini every day, but I was way past caring. The one named Chuck rummaged around in the front seat and emerged with a clipboard.

"It wasn't Mrs. Weaton, surely? She's on social security," Jazz wondered aloud.

Me? I had a sneaking and sinking suspicion about what was going on, and I didn't like it one bit. It was confirmed when Chuck handed me the pink billing slip with a California address on it under the name of Katherine Lyons. I didn't need to be a genius to figure *that* one out. Then my eyes glanced down at the totals.

"Holy shit!"

Jazz grabbed it from me. "Holy shit, is right. Are you coating the floor with diamonds?" She aimed at Chuck. "And who the hell is Katherine Lyons?"

"Jack's assistant, I assume," I informed her. "Her name is Katie." I was absolutely fuming and stunned all at the same time. Why would Jack do this? He knew I wouldn't be able to pay him back. But I would, of course, if I spent my whole life doing it. So much for erasing him from my memory. Even if that had been possible, it was certain to be delayed by a few decades now. I looked back at the invoice and saw a huge chunk of the cost had gone to the fancy dustless sanding process and floor repair. Presumably already done. Great.

Chuck just stood there, a little confused, scratching his head.

"You can't continue. You'll have to issue a refund for the parts you haven't done yet," I told him.

"No can do. It was a package deal. Ain't no way to divvy that up without you paying more for the part we already done." He rocked on his heels.

My stomach sank.

"You can take it up with my manager," he offered at my crestfallen expression. Pulling a pencil from behind his ear, he scrawled a number down on the bottom of the invoice.

"I will. Please don't come again until this is sorted out."

He walked away shaking his head.

I stomped up the porch stairs with Jazz on my tail. For once, she was at a loss for words as well. We walked into the house. Neither of us said anything as we moved silently from empty room to empty room, taking in the sight of the smooth bare floors.

All the furniture had been moved out of the way, some out onto the back porch. Even the stairs had been sanded. It was beautiful. It was *going* to be beautiful. My eyes were teary. It made me madder. When we got to Nana's room, it too was stuffed with some furniture from downstairs. I turned to Jazz.

"I kissed him. We kissed. We talked. We had the most . . . amazing day. When I heard your voice, I picked up his phone to bring it inside and accidentally saw a message from *her*. It said: *Thank you for calling me last night, I love you too, thank you for letting me fix this. I'm so sorry."*

"Oh, honey." Jazz pulled me into a huge hug.

I swallowed hard over the lump in my throat. If she said one more thing to comfort me, I knew I was going to lose it. But she always knew the right thing to do.

She stepped away. We weren't done discussing it, but for now she knew I needed a moment.

"I'm going to get your truck and stop by the package store. We're going to start on those margaritas a little sooner than anticipated," she announced and swept down the stairs and out of the house.

I heard her hauling my bike out from the small woodshed as I made my way over to the window in Nana's room. If you stood on tiptoes you could almost see the ocean. The view from this side of the attic, a floor above this one, was better. On a whim, I headed that way.

As a small child visiting my grandmother, whenever I felt I needed to be alone, I went up to that spot in the attic below the dormer window to hide or read. Nana had allowed me to take a few items up there; seat cushions from a discarded couch, a small rickety wooden plant stand I used as a table, and a reading lamp. Nana had her craft and sewing supplies in the attic as well and after my parents and I moved in with her, we both worked up there on various projects alone or together. Or sometimes I lay in my reading nook for hours engrossed in a book with the sound of her working away on some sewing project behind me.

I climbed the last few stairs and stepped into the crowded space. I walked the length of it, past the two worktables with my unfinished projects, and boxes of tools and books and things from my parents' move that had never been unpacked. My nook at the end was hidden behind two old gnarly eight-foot doors propped up against the rafters, and behind that I had tacked up old curtains. You might miss it, unless you really looked. That's how I liked it.

I hadn't been up here for over a year. I guess I had finally grown out of needing to get away. That was what happened when you were the only one still in a big house with no one left to get away *from*.

If only I had known then I had such a short amount of time with those I loved, I would never have hidden away.

It was an unrealistic and pointless notion, I knew.

CHAPTER NINETEEN

*E*verything in my little reading nook was just as I had left it. I sank down onto the old brown cushion that was tossed on the dusty wooden floor beneath the window and looked out at the view. There were two or three rays of sun still making it through the thick clouds. They sparkled on the water in the distance. It would be sunset soon.

I pressed my fingers to my lips as I relived Jack's kisses. My belly fluttered in remembrance. I wondered if any kiss in my life would ever be able to compare to the first feeling of Jack's mouth against mine.

"Oh, Nana," I breathed. I missed her terribly. She had always seemed so wise and always knew how to make me feel better. I couldn't imagine her being okay with me throwing myself at a boy like I had done with Jack, but I knew she was a romantic at heart.

She'd met my grandfather right before he went off to Germany to fight in the Second World War. She once showed me the amazing letters they wrote to each other over the course of four years. You could feel the love pouring off the pages and his worry he wouldn't make it back to her. With all my grandfather was enduring, he'd worried about her being alone. Never once had he thought she wouldn't wait for him. They had such loyalty and unshakeable faith in each other. Did people love like that any more? I'd asked her the same thing at the time. But no matter how hard I thought about it and wracked my brain to remember what she'd told me, as if it would be the one thing that would make me feel better, I couldn't.

I thought of my mother and father. The truth was I didn't even know if they'd had a good marriage. I never asked Nana, I wasn't sure why. Maybe because I knew they hadn't. I did know my parents met when my mom was very young and she got pregnant with Joey and married right away. I couldn't help the regret I felt wishing I'd paid more attention to my parents, spent more time with them, asked them as much as I could before they were gone.

Had my mother been happy? Did she feel she had never fulfilled her destiny? The facts were she was a wife and mother who'd moved in with her *husband's* mother. I knew Nana loved her, but whether or not my mom was happy with her life choices was a question I would never get an answer to. Joey and I were loved by them all though—we never wanted for love in our house. And how many people could say that?

I thought of Jack's mother taking her young son to another country and changing his name with no support system or other family to speak of. How lonely it must have been. I knew I only had Joey left, but I'd grown up surrounded by so much love.

The rain started spitting against the window. I hoped Jazz had made it to my truck by now. I looked around at the small space and at the jars I had placed on a narrow shelf. They were each filled with a different shade of sea glass found on beaches up and down the Atlantic coast. Nana had been collecting it for years, and then I joined her in the passion. It was hard to find now. I grabbed a greenish one and held it up to the fading light at the window. I quickly put it back and grabbed another darker one. I marveled at the green shades as they glowed. I put it down and went out to my worktable.

It had literally been over a year since I had worked on these projects. I fingered some of the old weathered wood, palmetto boots, wire, and line I had pulled up out of the waterways and marshes while I kayaked. The chandelier I had been working on was almost complete and I'd left it abandoned.

I had a startling realization right then that I really wasn't as okay as I'd thought I'd been. I'd happily agreed to stay here while Joey finished school, he had already started after all, and one of us needed to stay with the house. It was his turn, and then it would be mine, we'd always had that deal. But, somewhere along the way, I'd become . . . not okay with it. I'd started feeling lonely and trapped. I was going through the motions here in Butler Cove, but I'd lost something. When did I stop being creative? I'd loved creating things my whole life, and I just let it fade away.

It wasn't that I didn't love this place. I grew up here, I had the best memories of my life and my family here. In *this* house. I was suddenly mad at myself, and at my weakness, and in my ridiculous strategy of avoiding life so it wouldn't hurt me any more. It had made everything fade. I'd become paralyzed.

I thought of how Nana always used to say '*you only live once, so do everything twice*' right before she tried something new. Well, I had done everything exciting in *my* life exactly zero times. And what happened? 'Life' had arrived on my doorstep and taken matters into its own hands.

Or Nana had.

I smiled at that thought.

It would be just like her to send me my dream man to get me out of my comfort zone. She knew who he was after all. I used to sit right here in my reading nook reading the first *Erath* book while she worked at this very table asking me about what made Max so amazing. I wondered if she knew Jack had another girlfriend before she meddled with fate.

Also, Jack was *not* Max. That much was clear. Max was strong, honorable, and ruthless in his persistence to be with Claudia and keep her safe, despite being stuck in a parallel dream dimension most of the time. Jack couldn't even tell me the truth. Or Audrey for that matter. *She* thought they were getting back together, and he was in a swimming pool kissing *me*.

I actually felt sorry for her for a moment before I remembered she had publicly humiliated him by making out with an older man all over California.

Well, they were both messed up, and I didn't want any part of it. I couldn't do anything about them, but I could do something about myself.

I grabbed the jars and hot glue gun and my tools and pulled a stool up to the workbench. Thirty minutes later when I heard Jazz downstairs I yelled for her to bring the drinks and the iPod speakers to the attic.

Three margaritas apiece, a finished chandelier, and much giggling later, we were both maneuvering down the stairs with a little less grace. I was balancing the speakers and my glass. Jazz had her glass and the pitcher and we were both singing *All These Things That I've Done* by The Killers at the top of our lungs. Considering our recipe for margaritas was tequila, Cointreau, and fresh lime juice—no sweet and sour filler mix for us—three was ambitious.

I groaned when we got to the stairs leading to the second floor and saw all the bare wood waiting for me. Jack. What was I going to do about Jack?

"My heart hurts." I plopped onto my backside halfway down the stairs. "And maaaan, that boy can kiss," I added.

"I know," Jazz concurred, sliding down to sit beside me and setting the pitcher down. "I've seen it in the movies . . ." She giggled, slurring slightly. "Why can't we have the boys we want?" she whined. "We're pretty. We're nice. We're fun, right?"

"Joey?" I asked, even though I knew the answer.

She groaned and dropped her head back to the stairs behind us.

I followed her down, and we both lay propped awkwardly side by side, risers digging into our spines as we stared up at the ceiling. A deep rumble of thunder pressed in on the house, causing the windows to rattle. Apparently, the storm had hit. It was raging outside.

"There's a cute boy in my econ one class. Brandon. He is sooooo nice." She giggled again. "He's so hot, too. He has these deep puppy dog brown eyes . . . like chocolate. Mmm. I looove chocolate. He's asked me out about four times, and I always say no. Why, oh why, can't I say yes?"

"You should," I slurred, nudging her arm. "Joey's an ass. Why on earth would you want to *date* him?"

She sighed dramatically. "'Cos maaaaan, that boy can kiiisssss!"

"Ew!" I nudged her again. "TMFI!"

She cackled loudly. I thumped her. And we lay there for a bit longer, the music playing loudly, both of us lost in our thoughts.

"So did you see him?" I asked her eventually, feeling sober at the turn of my thoughts. I'd studiously avoided asking about my truck or whether she saw Jack when she went back to get it.

Jazz turned and looked at me. "The clothes you left are in the kitchen," she said, indirectly answering my question, and then went on, "he said . . . he said to say thank you and good luck with the house." She winced at the last words.

My breath whooshed out of me. It was crushing. I stretched my feet down the last few steps to the floor and let my body slide, bumping down to meet them. When I got to the bottom, I curled over, hugging my knees to my chest and buried my face. Oh God, it hurt.

"I really should have let you drag me out and about these last few years," I mumbled. "At the very least so I could get used to some rejection. This pain . . ." I took a deep breath. "This shit is real."

Jazz thumped down to meet me at the bottom and rubbed a soothing hand up and down my spine.

"I know. God, do I know."

"I'm crazy about him. Like, totally. Ugh. Isn't that the dumbest thing you've ever heard?"

"No, hon. It makes pretty good sense to me. How could you not be? We're all in love with Max. Then the real guy comes along, and he's nice. He's attracted to you. He makes you laugh. It's not like it's your fault he turned out to be a shallow dickwad."

I opened my eyes and looked around me. What the hell was I going to do about the floors? "Yes, he is a dickwad!" I grappled around in my pocket and pulled out my phone.

I pressed send on his number before Jazz realized what I was doing. She made a grab for the phone, and I scooted away just as it started ringing. I realized I'd never called him before. A voicemail clicked on, and Jack's voice caressed my ear and said simply, "Leave a message."

Grrr.

"You can't growl at him!" Jazz said, her eyes wide, before slapping a hand over her mouth.

I hadn't realized I'd done that out loud.

"Yes, I can. Grrrr," I said loudly for good measure. "Grr, Jack. I am pissed. I am beyond pissed."

I got to my feet and paced around the bare floors, my temper rising. "What the hell *was* all that, Jack? And what on earth did you hope to accomplish by getting my floors done? Seriously? Did you think I would be so indebted to you I would do whatever you wanted? Sweet, innocent, little Keri Ann can be your bit on the side while you figure your Goddamn life out? Buy her affection with an extravagant gift? I am going to pay you back every last cent. I don't owe anyone. I won't owe anyone, ever. And don't tell me it's *just* a gift, Jack. That's the kind of gift I can't accept."

I started laughing hysterically. "Perhaps you thought you could *buy* my virginity? Is that what kinky fetish is big in Hollywood these days?" I laughed again, though it sounded like a howl, and I realized I had tears running down my cheeks.

"Give me the damn phone!" Jazz hissed, practically tackling me to the ground. "You're not making any sense!"

But I wasn't done. Apparently I still had one last humiliating arrow in my quiver.

"You don't just walk around the place paying people to fall in love with you so you don't have to be lonely. *Be* lonely, Jack. It's character building. God knows you need it." And I hung up.

Jazz was staring at me with her mouth open.

"My God, I hope you dialed a wrong number."

I looked at her, probably with a similar look of dawning horror on my face.

"Oh shit," I managed.

"Oh shit is right. You just pulled a major psycho stunt. On the up side, you're drunk, and I think that'll be pretty obvious to him, so perhaps he'll just chalk it up to . . . you being drunk."

"And on the down side?" I asked. The up side was looking pretty dire to me right now. But the down side was that I had pretty much insulted him in every way I could.

A huge crack of thunder sounded outside making us both jump.

"Well, on the down side, you basically admitted to him you're in love with him."

Oh, *that* down side.

The lights flickered on and off.

"Oh fuckity, fuck. I think I'm going to need another margarita."

"Honey, you need a hot shower and some pj's before the power goes off. You're going to feel like shit tomorrow when you wake up anyway, no need to make it worse. I'm going to fix us some hot chocolate." Jazz pulled me into a quick hug, and then collected the offending margarita pitcher and glasses and stumbled her way to the kitchen. How did that girl keep a straight head on her shoulders? Oh man, I couldn't believe what I had just done.

CHAPTER TWENTY

The shower had done wonders. And the huge dollop of vanilla ice cream I was currently dumping into my hot chocolate would do a lot more. The power had gone out just as I went to blow dry my hair. So now Jazz and I were sitting in the dark living room in front of the crackling fireplace on a blanket eating all the available ice cream before it melted. My wet hair was scraped back, and I wore my most favorite flannel pajama pants in pink tartan and a black tight t-shirt with a huge skull across the front.

I loved Jack Eversea. I really did. Not Max, but the actual guy. This was really shitty. Maybe it was the way he took my nervously barbed insults with such amusement, or maybe it was the fact we traded movie quotes perfectly, or maybe because he was so damned hot . . . except I liked to think I was a little less shallow than that. But for the sake of honesty, it was fairly clear even Mother Teresa would have gotten a twinkle in her eye when it came to Jack. Or perhaps, it was that I . . . *saw* him. The frightened and lonely boy who had put himself in the limelight with a fierce passion for his craft, despite the fact he could have hidden in shadows after whatever it was his mother had run from. I wasn't a child psychologist, and I didn't know for sure what he or she had endured, but I knew whatever had happened would have crippled most people with a lifelong fear.

But he *was* flawed. Majorly flawed. Not flawed enough for me not to love him, but flawed enough I would be staying away. Very far away.

He didn't have the kind of bravery I needed if he was willing to lie to his girlfriend and keep a relationship alive for the sake of his career, if that was truly what was going on. And if it wasn't—he had lied to *me*.

I handed the tub of vanilla back to Jazz. "I really wanted him to deny it, Jazz. He should've seen the text and realized why I was upset and denied it. He should've told me it was a big mistake. Except it wasn't, was it?" I wasn't sure why I was stating the obvious.

"I know, hon. I'm sorry."

I took a long sip of rich hot chocolate and cool vanilla ice cream. "Do you have any magazines in your car still?" She literally couldn't buy a pack of gum without buying a tabloid magazine, too. I would bet the last scoop of *Turtle Tracks* she had picked up the latest one tonight while buying the tequila.

She nodded. "But I ain't going out there to get 'em."

Another rumble of thunder punctuated her words.

"Never mind. It was a dumb idea and will only prolong the agony. I just realized I've never really paid much attention to his life, and it's all out there." I thought of how private he claimed to be, and the secret he'd shared with me. "Well, most of it. The public stuff anyway."

"Yeah, don't start getting masochistic. This is a worst case scenario for a break-up to have all that tantalizing information out there."

"Break-up?" I snorted. "Apparently, we were never together."

"The only things I do know are that people are still wondering where he is, and Audrey put out a public statement."

"Really? What did it say?" I hated my weakness, but I was curious.

"Something along the lines of how sorry she was, and that it was a momentary indiscretion, and that she loved and respected him deeply et cetera, et cetera. But I am assuming she put out a public statement because she doesn't know where he is either."

I mulled that over a second before another thought occurred to me. "Dare I ask what the book is for book club tomorrow? I'm assuming the reason you forgot to tell me is because I've read it already?" I rubbed my temples at the tequila headache slowly coming on.

Jazz grimaced. "Yes, well the older ladies hadn't read them yet . . . and with the movie coming out soon . . ." She trailed off.

Tomorrow would suck. "Look, it's not like you knew we would actually *meet* the guy when you picked them, so don't worry about it," I said, instantly forgiving her.

"Yeah, but at this stage I wish we were reading *Anna Karenina*."

"Me too."

Jazz let out a huge yawn. "Wow, margaritas plus ice cream. I am going into a carb coma."

I yawned too, and then we both jumped at the sudden pounding on the front door.

"Shit, who's that?" Jazz said. "Should we get it?"

My heart lurched from the sudden fright. "It could be Mrs. Weaton, perhaps they didn't fix her roof properly today." Or not. Jazz grabbed a poker from the fireplace, and we both skidded on sock feet to the front door. I looked out of the peephole, but with no lights on I couldn't really see a thing.

"I can't see anything," I whispered, and then jumped back as another round of banging started.

"Keri Ann?" Jack's voice shouted over the wind and rain.

"Oh my God," I mouthed to Jazz.

Her eyes were wide.

"Do you think he got my message?"

"Shit, I don't know," she whispered back, her shoulders hunching up.

"Keri Ann? Please . . . please open the door. I really need to talk to you."

What the heck was he doing out there in the rain? Obviously, I was going to have to let him in. I could feel mortification and its crimson tide crawling up my chest to my neck.

Jazz shrugged with an apologetic 'this is your mess, I have no clue how to help you here' look on her face.

"Thanks!" I hissed at her.

"Keri Ann! Open the Goddamn door . . . please?" Jack's voice broke over the last word and my shoulders slumped.

Jazz rolled her eyes.

I opened the door as a huge gust of wind blew in and wrenched it out of my hands. It swung back hard banging against the wall. And there stood the tall, looming shadow of Jack, hands on either side of the doorframe, in jeans and a dark wet t-shirt that clung to his body. Water streamed down his beautiful face.

"For the love of shrimp 'n' grits, girl," I heard Jazz murmur next to me as we both took in the archangel standing on the threshold. "Good luck."

I shivered.

"Jazz." Jack acknowledged her with a nod as he took a step inside the door.

"Jack," she returned, her chin up and arms crossed. She couldn't have screamed, 'Don't mess with my best friend' any louder than if she'd said the words.

He seemed to get it because, as I closed the door quickly against the rain that followed him in, he directed his next statement to her. "I just need to talk to her."

"Don't move," she said to him and pushed me back through the arched opening into the living room.

I glanced at him to see his shadowed green eyes boring into mine.

Jazz and I stopped in front of the fireplace and she pulled me in close. We were far enough away from Jack, but she still whispered. "I am going to go upstairs and sleep in Joey's room. Are you going to be okay?"

I nodded.

"Are you sure?"

"*Yes!*" I whispered back, fiercely.

"If you decide to give up your vajayjay tonight, keep it down, okay?"

"Jazz!" I squeaked and practically choked on my own tongue.

"I'm just sayin'. . ." She shrugged with a wink.

"Well, don't 'just say'. I'm mad at him, remember?"

"Yeah, yeah, I know. But look at him." We both turned to look at Jack who was standing with one hand on the back of his neck and the other on his hip, his head tilted down at the floor he was dripping all over. His dark, wet hair was flopped over his furrowed brow, his jaw grim.

"You could always dump him in the morning," she murmured.

He looked up at us staring at him from the other room.

"What?" he asked.

We both started.

"Nothing," we chorused and turned away again.

"I can't *believe* you are encouraging me." I dropped my voice back to a whisper and thumped her on the arm. "Some good friend you are. You're supposed to be protecting me from my mistakes."

"*I am.* Can you imagine how pissed you'll be when we're old dames and you blame me for talking you *out* of having sex with Jack Eversea."

She made a good point.

"Are you still drunk?" I glared at her. "Anyway, I don't know why he's here. Probably to let me know about the restraining order after my phone call."

"Yeah, right. Guys don't just show up like this, especially after a phone call like that. And if he was really in love with Audrey, he would definitely not have come over here. You gave him the perfect out, and he's still here."

"Maybe it's just a booty call."

"Maybe it is . . ." Jazz winked. "Lucky you."

"You do realize it will be *you* mending the pieces of my broken heart in the morning?"

"I believe we were doing that anyway."

"Good point."

Jazz then stood tall, laid a hand over her heart and hissed out the corner of her mouth like some retarded ventriloquist, "I, Jessica Fraser, hereby grant my good friend, Keri Ann Butler, permission to embrace her inner strumpet, and I do so with the utmost promise of confidentiality and lack of judgment."

"Lack of *good* judgment you mean." I rolled my eyes at her, but inside, thinking about going to bed with Jack, my stomach twisted and turned in nerves, and not a little heat. However, he and I had some shit to sort out, so the chances of that ever happening were remote at best. I frowned.

"If you're done . . ." I crossed my arms and tapped my foot.

She grinned wickedly. "Just be safe about it, I am *not* ready to be a godmother." And with that effective cold bucket of water dumped on my stirring libido, she made a hasty exit, brushing past Jack and up the stairs.

Ugh! I stomped my foot. I couldn't believe she would encourage me, then scare the shit out of me in the same nanosecond. Typical.

"Uh . . . do you think I could borrow a towel or something . . ." Jack asked, his eyebrows raised in bewilderment at the long hissing exchange he'd just witnessed.

"Oh yeah, sorry. Uh, go sit by the fire, I'll bring you one."

"Here ya go!" came Jazz's voice down the stairs as a huge white bath towel flapped to the bottom.

"Uh, thanks," Jack called out, heading for it.

"No problem," she sang. "Y'all have fun!"

And we heard Joey's bedroom door bang shut.

CHAPTER TWENTY-ONE

I looked at Jack in my darkened living room. He was still standing awkwardly and soaking wet, but now trying to dry himself over his wet clothes. He should really take them off before he got a chill, but I was going to bite my tongue until it bled before I suggested that.

"How did you get here?" It suddenly occurred to me I hadn't heard his bike.

"I ran, slash, walked."

"In the rain?"

"Well, it was a bit dangerous to be out on the bike, and it didn't seem so far . . . but I wasn't thinking about what it feels like to try and get somewhere fast in soaking wet jeans. And damn, when it rains, it rains here."

It sure did. "And *why* are you here?"

He looked around the room, maybe for somewhere to sit, before settling down onto his haunches and looking into the fire. The firelight dancing across the planes of his face was devastating.

I swallowed and looked away.

"Yeah, sorry about there being no furniture," I said a little acidly, maybe to cover my nerves. "Apparently someone paid to have my floors done."

"There is such a thing as a gift without strings, Keri Ann," he said quietly. "Not that I've ever received one, but I certainly didn't expect anything from you for that. I just did it. Without thinking. I could. So I did." He shrugged, as if it had been the most simple thing in the world. Like buying a cup of coffee. "But, I'm sorry. The last thing I wanted to do was upset you. I understand pride. Trust me." He laughed, humorlessly.

My heart twisted at his reference to never having been given a gift with no strings. I was such a sap.

He seemed to gear up to say something else, like he was trying to find the right words to explain something. "I want to go and tell everyone to get screwed," he started. "But I owe them too much. I wouldn't be where I am today in my career without them. It makes me doubt my ability. But it's not actually *me* they care about, I'm alone in this. They care about me being in the right place at the right time, dating the right person," he looked at me before continuing, "God, I know I'm not making sense to you. I know I tried to explain this before . . ."

I could tell it was hard for him to admit to his vulnerability, but what he was saying was still making me mad. It just screamed weakness. I knew he was better than this. And all I wanted to ask him was, "Did you really call Audrey and tell her you were getting back together?" It was out of my mouth before I could help myself.

He took a deep breath. "Not in the way you mean. She issued a statement publicly apologizing."

"I know. Jazz read about it."

He nodded. "It was such a stunt. I haven't been taking her

calls so I guess she got desperate to communicate with me.
I should have, we've been through so much, I owed her at
least a phone call."

That was up for debate, but I stayed silent.

"I did call her last night, to talk. She didn't answer. But I
guess she took that as a sign I was ready to work on fixing
everything."

So, he didn't betray me, exactly. "Are you?"

"No. But I'm not sure how to move forward. I called her
again tonight. We're going to be traveling around the world
together for the next two months as the publicity tour starts
up. We are going to have to be together, we are going to have
to be seen as *being* together."

The emphasis to the word 'being' left no doubt in my mind
about what it meant. I envisioned photo shoots, red carpets,
interviews, public displays of affection . . . and shared hotel
rooms. Would it be rude if I excused myself to go and be
sick?

He stood up and turned to me. I saw goose bumps on his
arms as he tried to get warm despite his wet clothes. "That's
what I came here to say, Keri Ann." His green eyes looked
almost black in the dark room. "I came here to apologize.
First, for not trusting you and assuming the worst. Second,
for letting what we have between us develop into anything.
I should never have let it get so far." His words were stones
hitting the bottom of my stomach. "And I know seeing that
text from Audrey hurt you." He grimaced. "I'm sorry. That's
what made me realize how careless I was being."

Hot shame swarmed over me at the naïve, star-stuck, and
broken-hearted little girl he saw me as. And it made me
mad as hell. I just didn't trust myself to say anything. Or
move. I wanted to slap his face. And I had never wanted to

hit another person in my whole life. Except maybe Joey sometimes. And Jazz. Okay, maybe I did like smacking people.

He wasn't done though. He ran a hand through his dark wet hair and shook his head, seemingly unaware of the anger and shame thrumming through me.

"Look at us both, too scared to really live and do things the way we want to."

I snapped and shoved at his chest. "Do you think I just sit here working and struggling because I'm too scared? I'm here because I made a deal. My brother and I only have *each other* left and we made a deal, it's *his* turn. Then it will be mine. Maybe you don't know what it's like to make a sacrifice for someone else. I can only assume you made it in your career by always putting yourself first. Well, the rest of the world doesn't live in your empty vacuum. We have lives, and families, or *had*," I amended. "And choices. And we make decisions based on all of those things, not just the ones that put *ourselves* at the top. Maybe the reason you are so lonely is you never think of anyone else!"

He flinched like I'd followed through on my urge to slap him. I knew I'd gone too far. I hadn't really meant that. I was just so angry, and the words that streamed from me wanted to cut him and make him feel as bad as I did. Punish him for making me feel like a naïve, unambitious girl who wasn't good enough for him.

To my shame, I suddenly realized, as I had this afternoon up in the attic, that he was right in a way. I *had* been scared. I was using Joey as an excuse not to do something with my life. I wanted to apologize, but he spoke first.

"You're wrong," he said quietly. "I haven't thought about anyone *but* you since the moment we met."

The crackle of the fire was suddenly deafening in the silence between us. *Did he really just say that?*

"So," I started, unsure of how to interpret his conflicting words. "So, I still don't understand."

His hands came up to the back of his neck again as he looked down at the ground. The action drew my attention to his broad shoulders. Oh, how I wanted those arms wrapped around *me*. When he looked up again the stark emotion on his face was unlike anything I had seen. I had read books and books about men and women betraying a world of emotions with just one glance. I used to chalk it up to artistic license, but this was really happening. I swallowed.

"Did you mean it today when you said you were sorry you kissed me?" he asked, his eyes searching mine.

Never. I was going to hang onto those memories forever. I managed to shake my head.

"Did *you* mean it, just now, when you said it was careless?" I responded, barely finding my voice.

"Touché," he said, his tone low. "I haven't lied to you, Keri Ann. About anything. When I told you I had never felt this way before I meant it. When you walked out today, I . . . it . . ." He bunched a fist up and planted it knuckles down in the center of his chest. "I shouldn't have let you go. Or maybe I should have, for your sake. I . . . shit, this is hard."

I waited. I was on that freaking tightrope again, except this time someone else was in control of it. I didn't like it one bit. The hope warring with the hurt in my gut was making me nauseous.

"I guess what I'm asking you, Keri Ann . . . is . . . knowing what you know, about Audrey, about the contract . . . about me . . . will you take a chance?"

I wondered if he knew how amazing he looked wet. I mean, what with the sweaty Jack, the paddleboarding Jack, the swimming Jack, and now the rain-soaked Jack, I really wasn't being given much in the way of strength to say no.

I walked over to the blanket near where he was standing and sat down facing the fire. I hugged my knees to my chest. I needed my hot chocolate. Seeing it on the mantle next to him, I pointed at it.

"Farmboy, fetch me that pitcher?" I was hoping the *Princess Bride* reference would help ease the tension a little.

He paused a moment at my non-sequitur, and then the dimple appeared with his faint smile, and he handed it to me.

"As you wish."

I smiled back and took it.

"Thanks."

I took a sip, thankful it was still warm. I held it out to him, and he crouched down again next to me.

"Taste?" I asked.

He took it from my hand, but instead of taking a sip, he set it down on the floor out of reach. Then his hand cupped my face and turned me toward him, his eyes searching mine.

"Say yes, Keri Ann."

I sighed and closed my eyes against the feel of his skin.

"Yes." It was the easiest thing I'd ever said.

He shifted, dropping his knees to the floor in front of me. His other hand came up to cradle my face, his thumbs running over my jaw and cheekbones. I watched him under my lashes as his eyes roamed my face, and then his mouth descended to my forehead, each eyelid, one cheekbone, then the other, and finally, my mouth.

I clutched his wrists for balance as his tongue lightly ran over the seam of my lips. I opened to him, and he groaned.

"Mmmm, chocolate." He took another taste. "And marga-ritas." His tongue slid along mine again. "And Keri Ann. A heady mix."

It was for *me*. My heart pounded deep throbbing beats through my body. Still holding his arms, I came forward to my knees and we both raised up our bodies meeting from leg to chest. My hands worked of their own volition winding up his neck and into his wet hair, and I pulled his mouth more firmly down against mine.

His lips were warm and soft next to the rough skin of his chin, and I drew closer to him like a magnet, needing to press my body, my skin, against his. But there were two layers of fabric between us, and I became aware of the cool press of his wet t-shirt.

Letting go of his neck, I brought my hands down to slide under the hem of his shirt. He inhaled sharply as my warm hands made contact with his skin.

"You need to take this off," I managed. My voice sounded raspy to my own ears as I made to lift the fabric.

He let go of me and reached behind his neck. Gathering a handful of shirt, he peeled it forward over his head.

My breath left me as I came face to chest with his perfectly sculpted body. The firelight played across his skin and his flexed abdominal muscles as he leaned back on his haunches slightly to lay the shirt out by the fire.

Without thinking, I brought the flat of my hand up to the center of his chest below his collarbone. His skin was cool to the touch and smooth.

He stilled where he was, leaning slightly away from me on his knees and brought his eyes to mine.

I very slowly ran my palm down over the ridges and planes of his chest, pausing for a moment when I noticed the hard beat of his heart. His eyes got darker and broodier as my hand continued its slow journey downward. His breathing changed, as did my own in response. My eyes dropped to follow my hand as it reached the belt buckle of his black jeans.

I took a deep breath. "You should take these off, too." My words came out as a whisper.

His jaw tightened, his dark eyes watching me.

I went to undo the buckle but his hands stilled me. For a moment, I thought he was going to keep his wet clothes on. As much as he needed to take them off so they could dry and he could get warm, I was hyper-aware of the combustible situation that existed between us. I knew he was too.

He shifted away and brought up one foot, then the other, to undo the laces on his black boots. His socks came next, and he laid them by the fire. I was mesmerized by every action. His hands returned to his buckle as he stood and undid the belt and his buttons, revealing the waistband of his black boxer briefs. Then, leaning down, he shucked his jeans off each leg and stood back up.

My shallow breathing was loud next to the soft crackle and pop of the fire, and I swallowed the lump in my throat as my eyes took in how aroused he was. He was glorious in his perfection, like a dark angel.

He reached for the towel and wrapped it around his middle covering himself, and I realized my face must have shown my trepidation. I looked up at him.

"It's okay, Keri Ann. I'm not going to take advantage of you."

Oh, but I wished he would.

CHAPTER TWENTY-TWO

"I'm not the one who's undressed. You should be worried about me taking advantage of *you*." I grinned sheepishly.

Jack chuckled and came over to sit beside me by the fireplace.

I pulled the blanket up over our legs.

The storm picked up again and there was a flash of lightning followed by a sharp crack of thunder that was a whip on my tightened nerves. I jumped.

"You don't like storms?" he asked, wrapping an arm around my shoulders and tucking me in against him. It felt good and unexpected.

"Actually, I love stormy nights. Hot chocolate and firelight and now barely dressed men have probably made them my all-time favorite." I nudged him playfully, my awareness of him still simmering insistently in a warm pool inside me.

He laughed and squeezed my shoulders.

I realized he was telling the truth. He really wouldn't take advantage of me.

I took a deep breath and turned to him. Drawing his face down to mine, I kissed him.

He held his body tense as I touched my lips to his

It was slow and soft, his lips giving way to mine and moving in gentle rhythm, tasting my lips with his lips. The kisses were delicious, but I wanted more. I wanted passionate Jack who couldn't control his breathing or his reactions when he was kissing me.

I turned more fully toward him and tentatively ran the tip of my tongue along his lower lip like he had done to me.

Jack's reaction was swift. It was like he'd been waiting for permission. One minute we were sitting side by side, the next he gave a soft growl and had me on my back with half his body covering me.

I gasped under the sudden move and his weight before he lowered his mouth and plundered mine. Heat speared through my core, and my body arched of its own accord, to meet his.

Jack's lips moved with greed, his tongue sliding in and claiming me, leaving me almost light-headed.

Reaching up, I clutched the hair at his nape and sought to taste more of what he was giving me. The feel of his body along the length of mine was intoxicating. My hands roamed down over his bare shoulders, clutching at the tense muscles in his back. I wished I were wearing less. I had a demanding need to feel my skin against his. That annoying ache I had a feeling only one thing would fix had started up between my legs and was getting more and more intense.

Jack's kisses moved down toward my neck.

I sighed with pleasure and shivered involuntarily as his tongue trailed up over my earlobe.

"You like that?" he whispered in my ear, causing another shudder to run through me.

I nodded with an incoherent sound and felt his smile against my sensitive skin before his tongue darted out again. I moaned, tilting my head back and exposing more of my neck to his hot mouth. *Yes, please.* I wanted a lot more of that, too.

The movement had thrust my chest forward toward him and his hand came up to rest on the bare skin of my stomach where my shirt had ridden up. One of his legs was slung over mine, and I felt how hard he was for me. From experience that was limited to pictures I had giggled over with Jazz, or my imagination, he felt . . . big. A tremor ran through me.

He came up on an elbow, and I opened my eyes through the fog of desire to meet his intense, hooded gaze. I became aware of how rapidly I was breathing, but was completely helpless to stop it, especially as his hand at my waist slowly pushed my shirt upward. He held my eyes, unflinching, and I bit my lip with nerves as he slipped my shirt further upward and exposed first one breast, then the other. The cool air hitting my exposed skin made my already hard nipples pebble into painful peaks. My breath was almost coming in pants. God, I wanted him to touch me.

His eyes left mine and dropped to my newly exposed flesh. His jaw tensed, and his nostrils flared. He ran a fingertip up the channel between my breasts, and then around each one excruciatingly slowly.

"God, you're beautiful," he whispered. His warm breath across my skin was too much.

"Please—" I croaked and arched up further.

"Please what?" Jack lowered his head and looked up at me through his lashes, a glint in his eye.

I moaned again, I couldn't help it. "Please touch me," I managed, too far gone to feel embarrassed by my plea.

He pressed his lower body harder against me. His fingers brushed across a tight peak.

I inhaled swiftly. Then his warm hand palmed my whole

breast, capturing a nipple and rolling it between his finger and thumb. The sensation was incredible.

"More," I gasped.

He made a sound low in his throat, drew my hands above my head, and held them tight in one hand. The other arm came under my arched back, holding me up as he lowered his head and sucked a nipple into his hot mouth.

Holy shit, I thought, as lust hit me like a Mack truck. Every sensation I was feeling was more intense than the last. I was a complete slave to it and completely lost in it. The aching between my legs had reached an insistent sharp throb that was hardwired to every pull of his mouth at my breast. The lower part of my body surged toward him, trying to move his leg between mine.

Jack groaned and shifted, his thigh coming up to press against the apex of my legs.

I flexed, rubbing myself against him, trying to create some friction.

"God, you're killing me," Jack hissed.

"Likewise," I said between breaths.

He let out a low chuckle and took my mouth again, kissing me deeply. Then he rose up and worked my shirt up over my head and arms.

I went to help but he held my hands tighter.

"No," he said, pulling my shirt up over my head as far as my wrists and wrapping it securely around them.

My heart thumped, but I knew I could break free if I had to.

"I have to do this, because if you touch me right now, I won't be able to handle it."

My insides lurched at the heady feeling his words inspired. My upper body was now completely bared to him. I wanted to feel a shy embarrassment, but his hot, raking gaze was making molten heat pool through me.

His mouth found mine again, and I kissed him back fiercely, making up for the fact that my hands couldn't touch him.

"But I *want* to touch you," I said between breaths and kisses.

"In time," he whispered in my ear. He trailed wet kisses down my neck and throat to my chest.

Jack took his time licking and nipping at each nipple, driving me to a gasping point. I was writhing and arching against him.

One of his hands ran down my side and over my pajama'd thigh, hitching me up hard against his leg.

I whimpered as his fingers trailed over my bottom and between my legs. I was sure he could probably feel how hot I was for him through my pajamas. I tried to move against his hand.

He tensed and his breath came out forcefully. "God," he croaked.

I knew the feeling.

He pulled his hand back up to my chest.

I wanted to grab it and press it against where I needed it most. He kissed me again, slowly, deeply and pulled away, shifting off me slightly.

I opened my eyes to him watching me. He was flushed, his green eyes intense. It was a mesmerizing sight in the dimming red glow of the dwindling fire. Both of us were breathing hard. He ran a hand down slowly from my neck to my hip bone, and then dipped inside my pajama pants below my navel. I held my breath, but his fingers slid back out and up to my belly.

"Please . . . I want . . . I need . . ." I didn't know how to ask, but I needed Jack not to stop.

I knew that every pause, every slowing down, and every hesitation was him making sure I was still doing this willingly, almost like he wouldn't trust himself to stop if he wasn't paying attention. The knowledge made my heart swell in my chest.

Jack squeezed his eyes shut tight and swallowed before his mouth came down to mine again, kissing me deeply and slowly like he was deliberately trying to hold back the pace.

But thank God, he wasn't stopping. His hand slid back down my belly and inside the loose waistband of my pants.

My breath was shallow, my body tense, as he lightly ran his hand around my hip, cupping the bare sensitive skin of my buttock. Instinctively, I lifted a knee up.

I moaned a breath as his fingers trailed back around the top of my thigh and into the crease between my legs. Squirming against his hand, I tried to bring it to me, and he chuckled softly against my lips. I nipped at his mouth with my teeth in frustrated retaliation.

Everything moved pretty fast after that.

He growled against my mouth as his fingers found my wetness and slid down over my sensitive nub, plunging inside me.

I cried out and arched up.

"Fuck," Jack gasped. His tongue plunged into my mouth too, mimicking his fingers as they slid out of me and back inside, his thumb rhythmically sliding over my hot button.

I whimpered and moaned and gasped into Jack's mouth. My wrapped hands came down locking his head to me as we devoured each other, my hips thrusting against his hand shamelessly.

His breathing matched the quickened pace of his sliding fingers.

"Feels . . . so . . . good . . ." I panted out between kisses, and he groaned in response, sliding deeply into my mouth again. Suddenly it was too much. I was splintering apart on an explosion of sensation. I held tight to Jack's head with my arms as he captured my cries into his mouth, my body shuddering and clenching against his hand, his palm pressed hard against me.

"Shhh," Jack soothed. He gave small chaste kisses along my mouth and cheeks and neck. "Shhh," he whispered into my ear as I still shuddered through my release.

I clamped my lips between my teeth to keep from crying out any further.

His fingers slid slowly in and out, drawing out the sensation as I clenched around him. Jack's harsh breathing against my neck matched my own, before he leisurely withdrew his fingers and drew a trail of wetness up my belly.

My heart still thudding, my eyes flickered open as I watched him lean up and paint my moist arousal around one of my nipples. Then dropping his head, he drew it into his mouth. The shocking action punched another wave of heat through my belly.

There would be no going back from sleeping with Jack Eversea. If I hadn't been clear on that before, I knew it now.

All the experience in the world wouldn't have changed the fact I knew deep down to my soul the kind of heat created between Jack and me was stratospheric. It was the kind of energy women who read thousands of romance novels yearned for and rarely got and certainly nothing like the times I had touched myself. I wondered, fleetingly, if I would ever bother again. He felt it too, he had admitted as much. And that had been . . . before.

I broke my wrists out of the bonds of my t-shirt and clutched him to me.

He laid his damp forehead down on my chest, and I could tell he was forcing his breathing to slow down.

I ran my hands down his back. He must be painfully turned on if what had happened to me was any indication. For a moment I felt nervous. I wanted to . . . relieve him . . . but didn't know how to ask. And I wasn't ready for him to be inside of me. Not yet. I wanted it, but I wanted to delay that point of no return just as fiercely. I would belong to him then. Body, heart, and soul, and I still wasn't sure if he was fully mine in return. That thought terrified me and cooled the flow of lava coursing through me.

But Jack had asked me to take a chance on him. I tried to swallow my shadow of doubt.

"Are you okay?" he asked, looking down at me, a small furrow appearing between his eyebrows.

I nodded and smiled gamely. "After that? Who knew you were so talented with your hands, Mr. Eversea."

He winked, and his dimple appeared. "I told you I was good with my hands . . . you just assumed I meant for construction purposes." He pressed a small kiss on my nose.

"Oh my God, your elbows must be in agony from this hardwood floor!" I was suddenly very aware of the fact I had been completely caught up in a tsunami of feelings. If the roof had blown off the house, I wouldn't have paid the least attention. Embarrassment crawled up my cheeks as I came to terms with how I had just wantonly come apart in his hands.

"That wasn't foremost on my mind . . . but now that you mention it . . ." He rolled to the side. "Hey, *now* what's with the blush?"

"I . . . well, that was amazing . . . I'm sorry I didn't even . . . couldn't even . . ." Well, this was awkward. I had *no* idea what I was trying to say.

"Hey," he turned my face to him. "That was the hottest freaking thing I've ever experienced. I actually am physically trying not to think about it, because I'm dying here. Do you have any idea how fucking sexy you are?"

"Will you sleep here tonight?" I blurted on a whim to cover my reaction to his words, perhaps. "I mean stay in my bed . . . not . . ." I took a breath. "Just to sleep, I mean." God, where the hell was my mind? Somewhere stuck in the bunched up blanket I was sure, because it sure as heck wasn't in my head. I couldn't articulate a damn thing.

"I'm not in any condition to walk right now, anyway, although the rain could double as a cold shower." He laughed and kissed my forehead. "Yeah, I'll stay. I'd like that."

He helped me to my feet, as I clutched one arm across my bare chest, and handed me my shirt.

I quickly pulled it on.

"Is there anything down here you need to take care of?" he asked.

Apart from *him*? From under my lashes, I took in his body, head to toe. But my roving eyes and my traitorous blush gave me away again.

He groaned. "Seriously, Keri Ann. You'll be the death of me. And now that I understand what that blush means, the question is," he cocked his head to the side, "just what naughty idea were you having in my bathroom the other day?"

Damn, I knew he wouldn't let that go.

"I'll never tell," I said, shaking my head.

He leaned in, a smile on his beautiful face and gave me a quick kiss before sweeping me up, one arm under my knees.

I squealed and grabbed onto his neck.

"Hold on," he said, and headed for the stairs.

CHAPTER TWENTY-THREE

Jack took the stairs two at a time in the dark. I saw Joey's door was safely closed. I didn't ask how he knew where my bedroom was first try. He had been in my house alone for several days.

Luckily, I'd lit a candle in a hurricane jar next to my bed after the power first went out. I ducked my head into his neck and inhaled the scent that was fast becoming my all-time favorite as he entered my room and headed straight for the bed. I had never really felt dainty before, or wanted to for that matter, but being held in Jack's strong arms as he effortlessly moved about holding me, was a novel and not unwelcome feeling.

"Man, you have a lot of books," he said, depositing me on my bed.

"I like to read." I shrugged and nonchalantly grabbed the fourteen books caught up in my bedclothes and put them on the chest of drawers that doubled as another bedside table.

"Me too, actually. I get it. Can I borrow the light to go to the bathroom?"

I handed him the hurricane jar and told him where a spare toothbrush was, and then lay back in the dark room. The thought of sleeping next to him all night roused all those damn butterflies inside me. I wondered if I'd be able to sleep at all.

He came back, handed me the lamp, and I went to the bathroom to brush my teeth. Catching sight of myself, I did a double take and groaned. Damn. My hair had started drying and coming out of its pony. I looked horrific with wisps and kinks and teased pieces all over the place. I quickly pulled it loose and ran a comb through it. Since it was still damp, I'd probably look like a witch by morning. I hastily braided it to minimize the damage, brushed my teeth, and walked back to the bedroom.

Jack was lying under my comforter on his back with his eyes closed and his head cradled on his arms. I paused a moment to mentally capture the picture of Jack in my bed. It really didn't compute. He opened an eye.

"What?"

I lifted a shoulder. "Just looking at you."

"And what do you see?"

"A gorgeous man in my bed," I said simply. That didn't begin to cover it.

He reached over and flipped back the cover for me. "You see a lucky guy who gets to share a bed with a gorgeous girl."

I scoffed lightly. "Right. Plain girl next door is more like it." I climbed into the bed, keeping a few inches between us and rolled to face him.

He frowned at me. "You are more beautiful with your bare makeup-free face than most of the girls I know after four hours in the hair and makeup trailer."

I didn't say anything for a few moments. Finally, I managed a small *thank you*. Jack responded by reaching an arm out and dragging me to him, turning me, and pressing my back against his chest. He curled his muscled arm over my waist. I snuggled into the curve but stiffened when I felt his erection pressing against me. I bit my lip against the urge to turn in his arms and finish what we'd started earlier.

"Just ignore it. *I* am," came his muffled voice in my hair. "Night, Keri Ann." Then he inhaled deeply and kissed my shoulder. I sighed and closed my eyes, trying very hard to comply.

Sometime in the night I woke up utterly aroused and with Jack completely wrapped around me. My head was on his one arm, and his other was across my midsection. I listened for his breathing in the dark, expecting to hear the deep and steady rhythm that would tell me he was sleeping.

Then I felt the soft rhythmic caress of his thumb on my belly where my t-shirt had ridden up. That must have been what had gotten me hot and bothered and awake. I waited, willing him to continue. His body was hot at my back and one of his legs was hooked between mine, and then I felt his breath at my neck before he touched his lips to my skin.

I sighed, and with sleepiness making my inhibitions less bossy, gently moved his hand further up inside my shirt to cradle my breast.

He tensed for a moment before his thumb continued its movements, this time skimming across my taut nipple.

I bit my lip and involuntarily arched slightly into his hand as he hissed out a breath and pressed his hard arousal against my bottom, hitching his leg further up between mine.

His breathing was hot and heavy against my neck, matching my own, and I rocked against him as the deep throbbing inside me picked back up from earlier as if it would never be satisfied. He groaned, and his arms tightened around me and pressed me down against his leg.

An unrecognizable sound of pure need and lust escaped me. Why did I have to wear pajama bottoms and a t-shirt? Why wasn't I wearing some cute little spaghetti strap nightshirt with no panties? Before I could talk myself out of it, I untangled myself from Jack's leg to push down my pajama bottoms. There was just something about being in a dark room, and being in a drowsy state, that made all my inhibitions and nerves fade away.

"Stop, Keri Ann. Please," Jack whispered against my ear and stilled my hands.

It was like a bucket of cold water. I was instantly mortified.

"I want you too much. You have no idea." He squeezed me and kissed my shoulder.

I wasn't sure how to respond. His words were a soothing balm for my pride, but I still felt like a heel. Self-doubt crept in and left a heavy calling card in my heart, and I cringed at myself in the dark. *Nice one, Keri Ann . . . you offer to get naked for a guy, and he turns you down, with an 'it's not you, it's me' line.*

He rolled me over and kissed me softly on the lips before moving a little distance away. Although he still kept an arm across me, I felt bereft. I swallowed the lump in my throat, and thought about counting sheep.

CHAPTER TWENTY-FOUR

$\mathcal{I}$ woke up with a pounding headache left over from tequila and sugar. "Ow," I croaked and clutched my head. Water, I needed water. It was morning, but barely. *Jack!* It suddenly all came back to me.

"You okay?" came Jack's voice from the foot of the bed. I opened my eyes to find him sitting with his elbows resting on his parted knees, watching me.

He was still in just his boxers. He stood up and left the room. I heard the water running in the bathroom and the medicine cabinet open and close. He came back with a glass of water and two aspirin.

I accepted them gratefully and shifted up onto an elbow. "Thanks."

"No problem."

My cheeks burned as a collage of images of us in front of the fireplace downstairs fluttered through my head. Of course that was followed by the memory of my blatant invitation to him during the night that he flatly turned down.

I couldn't get a gauge on what he was thinking. He had come over last night to say getting involved with me was a mistake, I reminded myself. I swallowed the pills and water down nervously and decided on diversion as the best tactic. "Do I snore or something?" I asked.

"What?" His eyes widened a moment, then he broke into a laugh and shook his head slowly. "No."

When he didn't say anything else, I got up and walked past him to the bathroom to freshen up. Joey's door was open so I guessed Jazz had gone home early. She probably felt about as bad as I did. Jack hadn't moved when I got back. I stood uncertainly for a moment, and then got back into the warmth of the bed.

He didn't follow me, but stood and walked around the room looking at all my pictures and shelves crammed with books and frames and keepsakes, stopping at a few and commenting here and there. I watched his muscled frame with the snug black boxer briefs hugging his butt. That was a hangover cure right there, but the bundle of dread inside me, waiting for him to say what was on his mind, kept it in check.

"*Pride and Prejudice* and *Twilight* are next to each other?" he asked, looking at my bookshelf. "I'm assuming you don't have any kind of system?"

"Actually, I do. I keep books in the order I read them." I could map the timeline of my life by the order in which my books were kept.

"Seriously?" He looked back at them. I was waiting for some smart-ass comment about how or why I had gone from Jane Austen to *Twilight*. Not that I saw much difference between the yearning of a young girl for a seemingly unattainable guy in either story.

The irony of my current situation wasn't lost on me.

"So what period am I in right now?"

"Oh, um . . ." It was the summer my parents died, but I didn't want to bring the mood down. "Summer before my freshman year at Butler Cove High."

"Did you like the Jane Austen?"

"I thought the poor girl, rich guy thing would seem . . . trite, but then I read it and . . . well, it was good."

He nodded. "It was."

Of course he'd read it. Why not? My perfect guy was also a bookworm.

"*Slave Species of God*? I didn't know *anyone else* had read this!"

"You've read it?"

"Yep. Totally changed—"

"Every history class you were ever taught?"

"Yeah." He laughed and moved on.

"See any you haven't read?"

"Plenty. I don't do bodice ripping romances . . . sorry."

"Don't knock it 'til you try it."

"Don't tempt me." He winked over his shoulder.

I breathed a small internal sigh of relief at his implication, but I still felt like I was missing something.

He moved on to several framed pictures I had. One was of Joey and me taken a few summers ago in a two-man kayak. One was of us with my parents sitting on the front porch steps around the time when we first moved here. I was about ten years old, bracketed by my mom and dad, my hair an unruly riot of brown curls. I was wearing jeans and a white t-shirt that had a huge Hello Kitty on the front, and I was smiling a huge smile with teeth too big for my face. Joey stood tall and sullen on the other side of my father with a Tarheels basketball vest on.

"You haven't changed much," Jack commented with an

amused tone. I threw one of my small toss pillows at him. He smirked. "Are these your parents?"

I nodded. My mom with her bare face, long straight brown hair and light yellow sundress was beautiful despite her tight smile in the picture. My father had curling light brown hair and wore a completely straight face, neither smiling nor frowning. I often stared at that picture wondering what was going on in their heads, wishing I could remember anything that would give me a clue about what they were thinking that day . . . or any day. Were they happy to have moved here or was it a burden? Perhaps they'd had no other choice.

"That was taken right when we moved here."

"Where did you move from?"

"All over. My parents traveled a lot. My father always had some kind of business that needed tending to, and we would move. The last place I remember was North Carolina, but Butler Cove is the longest I've stayed anywhere. And I lived here every summer with Nana, so this felt like home anyway."

"What did he do, your father?" It was a natural question, based on the information I had provided. I hated this topic.

"He was in sales with a company in Savannah. Let's talk about something else." He was always selling something, always doing a deal, always about to make it . . . this time. Always up and down.

"A bit young for prom." He was looking at the picture Nana had taken of Joey, Colton Graves, Jazz and me.

"That was Joey's prom. He invited Jazz and me. That's his friend Colton Graves, Colt. They played football together."

He nodded and moved along a bit. "Time frame?"

"The books? Eighth grade."

He pulled out Book One of the *Warriors of Erath* series. "You read this way before the movies then . . ." he mused, like that satisfied him for some reason. "A bit young for this, weren't you?"

"I read it in secret, at least from my mother," I said with a sly grin.

"Really? How did you get away with that? A flashlight under the covers?" Jack left the shelves and started back toward me.

"I have a secret reading nook in the attic."

"Really?" he asked, climbing onto the bed. "Can I see it sometime? Are boys allowed?"

"Sure." I laughed. "It's a bit dusty and overdue for a make-over though. I went up there yesterday afternoon. To think."

He pressed me back and lay down by my side, his head propped on his hand. "What were you thinking?"

"That I'd never forget your kisses," I said honestly.

"I'm afraid to ask, given your headache this morning, but do you remember last night?"

Heat bloomed in my cheeks. Looking at his expression, I realized he may think he had taken advantage of me. It was no secret I'd been a bit intoxicated when I made that phone call.

"Every single thing," I whispered. My eyes flicked down to his lips as I thought about kissing him again. Then I remembered his original reason for coming over. "Do you regret last night?" I asked. *Please, please say no.*

"What? No. What makes you think that?"

"You came over to tell me it had been a mistake to get involved with me . . . and then during the night . . ." I trailed off.

"No, that's not what I meant by that . . . I mean it was, but not in the way you mean. I was trying to explain that I can't stay away from you, no matter what all the reasons are or should be."

I took a deep breath. "So don't."

"I can't." He ran a hand down the side of my face. My heart fluttered with hope.

Ugh, I was so easy.

I wanted to ask about Audrey. But I was too afraid of the answer. Jack had asked me to take a chance on him last night, and by my actions I had agreed to it. I needed to trust him. I would ask about her, I promised myself, but I didn't want to do it just yet.

Then he said, "I told Audrey I'd met someone."

I swallowed down the ridiculous wave of joy that had suddenly ballooned in my chest. "Really?" I managed as smoothly as I could.

"Really," he whispered, leaning forward to kiss me. I was glad I had gone and brushed my teeth. His lips moved softly over mine. It felt good.

He pulled away and looked serious. "A couple more things we need to talk about. Firstly, your phone call last night." He cocked an eyebrow at me.

Oh that. I covered my eyes in mortification. He gently peeled my hand off. "You asked me what it was all about. I didn't mean to lead you on, I couldn't help it, and it was two sided, wasn't it?"

I nodded.

He went on, "And I would *never* do something for you in the hopes you would feel indebted to me and sleep with me. I felt sick when you said that."

"I'm sorry."

"Don't be, I know you were mad and upset. I just . . . I need you to know . . . I find you sexy as hell." He kissed my hand softly. "And while most of the time I am so turned on around you I literally can't think of anything else apart from what it would feel like to be buried inside you—"

I gasped, but he went on as if he hadn't just shocked the hell out of me. "I am not going to do it. I don't want you to ever regret anything that happens between us."

I had grown hot, achy, and slightly breathless at his bold words, and now he was saying it was never going to happen.

I squeezed my thighs together and squirmed under the comforter. "Ever?"

"Shit, Keri Ann, you'd test a saint. I'm trying here."

"I just want to understand. You want to sleep with me, but you refuse to. Even if I decide that's what I want."

He nodded.

"Seriously?" I asked.

When he didn't say anything, I continued skeptically, "Is this some kind of reverse psychology?"

"No." He laughed. "I just know I'm going to have to leave here soon, and it's going to be hard enough to do that already." The reminder he was definitely leaving, no matter what happened between us, flipped my stomach over. And not in a good way.

But he was right, I had admitted to myself last night that taking that step with him would seal him in my heart and mind forever. For a moment I wished I had gotten my virginity out of the way years ago, in case he was worried about leaving a broken-hearted girl behind. Did he think I was a walking cliché; that as soon as he took my virginity, I'd expect marriage and babies? No, this was about me wanting to be with Jack specifically. In a way I had never ever wanted to be with anyone else.

"Why are we talking about this?" I asked, irritated at the turn of my thoughts.

"I just don't want you thinking that's all I want from you. I never want you to look back and think you might have been pressured."

"I'm a big girl, Jack. I think I can handle myself."

"I'm sure you can," he winked, "and also, I plan on persuading you to accept my gift of getting the floors finished, and I don't want you thinking I'm doing it for any other reason than if you refuse, I'm going to be left with this huge annoying credit at a flooring company, of all things, and nothing to spend it on."

I snorted. "So it would be me doing *you* a favor? Nice try." I rolled my eyes. "No. And I wouldn't think that, I was just mad when I called you last night."

"I wanted to do something for you. I don't know why, I just did. Maybe it was that for a second I got really excited about the project, and I had the means to get it done, so I did it. Or maybe it was that I was looking forward to seeing your face when something you had wanted to get done for so long was finally achieved."

This was quite persuasive, I had to admit.

"Or maybe it was because I imagined that when I saw your face light up, I wanted it to be me who made it happen."

Damn, this guy was good.

"No," I said again, but I sounded as shaken as I felt. I hadn't realized flooring could be so romantic. "I should have told you my face lights up over a bag of Lindor truffles. You could have saved yourself a fortune."

He got a wicked gleam in his eye and his lips descended to mine. "I did say I was going to persuade you."

CHAPTER TWENTY-FIVE

The rain had broken the stifling humidity, and while it was still warm, it was finally that perfect time of year. The time anyone who lives in the South dreams about all summer long with its bright sun and long shadows and a slight chill in the breeze.

Jack and I, despite his persuasive kisses this morning, had reached an impasse on the floors. There was still no furniture and book club was at my house. Consequently, our meeting would be happening outside on the porch.

I dropped Jack back at the beach house to read through a bunch of scripts Katie had sent him before heading to work myself. I wasn't there two minutes before Hector broke out in an operatic voice with 'O Mio Babino Caro' in the kitchen. I guess the flush in my cheeks and the ridiculous need to smile while asking about saltshakers and mustard had given me away. I rolled my eyes at him and tried hard to pull myself together.

By the time book club rolled round, I was a little calmer. Although my stomach did clench as I walked past the living room where the blanket was folded neatly by the fireplace.

Mrs. Weaton came through my back door fifteen minutes early bearing a huge basket of lemon squares and asked me to help her with the ice tea she'd made. We trotted back across the yard.

"So dear, he's a dreamy one, isn't he? And so charming," she sighed with a soft smile.

I laughed. "Yes he is, Mrs. Weaton, yes he is. Now you know you can't tell anyone, right?"

"I know, dear. And far be it for me to offer opinions, I was quite the little go-er in my day, but you best guard your heart, honey. And you know . . . that whole secrecy thing can make for a much more intense time than normal."

Go-er? I shook my head. Did that mean popular or slutty? I focused on the heart stuff.

"I'm trying, Mrs. Weaton. To guard my heart," I clarified. "But, just in case I fail, can you make sure and stock up on the lemon squares and maybe that chocolate caramel pudding with the sea salt?"

"Sure will, honey." She patted me on the arm. In the same moment, we heard the roar of a motorcycle going down the street on the other side of the house. She noticed my attention and raised her penciled-in eyebrows.

I shrugged. "He rides a bike, did he tell you that?"

She shook her head and sighed again. "As I said, dreamy. Let's hope he doesn't put on a tool belt. Then it's all over."

I sputtered. She just grinned.

I headed back up the steps, still laughing and held open the screen door for my aged companion. Jazz's car pulled up and disgorged her, Faith, and Liz.

"Who's minding the shop, Faith?" I asked with a smile, admiring, as I always did, the way she could pull off her elegant platinum hair and ruby red lips.

"I closed up early, there's hardly anyone around at the moment. And anyway, I made a huge sale today."

"You did? That's great."

Faith's store was an eclectic but super elegant mix of designer furnishings and one of a kind pieces—as well as jewelry she designed herself and accessories she saw here and there and couldn't pass up. She always joked it was the 'buy high' addiction for her and it was a good thing she had a shop to resell stuff in, or she'd be on an episode of *Hoarders*. We would roll our eyes when she said this, as her home and her store were as far away from impulsive and chaotic as one could get. I loved to go hang out there with Jazz just to sit in the serene, awesome candle-smelling-chic-ness.

I looked back and forth between Jazz and Faith, who seemed to be having an entire silent conversation. "What?"

"Well," said Jazz. "Please don't kill me . . ." She affected a fake sheepish look that told me she really didn't give a hoot if I liked what she was about to say or not.

"Oh, man. What, Jazz?"

"Well, uh . . . since you finished it last night, and Faith had been asking about your stuff, I decided to take the chandelier in to the store this morning." Her cringe looked a little less fake as she reached the end of her confession. Probably because my face must have shown complete horror.

"You did what?" I barely got the words out as the blood drained from my head. I wasn't ready. "It wasn't ready!"

Dear God, I felt like I had just woken up naked at a fair.

"Jazz, you had no right to do that. I wasn't finished, there was still so much, and the wiring . . . the wiring hasn't been tested, and I'm not sure I'm ready yet, what would I even charge for that piece of crap, and who the hell—"

Faith had said something, and her words finally penetrated. "It what?"

"It sold," Faith repeated with a shrug of her shoulders and a huge smile.

"It did?" I whispered. "How much?"

Faith and Jazz beamed, and Jazz bounced up and down as we all looked on.

"Well," Faith said. "I usually have a forty percent mark up on my home furnishings, and I wanted to make it worth your time, and mine, so I sold it for forty-one hundred dollars."

I made some sort of weird squeaking sound as I reacted in shock. "You what? Four thousand and one hundred dollars? Who in their right mind would pay that much for a glued together bunch of washed up stuff?"

"It was beautiful, Keri Ann," Faith pronounced, as Jazz nodded and murmured her agreement.

"You mean I made," I quickly paused to calculate, "about two thousand four hundred dollars today?"

I was breathless and a little shaky. Mrs. Weaton steered me onto one of the rocking chairs, and I made to sit down, and then stopped cold.

"Who bought it?" I asked.

Oh hell, no. I glared at Jazz. "Who bought it, Jazz?" She furrowed her brows in confusion.

"What do you mean?" she asked, and then she got it. "Oh." She looked at Faith. "I wasn't there when the sale happened. Faith, who did you say bought it? Did someone come in to the store?"

I grabbed onto Jazz's hand and she gripped me hard back. I didn't even want to acknowledge the kinds of feelings I would be having if she told me a guy bought it, or someone from California called. And it would be the latter probably, at his behest, if the flooring debacle was any kind of indication.

"Oh," said Faith, oblivious to the tension. "This lady is here with her husband on vacation from Ohio, some kind of second honeymoon, whatever. Anyway, she saw it and almost went into spasms of pleasure. She couldn't stop touching it, absolutely adored it. If she hadn't bought it, I was going to have to start charging her groping fees." She laughed.

My hand relaxed infinitesimally. The fact that I had automatically assumed it wasn't a legitimate sale wasn't lost on Jazz, and she'd give me a hard time about it later. But for now we grinned at each other stupidly. At least, *I* was grinning stupidly. Jazz would cluck like a hen if she could, such was the proud bearing of her shoulders and *I told you so* eyebrows.

"And I'd like to commission three more, all slightly different of course. Do you have any other things I can put in the shop?"

"She sure does," said Jazz. And the next half hour consisted of us bringing stuff down from the attic and Jazz showcasing all my various projects . . . from an old mirror framed with driftwood to sea glass-bejeweled photo frames . . . like she was hosting a promo special. I looked on in bashful wonder.

Finally, both Jazz's mom and Brenda arrived and we all got comfortable on the porch to start the book discussion.

"So, who thinks the parallel dimension theme is symbolic of the unattainability of the perfect man?" Jazz asked loudly. And basically, for me, it went downhill from there.

Between the pointed observations from Mrs. Weaton and Jazz about the heroine having to learn to trust and suspend her disbelief, and the references by the oblivious members of the book club about how perfectly cast Jack Eversea was in the role, I decided to stay out of most of the discussion.

Instead I opted to refill ice tea and offer snacks. It was the longest hour and a half ever.

At about six o'clock we were wrapping it up, and I felt my phone buzz. I waved goodbye to Liz and Faith who were catching a ride with Brenda and slunk into the kitchen for some privacy. A bubble of nervous tension lodged in my throat.

> *Late Night Visitor: Do you ever watch sunsets?*

> *Me: Yes, we get those here, too. You missing California?*

I wondered if my text responses came over snarky, or amusing.

> *Late Night Visitor: California, not especially. You, yes. I found a spot for a sunset—you want to come watch it with me?*

I put the phone down and was banging my head against the kitchen wall when Jazz came back in. She cocked her head at me. I pointed at my phone. She picked it up and looked at the text.

"Late Night Visitor? Interesting . . . Oh man, sunsets? Does he have a playbook?" She rolled her eyes. It would have seemed cheesy from anyone else but not from Jack for some reason.

"Jazz, I'm in so much trouble. I really, really like him. And he has to go back to Audrey."

I tried to explain Jack's situation to her as best I could.

"But just because they are photographed together, doesn't mean they actually have to be together? Right?"

"God, I hope not. But he hasn't really said. Am I being totally played, Jazz?"

"Look, Keri Ann. I don't think so. I mean, I saw his face yesterday when you walked out, it didn't look like it was easy for him. But what do I know? I don't want to give you bad advice. Nana always said 'love was taking a chance at life'. . . or was it 'life was taking a chance at love'? Hmm, oh well. Or maybe it's 'go for it, you only live once.'"

"Fat lot of good you are." I thumped her arm.

Nana always had a lot of wise nuggets and greeting card phrases tripping off her tongue. Most of the time we'd roll our eyes. Affectionately, of course. I probably should have paid more attention. I'd take a fortune cookie for help right now.

"Look," Jazz swung an arm around my shoulder, "I've been telling you this forever, but it bears repeating. You is kind. You is smart. You is important."

"Ha ha, Jazz. I'm serious here."

"So am I, K. Listen, you are gorgeous, you're funny, you're talented. I know deep down you believe in yourself. The facts speak for themselves, and I'm not just talking about the chandelier you sold today. There is no reason you wouldn't attract any man you wanted. I think you need to trust your gut."

A small kernel of quiet confidence deep inside made itself known as I heard, and really for the first time, started to believe the words, started to trust myself. And my gut said Jack had asked me to take a chance on him, and I should go for it.

Jazz grabbed her backpack and pulled out a bunch of files and papers, then headed to my fridge and pulled out a bottle of white wine and a block of cheese.

"What are you doing?" I asked.

"Packing a romantic picnic." She grabbed grapes, a box of crackers, and a knife. I handed her the bottle opener, and she stuffed it all in the bag.

"Wow, thanks, I'd love to spend the evening with you, where shall we go?" I asked her.

"Idiot. Do you have any plastic wine glasses?"

"No." I reached for two glass ones and wrapped each one in a dishcloth.

Was I really going to do this?

Yes. Yes, I was. I grabbed my phone and texted Jack to pick me up in twenty minutes, and then Jazz and I raced upstairs so I could get ready.

CHAPTER TWENTY-SIX

*F*ifteen minutes later, I flew down the front steps with the backpack as Jack stopped his bike and planted a leg on the ground. He didn't take his helmet off but handed me a spare one he was cradling between his legs.

"I had Katie send it," he answered my unspoken question.

At least I hadn't done much to style my hair other than braid it loosely. I smiled, put the helmet on, and adjusted the pale pink cashmere scarf Joey had given me last Christmas.

"Nice bike."

"Thanks, it's a Ducati. I hope you aren't nervous of speed."

My heart was beating a mile a minute, but it had nothing to do with the bike.

If Jack thought I wasn't dressed appropriately to ride a motorcycle, he didn't say anything. I grabbed his arm and swung a cowboy-booted leg over his bike, causing my short brown jersey dress to hike up around my bare thighs.

I scooted forward as far as I could, making sure my skirt was safely tucked under my behind and molded myself to him, gripping his jean-clad legs with mine. I wrapped my arms around his middle, and then inside the soft leather jacket that was open. His body was hard and strong under his t-shirt.

He cleared his throat. "You ready?"

"Yeah."

"Let's go for a drive first, then we'll stop. You up for that?"

"Sounds great."

He brought a hand down to my thigh for a second, then he gave my leg a brief squeeze and slid his hand slowly off. He turned the bike on. My hands gripped his middle tighter and I held my breath as I heard and felt the deep roar, and then we took off.

I had never been on a motorcycle before. It was scary and exhilarating and sexy as all hell. My blood pounded through me in waves as I reveled in the feeling of being wrapped around Jack's hard warm body, the deep throbbing reverberation of the bike beneath us, and the cold wind whipping over my skin.

The sun was low in the sky as we crossed the bridge to the mainland. I cast my eyes across to the yellow and silver streaks of the horizon. The reflection of the sky over the water of the Intracoastal Waterway created a gleaming sea of mercury. I would remember this moment forever.

When we reached the other side, Jack let out the throttle and leaned down, head into the wind. I gasped and pressed myself to him harder, laughing with exhilaration. My hands felt the rumble of Jack's chest, and I knew he was laughing too.

I had no idea how fast we were going, but I was pretty sure we were breaking about seventeen laws. There was hardly any traffic, and we were far away from Butler Cove in a matter of minutes. I couldn't believe he was taking such a risk, if he was pulled over, his cover would be blown immediately.

I wished I could press my face to his back, but the helmet was a bit of a problem, although I was grateful for it. Instead, I pressed my chest against him and splayed my hands out on his abdomen, trying for as much contact as possible.

It was clear he was a skillful and confident rider, his motions completely fluid and in tune with the throbbing machine between our legs. Every time he took a curve and we leaned to the side, I hugged him to me tighter. I began to wish for every curve even though the proximity of my knee to the pavement was scary as shit.

It felt so good to have an excuse to hang onto Jack. I was amused at myself as I realized what a pick-up gimmick this was. There were the classic three I could think of: inviting a girl over for a scary movie, playing guitar for her, and finally, giving her a ride on a motorcycle where she was obliged to hang onto you for dear life. But, strangely, I didn't mind. In fact, I realized how much Jack was sharing with me. And I didn't care that it was working.

I had a sudden memory of Jack's face above me, breathing hard, his lips taut, cheeks flushed and eyes glazed as I lost myself to him last night. I gasped at the hot, piercing lust that instantly shot through me.

The bike slowed down as we approached the last break in the two-lane highway before the interstate.

Jack turned into the break in the median and came to an idling stop. He shifted and turned as far as he could to me. There was no one around, so he pulled his helmet off and flipped up my visor. We were both grinning stupidly, although he couldn't see my mouth. His hair was sticking up all over the place. I was sure people paid fortunes to have their hair look like that. I couldn't say the same for what mine was going to look like.

"Are you okay?"

"Yes, this is amazing." I meant it.

His brow furrowed. "What happened back there? I felt you suddenly tense up on me. Did I scare you?"

My eyes flicked down for a second in embarrassment. I hadn't realized I had had such a physical reaction to my memory of last night.

I took a deep breath and decided to come clean. "I was thinking about last night in front of the fire," I said, looking him straight in the eye. "Thinking about how you made me feel. I want to do that again."

I literally saw him lose his breath. I knew what he looked like when he was aroused, and this had certainly done the trick. He wasn't laughing any more.

"Shit. Keri Ann," he croaked, his mouth firming into a grim line. He mashed his helmet back on his head and turned back to the road. "Hang on," he said and gunned the engine.

I hung on. I guessed I had gone too far. He looked seriously pissed off. We drove back toward the island at about the speed we had left it. But now that he was probably taking me home and putting an end to our evening plans, it wasn't quite as fun for me. We should have put an end to the whole thing this morning, or last night before I knew what it was like to be touched by a god. Or maybe even before then so my heart hadn't gotten tangled in the mix.

We didn't head home. As soon as we hit the end of the bridge, Jack took the next turn down to Broad Landing. He circled down under the bridge and pulled the bike to a stop. The sun was really low in the sky casting an orange glow over everything.

Relieved, I climbed off the bike, my legs feeling like jelly, and took off the heavy backpack and my helmet. "This is where I kayak from."

Staying astride the bike, Jack flipped the kickstand down and took off his helmet, too.

I caught his eyes for a moment. I wanted to apologize for being so forward, but his arm suddenly shot out and hauled me against him.

His other hand smoothed the hair from my face, and then tunneled into the braid at my nape, pulling it loose. His fingers worked through the strands, separating them gently but insistently as I gazed into his eyes. When he was done, his hand massaged my neck and scalp slowly. It felt good.

I had no idea what Jack was seeing in my blue eyes, but I could see a thousand questions in his. Questions I felt I'd never have the answer to. I stared up into his beautiful face. I wanted to tell him how amazing he was, how talented. How he was so much more, and he didn't ever have to doubt his worth or measure it against the adoration of his fans or the dictates of his handlers. Or ever be afraid of whatever had happened to him as a child. We were so close I could see small tiny freckles across his upper cheekbones and a small faint scar I had never noticed before in his eyebrow. An imperfection that made him all the more perfect.

I lifted a finger and traced it gently, then smoothed the small furrow that appeared between his eyes. "Jack . . . I was always told to live life, to grab it with both hands . . . I never have." I swallowed over my nerves, hoping the words were coming out right. "You were right, last night. I have been afraid to start living my life. Living means loving, and I know this sounds dumb, but all that has ever given me is pain. First losing my parents and then Nana. I know that's a stupid parallel to draw for never wanting to date anyone or . . . be with anyone."

Jack smoothed a lock of hair away from my eyes. I was absolutely pinned to the moment by the intensity in his gaze. I tried to go on without tripping over my words. "I don't want to be anymore. Afraid, I mean."

Jack's eyes flickered. "Sweetheart, there hasn't been one moment when I've considered you afraid. I look at you, and all I see is certainty. Courage. Bravery. God, I've never met anyone so sure and so strong in who they are." His mouth tilted up on one side. "It's . . . epic."

I was humbled, and to be honest, floored by his words. That was never how I saw myself. Ever. I was afraid of *everything*. I dropped my eyes a moment, but Jack's finger under my chin urged me to look up at him. I steeled myself to get it all out before I lost my nerve. "And I don't want any regrets. I've never been . . . frivolous, never done anything without weighing up the consequences. I feel like I've always had a heavy heart . . . Nothing—no one," I amended, "ever seemed worth taking a risk for." I took a deep breath and shored up my nerves. "This is. You are. I can't explain it. I—"

Jack's mouth parted slightly, although I had no idea if that was good or bad. His gaze roamed over my face to my mouth, effectively cutting off my words.

I didn't finish talking, but let my hand drift around to the back of his head and pulled him down to my mouth.

He didn't resist.

I let out a soft sigh as his lips met mine. It was so right. This felt so right. It was like it spoke to me deep in my soul. I opened my lips to him and accepted the soft slide of his tongue and heard him groan deep in his chest. I wound my hand into a fistful of his hair. I could feel this kiss through my whole body, and my heart swelled in my chest and my legs shifted to get closer.

I wasn't sure who instigated the move, but suddenly I had a leg across his lap and his hand on my thigh was dragging me astride him.

He'd lifted me effortlessly.

I let out a heavy breath as my skirt rode up, and I pressed my whole body to him.

"God," Jack groaned.

My head tipped back, gasping, as Jack's mouth found my neck.

He was hard and swollen beneath me. Moaning, I rocked forward against the rough ridge of his jeans.

"Christ," he hissed out. His arm locked around my waist and pressed me down hard against him.

I whimpered. Couldn't help it.

He dragged his lips up to mine and plundered my mouth as we rocked against each other. There was no argument in the world that could have convinced me Jack shouldn't be inside me at that moment.

"Take me home," I managed, between kisses. He pulled his mouth away from mine, breathing hard, and searched my eyes. His gaze, made luminous by the sunset we were missing, was piercing. I knew what he'd said to me last night and this morning, and I knew I faced rejection again, but I had to try. I wanted this. I wanted him. And I wanted him sealed in my heart forever. No matter what happened.

"Please . . . make love to me, Jack."

He closed his eyes tight and let out a breath, dropping his forehead to mine. After what felt like an eternity, he drew me into a tight embrace, his face buried in my neck. I wound my arms around his head and shoulders, holding him tightly back. If this was all I could have of Jack, I would take it with my heart wide open.

He was going to say no. I mentally prepared for his answer and tried hard not to let the feeling of rejection unfold inside me. I knew I should take the words back and take the decision away from him before he had to tell me no again. It wasn't fair of me to ask him to reject me again when we'd already talked about this.

I pulled back. "Never m—"

"Yes," he said at the same time.

"What?" I whispered.

"Yes. Let's go."

CHAPTER TWENTY-SEVEN

We roared past my house. Jack had asked me if I needed anything from home. I didn't. The short drive to the beach house took hours. I tried not to think of the last time I left there. It was only yesterday afternoon and it felt like eons ago, like I was just a little girl back then.

Finally, we stowed the bike, took our helmets off, and laughing, raced up the stairs to the house. Jack fumbled with the door lock, but finally we were inside.

I laid the backpack down, and he hauled me back and spun me around, pinning me against the wall with his hard body. I did some crazy moan-gasp thing and, looking me deep in the eyes, he hitched my leg up against his thigh and pressed against my center.

Holy shit.

My heart was beating hard in my chest, almost in my throat. I clutched at him. I wanted to feel his strength, so I pushed his jacket off his shoulders.

He let go of my bare thigh for a moment while he shucked off his jacket and let it fall to the floor.

I kept my leg hooked around him, reluctant to lose contact

for even a moment. I reached for his t-shirt, but he grabbed it behind his head and pulled it off, our gaze only breaking for a millisecond.

My cold hands found Jack's warm, smooth skin.

He tensed under my touch, his eyes now slate gray in the darkened hall.

Jack's hand came up to my face, and his thumb brushed over my lips like when my tongue had accidentally found him. This time he pushed it against my lips, seeking entry. I hesitated a split second before sucking him into my mouth to taste the tang of his skin. Jack's breathing hitched as he fed it to me, sliding it in and out against my tongue. His mouth grew taut, his nostrils flaring slightly, his gaze pinned on the action.

Watching his reactions, my own breath had grown shallow and irregular. My pulse was spiking, the heat inside of me swirling up between us like a fever.

Slowly he pulled his thumb out and rubbed the wet pad across my lower lip, pulling my lip down.

The laughing was over.

Every point of contact my body had with Jack's was like a conduit for an ever-increasing maelstrom of feeling. The feel of his rough denim-clad hips under my bare thigh, the press of his hardness against my apex, and the warm skin of his hand as it roamed up my thigh and waist to my neck, to my chest. His mouth. My heart.

Jack tugged my scarf from its loosely wound place at my neck. In moments, his hand cupped my breast through my dress, his thumb running across my nipple.

My breath came in ragged gasps. "Jack . . ." I managed, my chest involuntarily thrusting forward into his hand.

His lips quirked. "What about this?" he whispered roughly and slipped his fingers under the low neckline of my dress, tugging it and my bra down. He feathered a light touch around my bare nipple in the cool air.

"Gah . . ." I managed.

He chuckled, and then his warm hand palmed my breast more fully and I moaned.

His eyes flickered. Sliding down my body, he bent his legs and hooked my other leg around him. He stood up quickly, taking my weight, his hands on my bare thighs and pressed me firmly back against the wall.

I gasped and grabbed onto his broad shoulders to steady myself.

Jack's face was intense as he lowered his mouth to mine. He stopped millimeters away, his breath softly fanning my lips.

"Are you sure?" he whispered.

I nodded. "Yes."

He captured my mouth into a deep kiss and pressed himself hard against me.

I moaned and pressed back, sliding my tongue into his mouth and kissing him with every ounce of feeling I had inside me. Showing him how I felt.

A rough sound emanated from deep in his throat. "God, Keri Ann," he murmured, his mouth leaving mine and leaving a hot, moist trail down my neck and under my ear. "You have no idea how you make me feel."

I shivered.

I knew what he was making *me* feel. Was he feeling the same? I was on a tidal wave of sensation that was almost too much. I felt like I was quaking inside.

"Hang on tight," he said guiding my arms more firmly around his neck. He pulled away from the wall and headed for the stairs.

"You have a habit of carrying me up stairs." I laughed nervously as he effortlessly ascended.

"I'm part caveman, you know, I can't help it. Something about you brings it out in me."

"Oh wait," I said, as we got to the top of the stairs. "We might need the backpack."

"Why?"

I hid my flaming face back into his neck. "Protection."

"What?"

"Protection," I said a little louder, mortified.

In his bedroom, rather than setting me down, he tossed me onto the soft covers. "I knew it."

"What?"

"I knew you'd be blushing. I heard you the first time, I just wanted to see your face," he said devilishly and darted back down the stairs.

I quickly snapped my knees together, aware of how I'd landed.

He was back in a flash, holding a box.

My nerves started getting the better of me. There he was with his magnificent body, bare chested, jeans hanging on his hips, his hair unkempt both from the helmet and my fingers running through it. A god like this had probably had his pick of women for years and had probably picked all the flawless ones.

"A bit presumptuous, weren't you?" he teased.

"Um . . . I . . ."

"I'm glad. I was thinking I was going to have to tear Devon's bedroom and bathroom apart looking for some." He moved toward the lamp on the bedside table.

I swallowed. "You could probably keep that off . . . if you wanted."

He switched it on and came back around, putting a knee on the bed between my feet and cocking his head to the side.

I made to sit up but he stayed me. "Not on your life. You're gorgeous Keri Ann. I've been fantasizing about you naked since we met. You don't think I'm going to miss my chance, do you?" He raised a naughty eyebrow.

And just like that, the wave of nerves subsided.

"Come here, then," I whispered more huskily than I'd intended. Complying immediately, Jack's mouth was on mine.

I welcomed him eagerly, returning the passionate thrust and parry of his tongue and arching up to his body. We drank and nipped at each other hungrily, hands roaming and bodies straining.

Breathing hard, Jack pulled back enough to pull my cowboy boots off, then he pulled me up to my knees and grasped the bottom of my dress.

I lifted my arms to assist him, thankful for Jazz's assistance in picking out my hot pink bra and panties set.

"Seriously?" Jack asked, his voice strained. "You're killing me." He braced stock still watching me from beneath his dark lashes. His jaw was clenched hard.

Just like last night, I ran my palm down the planes of his chest, but this time when I got to his jeans, he didn't stop me.

My heart pounded as my fingers worked to unbutton Jack's jeans. The bulge under my hand was making them a little hard to manage and every time my fingers brushed against him, I heard his breathing change. I didn't know his reactions to my hands on him could cause such a corresponding reaction in *me*. I was hot and throbbing and desperate to have him naked.

Shaking, I finally released the last button revealing his

boxers. Instinctively, I slid my hand inside and curled it around his length. Call me a hussy, but I needed to know what I was in for.

Oh, my.

Jack hissed out a breath and grabbed my wrist.

"I want to touch you." I pouted with a small smile over my nerves.

"You will. You can. But I promise you I don't need any help right now. I'm so fucking turned on, I can hardly see straight."

His words punched into my gut and set my slow boil into overdrive. I could not believe, in this moment, that I held so much power. I hurriedly pushed his jeans down his thighs, and before he could move to assist me, I shoved his shorts down, too. A dark swirling tattoo snaked around his hip, but I didn't pay attention to that. I was more interested in what else I had revealed.

Jack immediately pushed me back on the bed and kissed me hungrily.

I gasped into his mouth at the amazing feel of his skin against mine, his weight settling on me and between my legs.

Pushing down my bra, Jack's tongue found my nipple. Within moments I was literally writhing under him. I arched up, whimpering more as the movement caused his erection to press against my damp core.

He rocked against me and it felt like heaven. Then he made his way south, kissing down my stomach, stopping to dip his tongue into my belly button. My nerves ratcheted up.

Dead focused, Jack slowly peeled my panties down my legs. The look on his face sent my pulse into overdrive.

I was panting and completely not in control of my body's reactions. I stilled, and he unhooked the last foot from my underwear and slowly ran his hands up my legs, parting them firmly as he went, his eyes, and then his mouth following the movement. His touch was a trail of fire up the inside of my thigh.

Shifting, Jack settled himself more firmly between my legs. Okay, now I was a little embarrassed. I squirmed and tensed as I watched his green eyes drink in the sight.

"God, you're beautiful," Jack groaned, and before I could have second thoughts, his mouth came down on me.

I cried out, bucking against him, causing his hands to grip my thighs more firmly to keep them in place. His tongue flicked over me.

Oh my God!

I squeezed my eyes shut as if that would help contain my reaction. It just served to focus all my senses on what he was doing to me. I was almost catatonic with pleasure and sensation, my body tight and prickly as if my skin couldn't hold the feelings inside me.

His mouth was hot, his tongue coaxing and exploring. And then his hands joined his mouth, and he eased a finger inside me.

I grabbed fistfuls of the sheets. I wanted him to stop but I didn't. I wanted to watch him, but I couldn't. It was like sliding headlong toward the edge of a cliff hoping to hell there was a soft landing. I was completely lost to sensation as he loved me with his tongue and his fingers.

He seemed to touch some deep and magical place inside me, because suddenly the cliff was there, and I was crying out as I flew out over the edge, arching my hips up into his mouth.

"Oh God, oh God, oh God," I gasped.

"No shit," Jack said, his voice rough, his breath sawing in and out, matching mine.

He placed a lingering kiss on my thigh, left the bed a moment, and then he was back, holding me as I still shuddered, kissing my eyelids until I willed them open.

The sight of Jack above me, his gray-green eyes darkened with passion and staring into mine, his weight on me, was too much for me to handle. I tried to swallow over the lump in my throat as I reached up and ran a hand across his beautiful cheekbones. He closed his eyes and let out a long breath.

"Where'd you go?" I whispered.

"Protection." He swallowed hard and loud and opened his eyes. He held my gaze as his body rocked forward and I felt his heavy arousal sliding against my wetness. "I'm scared I'll hurt you."

I opened my legs wider and wrapped one around him. "I was never one to pull a band aid off slowly. Besides, we could be struck by lightning right now and I don't think I'd feel it or care. I want you inside me, Jack. Now. Not slowly, but like right now."

"Aahh, God, Keri Ann," he croaked. Then he lowered his mouth to mine and at the same time he rocked back and then forward as he eased himself into me, stretching me, filling me. I forgot to breathe. It felt amazing, like coming home, and I wanted more. I knew he was afraid to hurt me, and I knew he might, but I didn't care. I rocked up, throwing my other leg up around him so he had no choice. He gave in, groaning and plunging his tongue into my mouth in a searing kiss that tasted of my passion. At the same time his hips rocked forward, taking me completely.

"Jeeesssssus," Jack rasped.

A sharp pain wrenched my mouth from Jack's. For a moment I was winded, but I kept him locked to me with my legs. I didn't want him stopping.

"God, Keri Ann, I'm so sorry."

Jack kissed me back and I slowly rocked my hips against his until he responded. His mouth left mine and his warm tongue licked the place my tear had escaped.

"Open your eyes," Jack whispered.

I complied and met his deep and searching gaze.

"You okay?" His breathing was irregular, and I could feel the quivering tension in his body under my hands.

"Yes," I breathed. "More than okay. This feels . . . you feel . . ." I wasn't sure how to describe what I was feeling.

"Amazing," Jack finished with a small smile, rocking into me again, harder this time. I gasped and captured my lower lip with my teeth, nodding in agreement.

He held my gaze, his hips moving back and forth, and I stared into his eyes with wonder, matching his strokes, as this new sensation took hold of me.

I noticed all the small changes of his face as the things he was feeling became etched across his features. I saw the tiny beads of sweat on his upper lip and the flush on his cheekbones. I saw the crease in his brow and heard his breathing as he gritted his teeth. His arms and body quivered with tension and restraint as he braced himself above me. Then his movements picked up speed and became slightly erratic.

I wasn't sure what was more erotic, the feeling of Jack sliding in and out of me or watching him lose the last vestiges of his control, but suddenly it didn't matter because I was right there with him. I tried to keep my eyes open, but the tide of feeling building inside me was as familiar as it was utterly foreign. I gasped under the onslaught, squeezing my eyes shut and writhing up to meet his thrusts.

"Look at me," Jack rasped out. I snapped my eyes open, not really seeing anything beyond what I was feeling. Except,

I saw him shift up slightly and felt, as his hand came between us, his fingers sliding over my sensitive and swollen flesh. The last thing I heard was Jack's rough voice saying, "Come for me, Keri Ann," and then, as I complied, "Holy shit."

Jack was no longer holding back as I rode out the waves, gasping and clenching around him as he slammed into me several more times before letting go, his face contorted in harsh and beautiful pleasure.

"Oh, God, Keri Ann."

I drew him down to me, holding his shuddering body tightly as I struggled to get my breath back. I knew the vision of Jack's face above me as he climaxed would be etched in my mind forever. After a few moments, he relaxed and wrapped his arms around me, letting out a deep sigh.

CHAPTER TWENTY-EIGHT

$\mathcal{J}$ watched Jack cross the room as he returned from the bathroom, and my eyes were drawn to the crazy swirling black dragon on his hip and glute. It looked like it covered some kind of scar. I had felt the ridges of his skin beneath it with my calf as we made love. I wanted to ask about it.

Jack crawled back into bed next to me and gathered me to him. He brushed my hair off my forehead and kissed it.

I sighed and snuggled up to his side, curling into a ball. "Hmmm, so this is what it feels like to be a woman, finally. Thank you for divesting me of my virginity."

A laugh rumbled through his chest beneath my cheek. "I knew you were using me. So are you done with me now?"

"Not even close." I let my hand roam across his chest.

I wondered if boys' nipples were as sensitive. On a whim, I pushed up and nipped gently at the flat of his nipple with my teeth.

His even breathing stumbled, and grabbing my hand, he slid it down his stomach under the sheet. Pressing my palm against his stiff erection, he murmured, "That's good, because it seems I haven't gotten nearly enough of you yet."

"Wow," I whispered at the hot silky feel of him and then swallowed audibly. Like a gulp. *Smooth, Keri Ann.* "I didn't know that was possible . . . that guys . . . I mean that you could . . . so soon."

"Trust me, it's new for me, too."

I grinned at him and sat up, sliding the sheet down. He had seen all of me—it was only fair I should be allowed the same privilege.

He placed his hands beneath his head, watching me with a lopsided grin, his eyes roaming over my nakedness in return. I resolutely ignored the urge to cover myself.

On a whim, I leaned forward quickly and kissed the dimpled crease on his cheek. "I love your dimple," I whispered, smiling at him.

His eyes flickered briefly.

I sat back again letting my eyes roam across his bared body. He was magnificent. I didn't have a lot to compare him to, but as far as I was concerned, he was perfect . . . and so very male. Running my hand toward his side, I made for the tattoo.

Jack grabbed my hand, but didn't remove it.

I waited a beat, not looking at his eyes, and then continued. Jack's hand rode mine, not stopping me, but accompanying me as I traced the skin covered by the swirling and black flames and fearsome eyes and teeth of a monster. He was tense beneath me.

"My father," he whispered so quietly, I almost didn't hear him. He cleared his throat. "My father . . . he beat her. My mother."

I waited quietly, wanting but also fearing the story.

He went on. "Nobody knew he was my father, we lived away from prying eyes, and he was never there. He was a public figure, in politics and . . . titled, and I understood later we were . . . a shamed secret."

He continued haltingly. "The last time . . . I remember waking up early in the morning. I'd heard them again in the night and hidden under my blankets and pillows so I didn't have to hear my mother crying again.

"He wasn't a drunk. He was a stone cold asshole. It would be weeks and sometimes months between his visits. He always came to see her, not me, for some reason. Although I knew it was always me they fought about. She'd made me promise not to come down if I ever heard him. So I didn't. I must have fallen asleep that night, normally I didn't, but they must have stopped arguing and it was late."

I kept very still as Jack talked. He stared at the ceiling and then closed his eyes before continuing.

"The quiet woke me up that morning. Normally, I could hear my mum in the kitchen or calling me to wake up and come down. I looked at the window and saw it was light enough that I should have been up and having breakfast before school. I went down the stairs in my pajamas calling for her and not getting an answer."

His hand on mine gripped hard as his voice strained. I got the impression he had never told this story before. My heart pounded in trepidation as he continued.

"I remember skidding around the corner into the kitchen and seeing *him* first . . . standing at the stove, all in black. I assume he must have been in a suit, but all I remember is the darkness and the fear of seeing him and thinking my mum would be mad at me for not staying out of the way. But then I saw *her* lying on the floor. She was naked . . . and not moving. In retrospect, I wonder why I didn't go to her, but I remember going wild and flying at him, trying to get to his eyes. His evil eyes. I wanted to scratch and rip those awful eyes out of his head and bite those awful hands that inflicted so much pain. The next thing I knew he struck me, and *I* was flying back across the room. I hit the table next to where my mother was lying. I couldn't breathe from the pain. I learned later my arm and a rib were broken."

I was glad his eyes were closed, and he couldn't see the tears sliding down my face.

"But he came at me again, and I felt real fear then. Fear he'd kill me and I wouldn't be able to get help for my mum. I didn't want to think she might not be needing help any more. He was holding a full pan of boiling water and he called me a little brat and threw it. I kicked my legs out, and by some stroke of luck, my foot hit a chair that protected me as it moved."

Jack gritted his teeth as if he was reliving it, right at this moment. "I remember it. In slow motion. I remember seeing the water hurtling toward me and partly splattering all over the chair."

He took another deep breath. "I threw myself to the side and covered my face before the rest of the water hit me."

My hand was still pressed under his, against the evil sight on his hip.

"I don't remember much right after that. Apparently, I screamed so loud a neighbor, and trust me, the neighbors weren't close, heard me. I still don't understand what a stroke of luck that was, but she found us and called the police and ambulance. *He* was gone, of course. My mum was okay, though concussed and badly injured.

"We filed a police report at the hospital saying someone had broken in and attacked and raped my mother. We basically told the truth except for the part where we knew him.

I'm not sure the police really believed us. I know the neighbor didn't. Mrs. Eversea was her name . . . she was basically the one who saved our lives. We stayed with her. Her husband worked at this boarding school nearby and persuaded the headmaster—"

"Mr. Chaplin." My voice sounded choked and foreign to my ears. Jack opened his eyes and looked at me, seeing the tears I hadn't meant to show him. I was sorry I'd spoken, I hadn't meant to.

"Yes, Mr. Chaplin—persuaded him to hide me at the school. I guess I wasn't that safe because after a few years we had to move." He took a deep breath. Surely there couldn't be more but he went on. "It was me he wanted. That's what they fought about. She hasn't told me all the details, but in addition to his love of inflicting pain, she discovered . . . other things he liked." Jack rolled to face me, keeping my hand covering the physical evidence of his horror.

"Is he . . ." I swallowed. "Is he still out there . . . your father?" I whispered.

Jack shook his head and exhaled. "He shot himself. Ten years ago."

We were silent. I couldn't even begin to articulate the emotions careening through me as I thought of Jack as a small boy enduring such terror and pain. I was angry. More so knowing his father was dead. I wondered if Jack felt the same frustration that he could never lay this ghost properly to rest.

"I'm an Earl, you know," he laughed, humorlessly. "He threatened her if she ever tried to divorce him. The public scandal would be too much. The bastard made sure before he killed himself to recognize me as his rightful heir. Even in death, he didn't want to let us go. There's a stately home and everything. The missing earl, that's me, donated it to the National Trust. There's one lawye*r, one*, who knows who I am now, and he's in love with my mother, so my secret, and hers, is safe." He snorted. "That was the one damned good thing that came out of it, *she's* happy and safe now. But my God, it was hard for her being a single mom to me. When I was older I certainly didn't make it easy on her. I had some demons of my own I had to work through." Jack shook his head. There seemed to be another story there, too.

"And Mrs. Eversea?" I asked, softly. How wonderful they had picked her name when she had basically saved them. Saved him.

"My mum and she are still friends, as far as I know." He shrugged and gave a small grin. "She made the best Digi Cake."

"The best what?"

"It's cake made with chocolate, syrup, crushed cookies and butter. A heart attack on a plate."

"Sounds amazing." I pulled my hand away from his hip and slid it through his hair, then across his face and down the side of his body and back to the beautiful artwork. Running my fingers over it, I followed every line and curve and ribbon, and then without thinking, I lowered my mouth and kissed every section of it. I ran my tongue over the angry raised ridges here and there like I could erase them away.

Jack was tense and still as he watched but didn't stop me.

There was no pity in my actions. It was simply worship of the man who had been forged out of his past. I didn't care if Jack wasn't his real name, and I didn't want to know it. He was Jack to me. I wanted to take away his pain. "I can think of another damn good thing that came out of it," I whispered, noticing he was becoming aroused again.

"What?" he asked.

"You." I took a deep breath and pushed him onto his back.

Jack tensed. His hand came to my hair. "What are you doing?"

"Show me?" I asked nervously and proceeded to make love to him the way he had to me.

"I don't think . . . I need to," Jack stuttered out, and this time it was *his* hand, white knuckled, grabbing fistfuls of sheet.

CHAPTER TWENTY-NINE

The next morning when I awoke with the bright sunlight streaming in Jack's window, it was to find myself with Jack still wrapped fully around me, in a very similar position to the one we'd fallen asleep in. I smiled groggily, closing my eyes against the bright glare and reveled in the feel of us cocooned together.

My heart was floating somewhere far above me. I couldn't remember the last time I had woken up with such buoyant happiness. I had to work later today, but perhaps Jack and I could kayak this morning, and I could see what other materials I could find. If I was going to start creating things again, I needed to start collecting more raw materials. And oh man, I was hungry. We never had gotten around to dinner or even eating the cheese and crackers Jazz packed.

My stomach chose that moment to growl, loudly. The sound was followed, immediately, by the bed vibrating as Jack laughed at me. I guessed he was awake. I reached my hand behind me and smacked where I expected his butt to be.

Quick as a flash, he rolled onto me, pressing me, belly down, into the mattress as his voice growled playfully in my ear. "I wouldn't do that if I were you." And then his stomach growled, too. I burst out giggling.

"I guess that makes us even." He laughed and reached for his boxers. "Time for food."

"I have no idea where my underwear ended up," I said, looking around the bed and holding the sheet up to cover my nakedness.

"I ate it."

"Ha ha. Seriously, these girls need confining, where's my bra?"

Jack laughed and dropped to his hands and knees at the end of the bed then came up and snapped my bra at me, followed by my panties. "Nice color."

"Thanks," I mumbled, my cheeks flushed again.

He pulled his jeans on, and then came and pressed a lingering kiss to my lips before heading to the bathroom.

I dressed quickly, opened the French doors to the view, and inhaled the cool ocean air. Glad I had a moment in the fresh light of day to think for a second and compose myself, I thought about what Jack had told me last night. It was such a big secret, and he had trusted *me* with it. I was humbled at the same time my heart broke for him. It explained so much about who Jack was. The fact that, as a scared six-year-old boy, his instinct had been to fight his mother's attacker rather than run and hide was a testament to his courage and strength of character. I had sensed all this about him, but knowing what I knew now, while it underscored what I felt for him, was no great comfort.

I took a deep breath and focused on the beauty laid out before me as Jack came up behind me and propped a chin on my shoulder. He snaked his arms around my waist, the warmth of his bare chest at my back. I smiled and leaned my head back against his.

"Hey, do you see the staked-out squares down there in the

dunes?" I pointed down to the left about twenty yards along the beach. "Someone found a turtle nest and marked it out. When those turtles grow up, they'll always return to this beach."

Jack nuzzled his face toward me and inhaled. "Keri Ann, will you consider coming out to California after I get done with this whole promotional tour thing?" he said to my neck.

His arms were tense around me, and I knew this was a really big deal of a question for him. Heck, for me, too. My heart danced around in joy, and I wanted to turn around and hurl myself into his arms shouting *Yes! Yes! Yes!*

But instead, I took a deep breath, and clearing my throat, said simply, "Yes, I'd like that."

His shoulders relaxed at my answer, and he gave me a quick squeeze. "I'm going to investigate what I have left in my fridge from my personal shopper. See you downstairs?"

I exhaled. "Then will you drop me home? I was thinking of going for a kayak. You interested? You can use Joey's."

"Sure. After we eat I'll drop you and bring the bike back here, then you can come get me. Work?"

I nodded.

"Oh wait!" Jack suddenly let me go.

I turned to find him fishing around in his jeans pocket, his brow furrowed. I mimicked his expression, wondering what on earth he was looking for.

He grinned as he pulled his fingers free and held his hand out to me. "Look what I found yesterday."

I stared, dumbfounded. In his hand was a piece of red sea glass, about the size of a quarter. I swallowed and gently took the dull, frosted piece, holding it up to the light. "Wow," I whispered, seeing small hints of amber in parts. "Do you realize how rare this is?" I glanced at him. "Sorry, I probably sound like a nerd."

He laughed. "I wasn't sure what it was at first, but when I realized it was sea glass, I knew you'd love it." I smiled curiously at the look on his face. He looked proud of himself. "And I don't think you're a nerd. I think you're amazingly talented."

I was quiet, processing his words and the enormity of the gift. To me, this wasn't just a piece of sea glass. To me, it meant Jack really *got* me. Did he realize that? I wasn't sure. "Thank you," I said, closing my hand around the glass.

Jack nodded once.

I turned back to the view outside before confiding my piece of news. "Guess what? Jazz took that chandelier I made to Faith's boutique yesterday. It sold. In one day." I couldn't keep the incredulity out of my voice, and it sounded even crazier now that I'd said it out loud.

"Seriously? That's fantastic, Keri Ann. Congratulations!" He turned me around. His huge grin was infectious. "It was gorgeous, and I didn't even see it finished. I'm not surprised. You should have told me, we could have celebrated."

"We did, anyway, didn't we?" I grinned back at him stupidly and cocked an eyebrow. He laughed, kissing me with minty lips and gathering me in a tight hug. "Yeah, I guess we did."

I was due to pick Jack up in about twenty minutes. The two kayaks were in the back of the truck ready to go. Once I got out of the shower and toweled off, I texted Jazz a not-so-cryptic message.

Me: Thank you for the small package addition to the backpack . . .

The phone pinged back immediately. I laughed.

Jazz: OMG, OMG, OMG. You okay?

Me: More than okay! We're going kayaking, I'll chat with you later. Just . . . thank you.

Jazz: xxx

When I neared Jack's house a few minutes later, I had to stop to allow a black executive sedan from an airport car service pull out of Jack's driveway. A weird feeling flipped over in my gut as I waited for it to pass, nodding to the suited driver. I fingered my phone for a second, wondering if I should call Jack. It could have just been a delivery but I had a feeling it was a person. The owners of the house, perhaps? His agent? Katie?

I took a deep breath and turned into the driveway. Perhaps the car had only been turning around. I climbed out and headed up the stairs. Jack had told me to come straight inside when I got back, but I knocked just in case. I heard voices inside, and then Jack flung open the door. His face was grim, and he hauled me inside.

"I'm sorry, Keri Ann. I didn't know she was coming."

"What?" I stumbled forward into the house and faced my worst nightmare. Jack's firm grip on my hand didn't detract from the impact of Audrey Lane, dressed casually in jeans and a white t-shirt, her long, glossy black hair swung over one shoulder. She was beautiful. I swallowed hard against the bile threatening to come up and glanced back at Jack with confusion. Why had he pulled me in here? I wanted to be as far away from this awful realization of my worst fears as fast and as soon as possible. I took a step back, trying to untangle my hand from Jack's.

"Auds," I heard Jack's voice from far away, "this is Keri Ann. Keri Ann, this is Audrey Lane."

"Carry-Anne? How southern." Audrey's voice was soft like honey and way too familiar from her movies. "This yours?" She dangled my pink cashmere scarf on a finger, and then flicked it toward me.

"Don't be a bitch, Audrey." Jack's voice lowered dangerously. He quickly picked it up and handed it to me.

"Why, Jack? How much does she mean to you? You've known her, what, a few days?"

How did she make it sound so trite and sordid? I ground my teeth but tried to remember she was fighting to save the man she loved. Wait, she'd cheated on him.

She turned her gaze to me and her eyes grew frosty. "Look, Carry Anne, I'm sure it seemed really special and everything, but just because—"

"At least he didn't cheat on you," I snapped and made to turn. I had had enough of her snide attitude, and I didn't want to stick around any longer while they sorted this out.

Her brittle laugh grated my nerves. "Is that what he told you? Hilarious. That's all he did to *all* his girlfriends. He was cheating on someone when he got together with *me*. The tabloids don't always have it wrong, you know."

A vague memory of Jack Eversea, the playboy, tickled my mind. *No.* I didn't care, it wasn't the Jack I knew.

"Besides," she went on, "he really hasn't broken up with me, so I guess that makes *you* the trashy piece on the side. Waitress, right? So cliché."

"Fuck off," Jack hissed at her. For a moment, Audrey looked shocked, but she recovered quickly and appraised us both.

"Oh God, Jack. You haven't *slept* with her, have you?" She rolled her eyes like he was an errant little boy. And just like that I wanted to be sick. It sounded like they'd had this situation before. I knew she was a good actress, but surely not *this* good.

I swallowed. "Um, Jack . . . I . . . I better go. Let you two sort this out."

"No," Jack snarled, gripping my hand tighter. "Stay."

"Jack, please," I whispered. I was going to liquidate Amélie-style or lose my breakfast.

"You should stay, Keri Ann," Audrey purred. "You may be interested in this, too."

She walked toward Jack and ran a traitorous hand along his cheek. *My* cheek. He was *mine*. She took a deep breath and smiled a huge, winning, Oscar-worthy smile. "I'm pregnant, Jack. Pregnant with your baby."

A tidal wave crashing through the plate glass picture window bringing a man-eating shark to flop around on the tile floor couldn't have caused more shock. I wasn't sure I'd heard the words right. But Jack's hand on mine went slack. His face turned chalk white.

Audrey smiled gently, running her hand down Jack's arm, disengaging his hand from mine and placing it on her belly. "I know how you've always wanted a family. A family like you never had growing up."

I stumbled back, eyes darting between them like I was in a ridiculous daytime soap opera. I waited for Jack to look at me or get mad at her, or say there was no way it could be true. I thought it was only contractual. But he had mentioned a time when it was real. I just didn't know it was . . . recent.

The moment stretched out, and I wobbled slightly before I turned and stumbled to the front door.

This time, Jack didn't try and stop me.

CHAPTER THIRTY

*H*aving been through grief several times before, I could honestly say the first stage of *this* traumatic loss was to be severely and violently sick.

I did manage to make it back to the truck despite the roaring in my ears and sudden lack of muscle tone in my legs, and I drove as far as the intersection of Palmetto and Atlantic before opening the door and heaving my guts onto the sidewalk. Great.

I wanted to blame the water leaking out of my eyes on the vomiting, but I could feel the traitorous sting. After retching nothing a few more times, the kind where it felt like my eyeballs were going to bug out of my head, I finally rose up in time to see a blurry vision of Brenda running toward me from the grill, holding a bucket and a glass of water.

"Oh my God, Keri Ann, are you okay?"

I gratefully took the water as she put an arm around my back, rubbing my arm soothingly. "Fine . . . must be something I ate," I croaked, swallowing and squeezing my eyes shut.

"Honey, are you pregnant?" she whispered, concern lacing her words.

"God, no!" I was about to make some quip about an immaculate conception, but bit my tongue, as I no longer qualified for that status. "Not me." Not *me,* anyway.

A fresh wave of anguish lurched through my belly, leaving me breathless. "Shit. I need to get home."

I eyed the bucket of water. At least I could clean up this mess. Brenda stayed my arm. "I'll take care of it, honey, you get on home. I'll take your shift tonight."

I nodded, grateful, and climbed back in the truck, making the last few minutes of the trip in a daze.

At home, I wandered through my empty house before heading to my room. I tried lying down, but just as I turned to curl onto my side, the smell of Jack wafted from a pillow.

Oh, God.

For a moment, I lay motionless. Then I buried my face in the pillow and inhaled deeply before hurling it across the room. The crash of upended pictures and trinkets and the sound of breaking glass was loud in the silence.

The thing I remembered most about the night my parents died was the terrible silence. We hadn't needed to go to the hospital, there was no one to visit. Mrs. Weaton had come over while Nana left to identify the bodies. No one spoke, and no one said I should go back to bed and get some sleep. I mean who could do that anyway? The quiet in the house, as one would expect in the middle of the night, was that night, heavy and deafening.

Eventually, at about four in the morning or so, without saying a word to Joey or Mrs. Weaton, I walked up to my parents' bedroom, crawled under the floral quilt on my mom's side, and slowly breathed her scent in and out.

I must have fallen asleep because when I woke up, Joey was asleep in the bed next to me on dad's side, and Nana was sitting in the chair by the window.

She smiled at me sadly.

To say there was a gaping hole inside me where my heart had been savagely and painfully ripped out was an understatement. It was a crushing and physically painful emptiness that gave way to a sense of sheer panic as I realized I couldn't smell my mother any more.

I sat up gulping for a fresh breath, and then threw my face back to her pillow, trying to catch the scent again. I tried this several times with increasing hysteria.

Joey woke and tried to hold me and I lashed out, pushing him away, realizing the awful broken howl I could hear was coming from me.

Eventually, both Nana and Joey had me, and we were all hugging and crying and rocking.

I slept in my parents' bed for the whole summer and didn't speak to Nana for eight days when she finally washed the sheets a few weeks later.

I stood up and walked past the mess I had just created in my bedroom and headed up to the attic where I found my place to curl up again.

I came out of a deep and dreamless sleep to Jazz sitting next to me on the floor.

She reached out a hand and smoothed my hair back as I opened my eyes. "I'm sorry."

"What for?" I whispered.

"Jack called the shop and told me Audrey was here and that I needed to check on you. What happened? I'm thinking the worst here, but he wouldn't say anything else."

"It's the worst," I confirmed tonelessly. "He's not leaving her."

I let out a breath and shifted onto my back.

"Oh, God, Keri Ann. I am so sorry."

"Don't be. It's not your fault. I mean, seriously, how could I have imagined this would work out any differently? I should have stayed far, far away. Why would a movie star want to be with a small-town girl like me? Why would a movie star with a gorgeous girlfriend leave her for a girl like me? Why would—"

"Stop it!" Jazz interrupted, looking pained. "Just stop it!"

"Why should I?" I yelled back. "It's fucking true! And this has nothing to do with my self esteem and everything to do with how fucking blind I was." I sat up. "My point is not about not being good enough for him, it's that I was too stupid to see the signs. He told me! He freaking told me it wasn't over with Audrey! *I* chose to believe otherwise. No one but *me*. Anyone who gets into bed with an unavailable man should expect this. Why would this be any different? And now that she's pregnant? Well, that just accelerated the inevitable, didn't it? I should be fucking grateful this happened now before I became some sleazy tabloid byline."

Jazz's face turned pale. "She's pregnant?"

I laughed hysterically. "Yes! Isn't that great?"

"Did he know?" she asked, incredulously.

"No. But that's not the point, is it?"

"Well, it changes things a little."

"No, it doesn't. You're missing the point, Jazz. Regardless of whether he knew, he was cheating on her. With *me*. And

I chose to ignore it. And apparently, it wasn't the first time. They may actually deserve each other. I went against every principle I thought I had. Seduced by a six-pack and a dimple and an entire personality of honor that was based on a ficti- tious character." I was yelling again, and to my horror, crying at the same time.

I thought back to Jack sharing his painful past with me, and for a moment, doubted myself until I firmly shut that thought back inside my head. I also again remembered past stories of Jack Eversea's exploits in nightclubs with fast girls. Back when Jazz first became a huge fan and would talk about him the way only a sixteen-year-old with a massive crush can, he was endlessly linked with bevies of beautiful women, leaving a trail of broken hearts.

The conversation I'd overheard on the phone in my kitchen, where his agent had all but assumed he was messing around with someone on the side, should have been the biggest clue.

"I'm so, so sorry," Jazz said again.

"Stop saying that, Jazz, it's not your fault."

"But it is. I encouraged you, I even told you I thought he cared for you. This is totally my fault." She winced. "I was living vicariously through you, wanting you to do what I would have done. It was unfair to you. I'm so sorry."

"I keep telling you all, I'm a big girl. It was my choice, Jazz. *Mine.* And the worst part is that he was so cautious . . . so hesitant . . . at *every* moment. It was *me* who pushed, *me* who closed every gap. It was *me.*"

I pressed my finger hard to my chest.

"It was me," I finished quietly and firmly.

The fault was all mine. He couldn't have played it better, really.

It was the perfect hustle.

CHAPTER THIRTY-ONE

If I'd thought Jack might come and find me, to either apologize or explain himself, I was mistaken.

Every day that went by with no contact from him stretched my nerves tighter and tighter. Somehow, I made it through the next week trying to block the entire episode out of my mind. I was a little numb, which made it easier, but not effortless. I tried hard not to think about whether Jack was still in Butler Cove. I knew if I even let myself start, it would all come pouring out.

Jazz checked on me constantly, and stayed over any chance she could, leaving early to get to work or class. I kept telling her I was fine, just annoyed, but I could tell she wasn't buying it. I had overheard her talking to Joey on the phone one night in hushed whispers. I didn't bother answering when he called me. I knew he knew, and I didn't feel like talking about it.

The thing really threatening to make me lose my mind, with frustration, was that most of the household furniture was still out on the deck or upstairs. On the second morning of walking past the bare floors and glancing at the fireplace,

I put in a call to Faith for help. She agreed to pre-purchase two of the three chandeliers she had asked for.

While stuffing my face with the chocolate pudding Mrs. Weaton had kindly brought over, I called the flooring company and asked them to reimburse some of the balance to the credit card used and take *my* money instead. They finally agreed and had an opening within days to come out and finish. I would still owe Jack for a large part of it, and would be working flat out to repay Faith, but for now, I could get my house back together.

I was functioning enough that I felt working and keeping busy were the only things that would help me heal without having to do too much thinking. Perhaps the healing could continue in the background while I went about my life. Hopefully, one day I could turn my full attention to the subject of Jack Eversea and feel only a slight annoyance. Perhaps a bit sad and maybe also a little chagrined that I fell for a pretty face; hook, line, and sinker, but the raw pain would no longer be there.

The following Thursday night, the grill was heaving with locals. I was busy and had perfected a happy mask on my face to all but the closest observers. Hector, of course, was ridiculously and uncharacteristically quiet. I had given him the stark news Jack was with his girlfriend and would no longer be in Butler Cove just as I had with Mrs. Weaton. I could tell he wanted to press me for details but wisely kept silent. Instead, he grabbed me in a swift, tight hug, and then set me away from him and work continued on as normal.

Jazz had managed to find a reason for her or the group to get together at each of my evening shifts. Tonight she was sitting with Liz, Cooper, Vern, and Jasper at a round table in the perfect spot to keep an eye on me.

I headed that way to offer drink refills. It was nearly closing time.

"You look like shit," Jazz said to my brittle smile. "And I mean that in the nicest possible way. Please let's talk about this tonight after work. You need some sleep, missy. I'm not above stealing a Xanax from my mom."

"Jazz. Please. I've said everything I want to say." I swallowed. "And I don't need to be drugged." Although, a night of oblivion and deep sleep, rather than the fitful and tormented slumber I'd been attempting, sounded like heaven. "I'll get over it."

"Oh, my God, are you serious?" Liz's voice broke through our tête-à-tête.

"For real." Vern's voice was dramatically conspiratorial. "He and his girlfriend are staying at the Mansion on Forsyth."

The historic mansion, turned high-end hotel, was one of the nicest places in Savannah. A nagging dread unfurled in my belly as I predicted the next words out of Liz's mouth.

"Jazz, did you hear that? Jack Eversea and Audrey Lane are staying in Savannah. Oh my God! We should totally go and have drinks there, it would be so cool to see them in real life."

I could see Jazz struggling to act surprised and excited so as not to arouse suspicion. At the same time, she gripped my hand as tight as she could. As for me, the blood had left my head again, and I swayed into the chair next to Cooper.

"Hey, girl, what's up? You okay?" Cooper asked in that soft way of his. His brow furrowed.

"Tired," I managed. I needed to collect myself and get up. For days everyone was told I was recovering from a stomach virus, but I couldn't pull that off forever. They would think I had *E. coli* soon.

Vern was informing everyone he was a host at Cosimir's Lounge at the Mansion. He had been cagey about his new job for weeks, but now he was coming clean. He said he could totally hook us up if we all wanted a night on the town. I shot a look at Jazz and shook my head.

"What the heck is wrong with you two?" Jasper said, watching our weird exchange. "A fun night out in Savannah sounds awesome. When was the last time we all did that? Beats sitting around drinking PBR every night." He took a swig of his beer and shifted an eye back to the animated Liz who was loudly wondering if the tabloids had been lying about Jack and Audrey breaking up. Every word was a needle sliding into my skin.

Of course Jasper would want an excuse to get us all out on the town. He wasn't going to ask Liz out on a date outright, but an excuse to go out somewhere fancy in a group with her was probably a dream come true for him.

"Nothing's wrong, Jasper," Jazz said. "Keri Ann has to work tomorrow night so there's no way she can go. And I have a ton of studying for midterms."

Jasper's face fell, although he still held a cocked eyebrow at the obvious undercurrent.

If I hadn't felt like I was under a lead weight, I would have laughed at him.

"Wait, Vern." Liz was looking at him with wonder. "Why were you so embarrassed to tell us about your job at the lounge, that's awesome. How cool."

Vern ducked his chin sheepishly. "Well, it's a little exotic . . . and I . . . well, I dress and . . . act exotic there, too," he finished quietly.

Cooper nudged him in the ribs. "Dude, we know you wear eye-makeup and shit. It's cool. Whatever."

"Seriously?" Jasper eyed him over his beer, like he was noticing Vern for the first time. We all were.

"It's a job," Vern defended. "And actually, I like it." He shrugged and cocked his chin up.

Jazz rolled her eyes. "It's fine, Vern. I always thought you were too pretty to be a boy anyway." Vern did, indeed, have doll-like and fragile features that didn't always add up.

We all chuckled as he threw a straw, followed by a wadded-up napkin at her.

"I'm not a cross-dresser," he huffed. "I just dress up for work. Think—emo rock star—without the band, of course."

"We need to *get* you a band, Vern," I said firmly, and everyone nodded. And maybe a boyfriend, but I didn't voice that out loud. If he wasn't ready to talk about it, we would all wait patiently.

I was thankful for Jazz's intervention in heading off the group outing to Savannah. I wanted everyone else to go, though. They would have fun, and the chances of meeting Jack Eversea were slim to none anyway.

Using that logic, a part of me wanted to say *screw it*, why shouldn't I go out and have fun with my friends, especially if I wouldn't run into Jack? But I knew that the mere proximity and inkling of a chance of bumping into him and Audrey was too much of a risk for my fragile psyche right now.

"Oh guys, pleeeeease," begged Liz, her hands clasped together in prayer, her big eyes pleading with us one by one. "Please? I never get to go out. My mom would be totally cool with watching Brady tomorrow night. Please? Please? Pretty please."

Jasper cleared his throat. "Um, I'm up for it, Liz, I'll—"

"Yes! That's one. Come on, Jazz and Keri Ann, please?"

"Sorry. No can do guys." I shook my head and stood up to head back to work, leaving Jazz to make up her own mind. I hoped Jasper would have the courage to follow through anyway. If it had been any other time, I would have rallied to help him out, but no, not this time. I felt bad, but I couldn't do it.

I turned around and bumped straight into the broad chest of my brother.

"Joey!" I yelped and threw my arms around him.

Taking a step back under my enthusiasm, he laughed and tucked me in tight for a hug.

"Hey, kiddo," he said, kissing my hair.

I squeezed my eyes shut, hanging on, and suddenly I was not all right. I didn't care why he was here, just that he was. The dam burst inside me and I pressed my face against him, knowing if I stood back I'd embarrass myself in the middle of the restaurant with a huge, desperate sob.

Either Jazz saw, or Joey felt my heaving shoulders because I was instantly in the back of the kitchen being held tight in Joey's arms while huge gasping convulsions wracked my whole body. I couldn't stop. Jazz stood off to the side rubbing my back soothingly. All at once, I was a small child crying her heart out.

Somehow they got me home, and as I walked through the door into the house with the newly varnished dark brown floors, I just couldn't take it any more.

"Oh, God, why?" I wept. "Why me? Why did he have to come here?"

"Shhh. It's okay, sweetheart," Joey tried.

"No, it's not fucking all right," I yelled. "I was fine on my own, I was doing fine, I didn't need this shit. I didn't *ever* want to feel this shit."

As I looked around the house, a thought suddenly occurred to me. "Nana!" I shouted. "Nana! Can you hear me?" My voice built in hysteria until I was almost screaming, "Nana! Was it you, Nana? Why? WHY? Why him, Nana?"

My voice broke over my high-pitched wail. I was so angry. "You knew I wouldn't be able to say no. Why did you do it?" I screamed again, my voice cutting off into a whisper as the last of my vocal chords gave up. I went boneless and sank to the floor at the foot of the stairs, out of the grasping hands of Joey who was trying to cage me into submission.

And all the things Jack had told me guaranteed that this orphaned girl would take pity on him and fall in love with the poor wounded boy. And, by all accounts he had shared it all with *Audrey* too, and who knew who else? And what if it wasn't even real? I wasn't that special, it was all just fodder for the perfect lay, to make sure I was fully there, heart and soul. Suddenly, I was so terribly sad for the pathetic man who was Jack Eversea—the man who had to use his past to play on the emotions of others and make girls fall in love with him to feel secure.

I ignored the fact that my feelings had been there before he told me about his childhood. I would work out the whys there too, just not now. It didn't fit right now.

I subsided into staccato gasps and hiccups as the stupidity of how I was acting hit me, and I felt pure and pathetic shame. And tiredness. I was so damn tired. I lay down at the foot of the stairs and closed my eyes.

CHAPTER THIRTY-TWO

"My God, you look unbelievable!" Joey stood at the bottom of the stairs as I teetered down. The sound of merriment came from my kitchen. I angled my body to the side as I took each step in the pair of gold Chinese Laundry stilettos I had bought on a whim one day and never worn. My tight black spaghetti-strap dress threaded with gold was a tad short. And by short, I mean it was like wearing a belt. I'd bought it with the idea of branching out from my usual Keds and jeans and pairing it with leggings. But no, not tonight. If I dropped anything, it was going to stay on the freaking ground.

My hair was ironed straight, sleek and smooth, falling about an inch longer than usual without all the waves. My eyes were rimmed with just the right amount of eye-makeup to accent and look slightly smoky without making me feel vampy, and a sheer slick of gloss on my lips flecked with gold matched the shimmer Jazz had added all over my body. I felt like a goddess . . . or at least a hollow statuette of one.

The look on Joey's face told me he almost didn't recognize me. And I liked *that* very much.

Tonight, I was going to don the façade of a young girl out on the town with a life full of promise. That's what I was. Or at least, should be.

I reached the bottom step, perched above the same spot where I had fallen apart on the hard wood two nights ago. My eyes flicked there for a moment, and then I took the last step slowly and deliberately, sticking my stiletto heel on the exact spot. A phoenix rising from the ashes, that's what I was. I would survive this stupid, stupid boy.

The idea of a night clubbing and drinking in Savannah had taken on a life of its own among my friends. I'd been back at work again after my embarrassing breakdown the night before, and bringing Jazz another drink, when something caught her eye on the screen. Jazz pushed her chair back and I turned to see what she was looking at. My stomach dropped.

A smiling Jack Eversea with his arm around Audrey Lane, her head nestled lovingly on his shoulder, both unaware of the camera, filled the screen. I tried to convince myself it was an old picture of the two of them from the archives, and not something recent. Except right at that moment, a breaking news banner scrolled along the bottom of the screen as the picture faded to Billy Bush mouthing the exclusive and breaking news that Jack Eversea had been spotted in Savannah.

Billy Bush was a handsome guy, but right then I wanted to punch his jaw as my eyes were pulled in by the closed captioning that was stabbing me word by word.

Jazz reached me and pulled me toward the kitchen, forcing my eyes to drag away from the screen.

"You okay?" she asked, as the door swung shut.

I nodded, numbly. "I feckin' hate Billy Bush."

"Yeah, well, he's also on my laminated list so don't shoot the messenger."

"He's married."

"Oh well," she shrugged. "Dreams are free."

I saw she was holding her phone, so I took it and quickly pulled up the Access Hollywood app I knew was on there.

"Are you sure you want to see this?" Jazz asked, concern all over her face.

I nodded, and we both hunched over it.

Jack Eversea spotted in Savannah at the swanky Mansion on Forsyth; cozied up with Audrey Lane as they try to repair their relationship.

"Ugh," said Jazz.

A source close to the couple says they have been in constant contact since Audrey Lane's heartfelt public statement and apology several days ago and they finally decided to meet on neutral ground to get away and sort things out. Still no word on where Jack disappeared to while nursing his broken heart or whether he will pull the plug on the rapid sale of his home they shared in California.

I hadn't known he was doing that.

A spokesman for Peak Entertainment said all of their current scheduled appearances for the upcoming Erath movie premiere are still going ahead, and it would take more than a few bumps in the road to keep these two apart.

How sweet. I wanted to gag.

"I need to get obliterated," I said to Jazz.

She nodded. "Brenda, love," she said, poking her head out of the kitchen door to the bar. "I know you covered for Keri Ann the other night, but would you mind very much if she had a shot of tequila right now?"

I'd resolutely stuck to my guns about not going, but on Saturday morning Liz texted Jazz with the disappointing news that Vern had called to say Jack Eversea and Audrey Lane had checked out. No doubt in response to the fact they'd been swarmed.

Jazz pinned me down after my lunch shift. "You need this," she said seriously. "Look, it's safe now. He's not there. You need to be out with friends, having fun. Pretend if you have to, but you need to get dressed up, feel good and God knows, you need to be flirted with."

"He's not there?" I hated my question, but part of me had felt a small bit of peace knowing exactly where he was. Now, he was gone to God knows where with *her* and their bundle of baby news. For a moment my heart wondered how Jack was coping with the news. It had been a shock to be sure, I had seen that clear as day. But I imagined, once the shock wore off, he would be ecstatic. And so would the rest of the world when the news went public. I would have to live with their joy on a daily basis. For Jack, I would be a distant memory.

I shuddered. "I can't stomach the idea of any sleazy guy coming on to me."

"Just take the compliments and brush them off nicely, but you need this. You need to know you are admired and desired and you need to just have some carefree fun."

"Don't you think I've had enough of boys' games of trying to get me into bed to last a lifetime?" I asked. "That's not the kind of male attention I need."

But the small seed was planted and started to grow and unfurl slowly as we talked. I wanted to do something, anything, to eclipse the dull empty gnawing ache in the pit of my belly. Perhaps it would feel good to practice the art of flirting a little. And maybe Jack wasn't such a good kisser . . . maybe I just hadn't kissed enough boys.

Now, as Joey's eyes left me and travelled back up the stairs to where Jazz made her way down, I felt an inner satisfaction with my decision. She looked amazing; all soft curves and spun gold hair. Her black pumps were about as impossibly high as mine, although her blue dress wasn't quite as short. She looked breathtaking, and Joey was trying to remember how to do that most basic human function. A flush crawled up his neck as he took in Jazz's outfit. This alone was worth it. I could do this for them, I could do it for Jasper and Liz, and I could do it for me.

"Holy shit!" came a familiar deep voice as Colton Graves wandered out of the kitchen, beer in hand. "Joseph, my man, we are going to be busy fending off the dudes tonight. You girls . . . just, wow." He whistled appreciatively. Dressed in black jeans and a blue dress shirt outlining his broad athletic frame, he hadn't changed much from what I remembered, and he was still handsome in that cropped hair, quarterback kind of way.

"Hey, Colt," I said, giving him a winning smile. *May as well start now, right?* "Good to see you. You look great." He'd moved back to Savannah after college and was working in a bank, although clearly trying hard to keep his high school physique, too. Joey had called to invite him on our outing which had taken on epic proportions.

"Well, you sure did grow up about as pretty as I thought you would," he said, winking at me. "And by that I mean, absolutely stunning."

A small fifteen-year-old teenager inside me who crushed on Colton Graves did a little backflip. The current Keri Ann gave him a small smile and a nod.

"Knock it off, Colt," said Joey. I glared at my brother.

Colt switched his raking gaze up and down the length of Jazz. "And Jessica Fraser, you are a vision of sexiness."

Jazz blushed appropriately, just as my brother's jaw got hard. I smirked. Against all odds, I may actually not have to pretend to have a good time.

"You'd better give us our space tonight, boys," said Jazz haughtily. "We're looking forward to the attention of strange men, aren't we, Keri Ann?"

Once everyone got over the laughable fact that we were heading for a night of drinking, and hopefully just a bit of sinning, in the church van that Jasper had appropriated from his father, we found ourselves forty minutes later being ushered up the steps of the old mansion in Savannah.

In the dimly lit interior, we were greeted by a version of Vern I hardly recognized. His dark hair was brushed and straightened low across one of his kohl-rimmed eyes. A small slash of emerald green eye shadow matched his green satin shirt collar that was popped up over a tailored black jacket and skinny black pants. A silver diamond glinted in one ear. Amazingly, I had never seen him look more perfect.

"Vern!" I clapped a hand over my mouth.

"You look amazing," echoed Jazz.

Vern preened. "Likewise, ladies, likewise,"

Cooper nodded at him. "Dude."

Jasper laughed and clapped him on the back.

"Hey, no touchy," said Vern, taking a step back, all business. "Now, I have the perfect table for y'all upstairs. If you'll follow me."

I looked around and took in the lavish refurbishment of the historic mansion. Dark wood floors gleamed and ceilings towered above us at about fourteen feet. The molding was brushed with metallic silver and on the walls hung large eye-catching pieces of exotic art.

We followed Vern through the restaurant set with linen tablecloths and gleaming silver. Drawn by a deep thrumming beat to a staircase carpeted in leopard print, we ascended into an exotic harem. Lush and opulent jewel-toned silk curtains framed windows and small intimate areas. The music was hypnotic and sensual as was every surface one's eyes could rest upon. The music, a cover of Alabama Shakes, was coming from a quartet set up in the corner, barely visible through some closely pressed and undulating couples.

A long mahogany bar lined one end backed by antique mirror panels reflecting the glittering and beautifully dressed people littering the space.

Vern led us to a corner room set into a turret with deep burgundy silk curtains swagged across the entrance. The room itself was lined with low, plush, curved benches, pillows and seats, a small low cocktail table with a Moroccan-looking lantern holding a candle in the middle. The entire place was a feast for the senses.

Joey and Colt, who had driven separately in Colt's BMW, had headed straight for the bar. They soon joined us with a bottle of Champagne in an ice bucket and seven shots of something vile, and we all got comfortable. After toasting to friendship, the future, world peace, and anything else we could think of, we were feeling suitably liquidated and Jazz dragged me out to the dance floor. I didn't want to get more buzzed than this as I knew the melancholy would set in and my internal protections to keep Jack out of my mind would melt down.

Heads turned to watch Jazz and me as we made our way across the room and it wasn't long before we had accepted offers to dance and declined offers for drinks from several earnest-looking business types. A few songs later, Jazz caught my eye with a twinkle, and I dropped my head back in a care-free laugh, capturing for a moment, how fun this actually was.

I was just turning nonchalantly out of the lecherous grasp of our latest admirer when Colt caught me around the middle and pulled me in close. For a moment, my belly fluttered in remembrance of how it felt to be dancing with him at his senior prom. I looked up into his handsome square face. He leaned down to my ear, swaying to the music. The house band had taken a break and Muse, with their deep rhythmic and grinding guitar, had come over the system.

"Hey, beautiful," he murmured. "You doing okay?"

His large hand, splayed on my lower back, was a bit too intimate but not unwelcome. Maybe it was the alcohol or maybe it was the yearning void inside me but perhaps I could just try and forget Jack with Colton. Jazz always said it was the best way to get over someone.

I nodded against his cheek and let myself sway with him. Why couldn't I have picked a nice normal boy to date? What had I been so afraid of? Staying in Butler Cove with a nice, safe boyfriend who worked somewhere like a bank sounded absolutely ideal. There was no fizzing in my veins and warmth pooling inside me at his touch, but that was a good thing.

The music worked itself into a sensual frenzy, and Colton's hands roamed my back, bringing me closer. I looked briefly over to see Jazz and Joey dancing together, although not quite as close as Colt and I.

Jazz winked at me and I gave her a small smile back as Colt's hand came up and sifted my hair, tilting my face up to his. Jazz towed Joey off the dance floor at Colt's move. There was no way he'd stand around and watch his best friend kiss his sister, and I guessed Jazz knew that.

It didn't seem like that thought had even occurred to Colt as he lowered his lips to mine. I took in his sandy brown hair and his kind blue eyes. And then I closed mine so I didn't have to finish the thought . . . *It's not Jack*.

His lips were warm and firm and not unpleasant. They moved over mine gently. It was a curious feeling to be so detached from the sensation, to really be able to analyze it.

I felt his tongue coaxing me to open to him as he tilted my head further. I pulled away gently, not wanting it to seem like a rejection, more of a slowing down.

His eyes earnestly searched mine.

I wondered how much Joey had told him about Jack.

"I wish you'd tell me who this chump was who broke your heart so I can—"

A loud disturbance broke our attention and we turned just in time to see people gaping and pointing as a figure, storming across the room, managed to push the last person out of his path and come like a hurricane at Colt. For a moment I thought it was Joey, but the burgundy ball cap and the voice . . .

"Get your fucking hands off her," it snarled.

Oh God . . . Jack.

CHAPTER THIRTY-THREE

All of a sudden a fist flew at Colt, landing square on the side of his face. His head snapped back at the blow, and he fell to the ground.

I was frozen and not even really processing, but within seconds Colt was hidden beneath not only his attacker, but also Joey and one of the suits who had been circling Jazz and me earlier. The suit, with his focused face barely containing his glee, looked like he had been waiting for just such a violent interlude all night. A burly security guard and a scared-looking Vern were already on the scene.

The insistent noise and gasping of everyone around me finally broke through as Jazz grabbed my arm and grounded me. Whispered variations of "oh my God" and the name "Jack Eversea" ricocheted around my skull not finding purchase. My eyes were glued to Jack, as Joey and now the security guard hauled him off Colt.

Jack's strength broke him free of his handlers within seconds, although they managed to get him back in hand, his hat tumbling to the ground. His eyes swung wildly around and homed in on mine. I was pinned. I was vaguely aware of heads, and now smartphones swinging between us, but most of my attention was on Jack. Jack's eyes, Jack's absolute fury, Jack's ticking jaw, Jack's heaving chest. Just . . . Jack.

Jack.

Jack. But where was Audrey? Why was he here? His eyes left mine and I looked around expecting Audrey's haughty face to appear at any moment. Instead, I caught Jazz's nonplussed expression and I followed her eyes in time to see Vern nodding tightly, and obviously against his better judgment, at something urgent Jack said to him. Vern turned and looked at me with undisguised curiosity.

Then Jack, in front of all the stunned onlookers, strode forward and grabbed my hand, jerking me forward. I stumbled slightly in my stilettos.

I swung my head at Jazz in time to see her restraining a fired-up Joey, who was about to come after me, and pointing to his best friend who was still lying on the ground. *Oh no . . . Colt.* I hadn't even checked he was okay.

Vern was leading us down a dark wood-paneled side hallway by the end of the bar and into a small dark room.

He turned on a lamp that washed the small office in low light before turning to me. "Are you okay?"

I nodded, dumbly.

Then he brushed past me, pausing for a moment to hiss in my ear, "Tomorrow, you talk," before leaving and closing the door firmly.

I was fine. I mean, I had just been kissed in a nightclub, had two guys fight over me, and now had the most famous and beautiful man on the planet drag me into a dark room. Oh, and I was in damn stilettos. I was totally fine. I would be on TMZ tomorrow, but I was fine.

Fine, fine, fine.

My focus shifted to Jack and the look on his face. I almost wanted to bring my arms up to protect myself against the physical onslaught his eyes were inflicting as they bored into mine. I settled for crossing my arms across my chest.

Oh, Jack. Jack. Jack.

I didn't recognize my yearning self, and hated myself for it, but I wanted to throw myself across the three feet of air between us.

No wait, I was not doing this. I was not this person, this pathetic girl who would fall at his feet. He should never have continued seeing me. He should never have slept with me. And he'd been right, I did look back and regret it. He'd said it all along, and I had chosen to ignore his warnings. My God, I pitied myself in that moment. You stupid, stupid girl.

"Keri Ann." Jack's voice was a choked whisper, his face a mask of anguish that made me waver. But there was something not quite right. I realized suddenly, as I should have right away, he was drunk.

As his body started toward mine, I threw up a hand, and it landed in the center of his chest. His heart pounded beneath my fingertips.

Jack stopped, a shutter closing down across his face.

"How dare you?" I whispered. Yes. I was proud of myself, because what I really wanted to do was throw myself into his arms and beg him to tell me it was all a nightmare, that he wasn't leaving, that Audrey wasn't pregnant, and that what we'd had was real.

Jack's eyes got hard. "How dare I? What the fuck does that mean? I wasn't the one letting some stranger stick his tongue down my throat." He leaned in toward me, pushing against my hand, his beautiful Jack scent polluted by the sickly sweet smell of whiskey. "Who are you? 'Cos *I* sure as shit don't recognize you. Is this how you spend your week-ends, dressed like a hooker, picking up strange guys in bars? Was sweet, innocent, virginal Keri Ann some kind of—"

My hand connected hard against his face, the slap reverberating around the small room. I was shaking with fury.

To his credit, his head listed a bit to the side, but he didn't grab his cheek. He just stopped and dropped his head, not meeting my eyes. Then, he slowly reached for my stinging hand and placed it back in the center of his chest where I'd had it seconds ago. He covered it with his own.

I swallowed, trying to ignore the feeling of my hand in his and the way he was pressing it so hard into his chest it was like he was trying to push it through to his heart. I hung onto my indignation by a thread. "Was that my appeal, then? The sweet virgin who would make you feel like a man?"

For a split-second, I debated lying and telling him he was right. That it was all an act he fell for. I could look on him with pity and pretend I didn't care. But I wasn't a liar. Jazz always said I sucked at it.

"God, no," Jack said, his voice sounding strangely strangled. He raised his eyes to mine. "Sorry . . . I'm so sorry."

"What for, exactly? Or should I say, which part?"

"For it all."

No. Not that. Please don't be sorry for everything. Just the part where you forgot to tell me you may have impregnated your girlfriend and that it obviously wasn't as over as you had intimated. Please, just the part where you leave me, not the rest of it.

"All of it?" I whispered.

"God, Keri Ann, what do you want me to say? I'm sorry I'm so fucked up I sold my life, my soul, and my future to the devil?"

His hand left mine, and he pressed it palm down in the center of *my* chest. "If I'd known *you* were in my future, I would have chosen differently."

His skin was hot against mine, and we both stood, each of us pressing a hand on the other's heart. It could have been ridiculous and childish if it hadn't been so Goddamn tragic. Not he *may* have chosen differently, he *would* have chosen differently.

I hung onto his words like a life raft. I felt a tear slide out of the corner of my eye. *No! I would not cry now.*

Jack stepped forward, our arms folding up to allow his advance, and I held my breath as his face came close to mine. His breath was cold where it touched my wet cheek, and then his warm tongue and lips were on my skin just like when we'd made love. I gritted my teeth against the onslaught of emotion the tender move caused, but my breathing hitched, giving me away. I gave in and turned my face, meeting his lips with mine. They were salty from my tears, tangy from whiskey, and hungry for me. The taste of bittersweet.

I accepted the slide of his tongue and returned it, pouring into my kiss words I would never say. I took his beautiful soft hair in my hands, trying to capture the memory of it, and then slid them down his muscled back, memorizing every nuance. Finally, breaking my mouth away from his, I pressed my face to his neck and kissed his throat. My mouth moved over the Adam's apple I had been so focused on the night he had almost kissed me. I tasted his skin and heard and felt the vibration of his groan beneath my mouth. And I inhaled the scent from his skin, deeply.

Then I brought my mouth close to his ear. "If you had chosen differently, you would have never found me," I whispered. That was the worst irony of all. And there was only one thing to do.

"Goodbye, Jack," I said and stepped sideways out of his arms.

Jack watched me, wordlessly. I eased open the door and slid through the opening into the arms of Joey, who had obviously been waiting for me.

One last look saw Jack closing his eyes and sinking to his knees before Joey took the door and closed it behind me.

CHAPTER THIRTY-FOUR

I couldn't believe it was possible to wake up and feel any worse than I did the day Audrey Lane arrived in Butler Cove and bombshelled the snugged-up little love fest I had going with Jack. But it was. It wasn't like anything had changed or gotten worse. Jack was still gone. Knowing he was suffering because of it should have given me a small amount of gratification, but all it really did was make the pain keener. Made the situation more tragic.

I wanted him to walk through the door and tell me I had rocked his world and that he'd never be the same. I wanted him to tell me that while he'd be there for Audrey and his child, it was me he wanted to be with. I hated myself for thinking that. For wanting that baby to grow up wondering where his daddy was all the time.

I was the other woman. I never wanted to be the other woman. Nana always said at the end of a day, a person's integrity was all they had to recommend them. I'd knowingly participated in every moment with Jack, and I hated my weakness. And what? Was I expecting him to move to Butler Cove, or me to California?

After Joey hustled me out of the room at the club, and away from Jack, we found Colt sitting on a barstool, next to Jazz, a bag of ice on his face. He handed his keys to Joey, and the four of us left in his BMW.

We dropped Colt home at his townhouse, Joey promising to return his car the next day. Colt didn't say a word to me.

Now Joey sat at the foot of my bed as I wallowed.

"You need to follow me to Colt's so I can drop his car. And we need to check on him." He pulled at the blond tufts of his hair. "Dammit, Keri Ann. Is Jack Eversea always like that? I mean, I know he'd been drinking, and he saw you with Colt, but that's no excuse to hit someone."

I just shook my head without answering. The truth was I didn't know. The night I'd met Jack, he was drinking whiskey. But I'd never seen him drunk, apart from last night. His father was violent. I shook my head again to clear that thought.

Joey pursed his lips at my silence. "What? No? He's not like that, or you don't know?"

"I don't know," I croaked. My tongue felt like wool.

"Well, either way, you shouldn't have any contact with him. I know I'm not really entitled to tell you not to, I'm just asking you. Please, as your brother. He's not good for you. That kind of intensity is just . . . it can suck you down."

I watched as Joey struggled with his overbearing personality. Even if I wanted to refute him, I didn't have the energy.

"Look, this probably doesn't help, but . . ." He placed a hand on my foot over the covers, presumably to soften the blow he was about to deliver. "I mean, even if his girlfriend had never shown up or whatever, I don't understand the two of you. Were you going to try and do the whole girlfriend of a movie star thing? Going to his premieres, parties, and not seeing him while he does God knows what on location?"

I flinched. "Stop, Joey. I don't need to hear this right now. I didn't think about it, okay?" Stupidly, I hadn't. I didn't know what I was expecting when Jack invited me to see him in California. I thought we were both kind of taking it one day at a time.

"I mean, that's just not you. I can't imagine you in that environment. And what about your plans? What do you want to do with your life?"

"Why are you going on about this now, Joey?" I couldn't keep the irritation and defensiveness out of my tone. "I feel like shit already. Why are you making me feel worse?"

"I'm sorry, kiddo. I guess I only realized last night how serious this was. I mean, he doesn't have the best reputation. I knew you were upset before, but after seeing the two of you together last night, and the way you looked at each other . . ."

"How did he look at me?" I whispered, suddenly craving validation of Jack's feelings from anyone but myself and my subjective imagination.

Joey sighed, resigned. "Like you were the last chopper out of Baghdad, the last IV in the field hospital, the last funnel cake at the fair, Jesus, I don't know."

I held my breath. Joey was usually more prosaic. His words were soothing my battered pride. It felt good.

"I just know that the way he was looking at you, he's coming back someday. I need you to be prepared for that and to know I won't let him mess with you again."

I swallowed. What would I do if Jack came back? Joey was right. I wasn't cut out to be a sometime girlfriend to a movie star and sometime mother to his baby. I needed to be me. Discover who *I* was. Jack's invasion into my life had at least shown me that. I had no direction, and I needed to find it.

I was like a piece of that sea glass lying forgotten in a jar upstairs. A discarded shard that had been washed and tumbled back and forth by the momentum of the sea, only to wash up in Butler Cove and stay stuck and forgotten without any hope of becoming something more. Something more beautiful. I needed to find my potential. Jack wasn't going to help with that. If anything, he would have completely eclipsed any chance I had of discovering what I was meant to do. The feelings I had for Jack were so strong they would have sucked me into a whirlpool straight down to the ocean floor.

Colt looked terrible. I apologized profusely. But what could I do? It wasn't me who threw the punch. He said he wasn't pressing charges. Mostly I think it was to keep me out of any publicity, and I think Joey had something to do with that. After saying our goodbyes, and promising to keep in touch, Joey and I headed back to Butler Cove in my truck with the windows down, the wind whipping through our hair. Both of us had too many thoughts and not much to say.

"When are you going back?" I finally asked Joey as we pulled onto the crushed oyster shell parking pad outside our historic home.

"This afternoon." He looked over at me. "Are you going to be okay?"

I nodded. "Jazz will keep me out of trouble."

His brow furrowed at the mention of Jazz's name. "Fine. Just call me if you need to. Columbia is only about a two and a half hour drive. You can always come up there and see me."

We sat for a moment. "I'm sorry I haven't been here for you, kiddo. I can see how selfish I was by continuing on with my plans for school. I didn't think about how being left alone must have felt to you."

"It's fine, Joey. I've been fine." I put a hand on his arm.

He shrugged. "I know you have. I just thought if I could get done first, then I could support *you*."

"Joey. This is nothing new. That was always the plan, and I was okay with it. I'm still okay with it—"

"I know! It's just that you shouldn't be. This is the prime of your life. You should be studying and figuring things out and making new friends. And dating. You should be dating! As it is . . . you were a sitting duck for the likes of Jack Eversea strolling into town."

I scowled. "Thanks a lot. Way to cheapen the entire thing and make me look like a fool."

"That's not what I meant. You know that. Just . . . please. I can't believe I'm going to say this, having been vehemently against it since I can remember, but Colt—"

"Do *not* finish that sentence, Joey."

"He really likes you, always has. And he's successful. Not Jack Eversea successful. But he has a good job, and he's doing really well."

"Stop it, Joey!"

"He's a normal guy. A nice guy. He wouldn't dare mess you around—"

"I thought you called him a man-whore because of all his one night stands," I reminded him. That should shut him up.

"That's just because he's never dated anyone like you."

I snorted. "Please."

"Okay. That sounded dumb. I guess what I mean is, just let him take you out. Take you on a few dates, or something. You never know."

"Joey. I can't, okay? I just . . . can't. I'm . . . raw. I just want to go back to it being only me for a long while. I don't want that giddy roller coaster ride of highs and lows. I'm in the low right now, and it's crushing me."

"But you wouldn't have that with Colt, it would be steady. He's steady."

"Joey." How did I explain how truly terrifying that sounded? "That would be worse than nothing at all."

He slumped in his seat. "I know that, I guess. I just—"

"Look, I get it, you're saying all this because you're worried. But, Joey, I'll be fine. I know I'll be fine. I felt like I'd never be fine again after Mom and Dad, but I was. And then after Nana. But I was. I still miss them every day, but I'm all right. I know I'll think about Jack every day for the rest of my life. He changed me. He made me want more. Made me want to be more. Those are good things. I'm hanging onto them. And regardless of what you think of him, and also how mad I am at him for how everything went down, he's a good guy. I have to believe I didn't fall for an asshole." I clenched my fists. "But I'll be okay. Not right now. But I will." And so I'd keep telling myself until I actually believed it.

We climbed out of the truck and headed up the porch steps.

With his hand on the railing, Joey stopped and looked about him a moment before fixing his eyes on me. "Okay, kiddo, one last thing. Don't wait on me. Please. Go ahead and look into some colleges or art schools, maybe even do something online for now. We can deal with the loans later. And fuck the town, they can just freakin' wait on the house. This is your life we're talking about."

I smiled and wrapped my arms around him. "I've been thinking the same, I just wasn't sure how you'd feel about it."

"Damn, I'm sorry," he said into my hair. "We should've

done that all along. Somehow, we should have figured out a way. I'm so sorry."

I hugged him tighter. "Stop apologizing. We did it the way we had to. And to be honest, I feel more focused now, more sure of what I want to do and study. I didn't feel that before. I always thought I should do a safe degree, but now I know I should follow my dreams. And at least I have a clearer idea of what my dreams are. I got lost for a while, I think."

Joey let me go and walked inside. He returned a few minutes later with two frosty glasses of sweet tea, and we sat on the top step of the porch in the fall breeze to enjoy the last hour of his visit together. It was cut short by two things, Jazz showing up and my phone buzzing a text.

I pulled it out of my back pocket, and upon seeing Jack's moniker, Late Night Visitor, lost all my carefully smoothed-out nerves. Breathing through the rolling wave of dizziness, I swallowed and read the words.

Late Night Visitor: I'm sorry. I'm sorry for how I was last night. I'm sorry for taking something from you I'll never be able to give back. I'm sorry I am telling you this by text. I'm just . . . sorry. You deserved so much more than me.

CHAPTER THIRTY-FIVE

Six Weeks Later . . .

$\mathcal{J}$ was sitting out on the front porch swing and enjoying my coffee and Mrs. Weaton's biscotti the morning of my birthday. She made it with salted caramel chunks. It was pretty spectacular.

Joey was due home later, having started coming home every other Saturday when his schedule allowed it, and today was no exception. He'd decided I needed a birthday party, which I'd vehemently opposed, refusing to change my shift schedule at the grill. Now it was happening anyway, and Brenda was coming in so I could clock out early and join the festivities at my house.

I pulled my sweater a little tighter around my body against the chilled breeze that had swept over the island, just as a sleek dark car pulled into the driveway and purred to a stop under the Live Oaks.

Colt had taken to coming over when Joey was home, although he never usually arrived so early. I couldn't help smiling when the door to his midnight blue BMW opened and several brightly colored balloons erupted out of the car and floated up into the Spanish moss-draped branches.

"Shit!" I heard, followed by several grunts. A pair of legs emerged, and finally Colt's body fought through the rainbow. "Sorry," he said, clutching the rest of the strings tightly in his fist, wrestling the bunch into submission. "I guess I lost a few."

My smile broke into laughter at the devastated look on his handsome face.

"Happy birthday," he said sheepishly. He leaned back into the car with his other hand and brought out a huge bouquet of white lilies. *Oh.* I kept the smile plastered to my face and tried not to let my nervousness show at his romantic birthday gifts.

Taking a deep breath, I left my spot on the swing and came down to meet him. "Thank you," I said, reaching for the flowers. "They're beautiful. Let's get them in water. You want some coffee?"

He gave me a rueful smile and tugged the front of his hair. "Yeah, that would be great."

Inside, I poured us both some coffee and placed the flowers in the sink filled with water while I hunted out a vase. I couldn't remember the last time I used one. Colt tied the balloons to a kitchen chair and trotted back outside to bring in a bunch of beer and drinks he'd brought for the party.

"Is there anything I can help with today?" he asked, coming back in and setting the boxes down on the counter.

I put the beer away in the fridge. "No, I think we're good. I have to finish up a bunch of tuition grant applications as they're due this week."

"Oh yeah. How did the meeting at SCAD go?"

I swallowed guiltily. Colt had asked me to text him when I was in Savannah to meet him for coffee. I hadn't.

First of all, the meeting Faith had somehow swung with the Dean of the School of Design had gone on longer than planned. Second, I was with Vern, and third, and frankly, more importantly, I was trying to avoid giving Colt even a hint that I might be interested in him. "It went great, but ran really long. Sorry I didn't text you, I was with Vern, and we had to get back." I smiled nervously.

He nodded and busied himself with the boxes. It was weird seeing the ex-Butler Cove High School QB looking less sure of himself than I remembered. I studied his handsome, sweet face and really wished I were attracted to him. He had shown himself to be thoughtful, funny, and a really good friend over the last two months. He made me happy. He made me laugh. What was wrong with me? Was it still too soon, or was it that Jack Eversea was a fire that burned brighter than the sun, and I'd been seared beyond repair?

I walked over and laid a hand on the soft gray sweater covering Colt's forearm. "I'm sorry, Colt. Thank you for being a good friend."

He winced. "I just want you to be happy, Keri Ann." Turning, he wrapped his big bear arms around me, and I sank into his comfortable embrace.

There was no chemistry. None. Surely he could tell that, too? I didn't really understand how these things worked. I felt him give me a warm kiss on my hair and smiled. "I know, and thank you."

Grabbing our coffees we settled at the kitchen table, and I filled him in on my progress with trying to get into school. Faith had become like a fairy godmother, helping me, guiding me, advising me, and pushing me to put myself out there.

We were both hoping I would be able to get one of the tuition scholarships SCAD offered. I was applying for state and private funds, too.

Being able to prove I was already selling pieces would go a long way toward getting a grant. Also the fact I'd been selected by the Picture This gallery in Hilton Head as a featured regional artist coming up in December, again with a wave of Faith's magic wand I was sure, would all be a part of my application.

Between work, creating pieces for Faith's store, and all the applications, I never had time to do much thinking.

My phone buzzed a text, causing a clattering across the table. I'd never responded to Jack's last text, and he never sent another. Even so, my belly always gave a small lurch each time my phone made a noise. I wondered if I'd ever get over that. I grabbed it and saw the name 'Jazz' and a link to Access Hollywood. "Sorry," I said to Colt. With a frown, I clicked open the link.

Jack and Audrey Split! Huge public blow up! I stopped reading.

I couldn't believe she'd send me this after agreeing never to mention his name to me again. We hadn't even talked about the movie when it came out. I hadn't seen it, obviously. I immediately called her.

"I know, I know!" she said as soon as she answered.

I eyed Colt who was looking at me with confusion. "Seriously, Jazz? Them being together or not has nothing to do with me—"

"Wait, I know it doesn't mention this in the article I sent you, but—"

"I haven't read it," I snapped.

Realizing the topic, Colt dropped his eyes and shifted.

"I figured you hadn't since you're already on the phone with me, and I *just* sent it—but just hear me out, ok?"

I sighed, and mouthing another sorry to Colt, went out the front door to sit on the porch swing. "Fine. Go ahead." I steeled myself to let whatever she had to tell me slide right off.

"Never mind. I'm coming over. Hang tight."

I ground my teeth together and breathed out in a huff.

"Oh, and happy birthday," she added and hung up.

I put my phone down beside me and drew my legs up. I hugged them tightly to my chest and waited, a medicine ball lodged in my throat. The amount of times I had thumbed gently across the Late Night Visitor entry in my contact list made me shudder with shame. My moments of weakness were more frequent than I cared to admit.

And when I allowed myself to think of Jack, my emotions ricocheted around like a three-ring circus.

In one corner of my mind, I had this memory that, despite the brevity of our time together, Jack and I had connected on some elemental level reserved for past lives and soul mates. We were just a boy and a girl who recognized each other across the deep blue universe. That corner of my mind found it hard to remember all the reasons that would preclude us being together. Like the fact he was a movie star and I was . . . not, or that he had a baby being carried by another woman.

The second corner called into question any real relationship at all. It was all based on lust and chalked me up to being blinded by Jack's celebrity status, his attractiveness, and his role as Max. This second corner had the added barbs of calling into question *my* role as anything more than a shallow groupie and willing female in the dark period of his life. In this corner, I only remembered our physical attraction. I wondered whether we had any connection at all. I couldn't believe I would have been that shallow. But the evidence was pretty convincing.

The third corner was deepest of all. The third corner simply stated that we were star-crossed lovers that should never have met. But we did. And in that game the evil jester called fate liked to play, we were attracted in an instant. The potential for love . . . for eternity . . . was, in a split-second, acknowledged, catalogued, realized, and set on a collision course with *never*. I could almost hear the snort of derision. *Ain't never gonna happen.*

A ripple on the fabric of fate. A joke that might have ruined my potential for any future happiness.

Now, I wanted it all. I knew I wouldn't settle for the sweet and steady Colton Graveses of the world.

No corner of my mind was a comfortable place to settle into. And now Jazz was stirring it all back up.

Her yellow car arrived in my driveway with a spurt of white shells. Flinging open the door, she climbed out. "Boot up the computer, we need to look through this together." Not pausing for breath, she marched up the stairs in her jeans and boots, her blonde hair flying all over the place in the wind.

"I don't want to know, Jazz!"

"You do. I promise. At least you can stop thinking he's been fine while you've been moping."

"I'm not moping."

"It's true you've been better. Okay, look, if you won't look yourself, just listen. That fight I emailed you about was confirmed on three different sites, but an 'insider'—"

"Dammit, Jazz, you know better than that." I turned my head away and stood up. An *'insider'*—Jack had told me once that was code for someone who wants to make up shit about you.

She grabbed my arm. "Listen! Something big went down. Even his agent's been fired."

"I don't care!" I yelled.

CHAPTER THIRTY-SIX

$\int$ couldn't remember the last time I was mad at Jazz. If ever. After about twenty minutes of us arguing back and forth, Colt strolled outside and immediately pulled the kayaks from under the house.

"You wanna go for a paddle?" he asked, pointedly ignoring Jazz. It was chilly out, but I couldn't think of anything I wanted to do more right then. I smiled at him gratefully. And in about five minutes flat, we were peeling out of the driveway in my truck, leaving an open-mouthed Jazz on my porch.

It was cold on the water, but since we were both in jeans and sweaters and life vests, it wasn't too bad. Our bare feet were pretty cold though. Neither of us thought paddling in our cowboy boots and loafers respectively was very wise.

"You want to talk about it?" Colt asked as soon as we were out on the water. I shook my head. Jazz's words were pounding through my mind, and all I wanted was for them to be quiet. I had shut her down as spouting trash, but in my gut I knew it was true. I had run through a million permutations in my head of what I'd feel in this scenario. Now that it was here, my reaction was not pretty. Rather than the surge of hope I thought I'd experience when I fantasized that Jack and Audrey's relationship would finally run its course, I felt absolutely terrified. I was filled with . . . dread, and I had no idea why.

It was beautiful and peaceful out on the water. And I found a little more peace inside me with every pull of my paddle. We glided and pulled through the marshes for over two hours until the combination of hunger, choppy water, and icy toes sent us heaving with exertion back to the dock at Broad Landing.

We arrived back at the house hungry and ruddy-cheeked to see Joey had arrived, and he and Jazz were talking in circles around each other. The tension was thick as pluff mud.

They managed to shut up for a few hours while we all ate and sat around for a game of spades after lunch, but they were back at it when I finally got ready to leave for work at the grill.

I had a feeling their arguing was based on more than disagreeing on whether Jazz should have told me all that shit about Jack. I was refusing to listen any time she brought it up, and I was still so mad at her. Some birthday.

"C'mon, I'll walk you over to the grill," Colt said, looking me up and down with appreciation as I stomped down the stairs, freshly showered and made up. I'd dried my hair into natural looking waves, and I was wearing a snug pair of jeans. I was already in my boots instead of the sneakers I usually wore and would later change out of my black tee into the sexy red 'cold-shoulder' top I'd appropriated from Faith after she said it was too small for her. I was as close to ready for my party as I would be able to get and still be comfortable at work.

Colt cleared his throat. "Damn, you smell good. And you look—"

Jazz came out of the kitchen. "Okay, Keri Ann. You win. I'm not going to say another word tonight. I wish you'd hear me out." She huffed and glared at Joey who wandered out behind her looking stoic. "I'm letting it go. For now."

"Good," I said. Then I walked up to her and pulled her into a hug. "You're an idiot, but I love you," I said into her hair.

"You're an idiot too, and you're stubborn." Her muffled voice came back. "Just like your bull-headed brother. But I love you, too."

I gave her another squeeze and winked at Joey over her shoulder, before pulling back. "We'll talk about it, I promise. Just not today. Not tonight."

"Liar," she huffed. "But anyway, hurry up and get home so we can celebrate. Plus, I can't *wait* for you to see your present." She looked me up and down and turned me round. "Damn, those jeans make your ass look like a Brazilian infomercial. Spectacular."

My cheeks throbbed with heat instantly, but I needed the confidence boost. I gave her a small smile of thanks.

"Come on," said Colt, slinging an arm around my shoulders. "Let's get you out of here so we can get this place decorated."

Colt left me at work promising to come get me at nine. I could walk myself home without a problem, but I didn't have the energy to resist Colt's attention after the strange day I'd had.

There was an Ohio State game on at the grill so it was relatively busy. After years of vacationing, far too many from that wholesome state had retired down here for it to be a quiet evening.

Time flew by. Brenda came in at about eight thirty, ostensibly to transition me out. But it was busy enough that we were both working hard at nine when I felt the breeze from the main door opening and heard the change in atmosphere. Thinking it was Colt, residents loved to see their high school football star return home, I turned with words to apologize for not being ready on my tongue, but froze.

Devon Brown stood comfortably in the entryway looking slowly around the restaurant. Dressed casually in a blue checked shirt hanging out of faded jeans and brown work boots, he looked comfortable. And actually not that different than some of the locals from the surrounding countryside who pulled in here from time to time.

But his shaggy blond hair and tanned and rugged features were too familiar for him to be mistaken for anyone else but the movie actor-turned producer who was rumored to have bought a house on the island.

Conversation had died down and then whipped up again.

His eyes scanned over Brenda then came to settle on me.

I still hadn't moved from my position near the bar where I'd been collecting more napkins for table seven. The adrenaline spike I'd experienced upon seeing him, my closest link to Jack, had now washed away leaving me feeling slightly faint and nauseous. My pulse throbbed heavily in my throat.

His brown eyes furrowed slightly then cleared, and he gave a tiny nod. What did he see when he looked at me? And how did he know who I was? Because I could tell he did. I had no doubt. No doubt at all.

"Would you like a table for one?" Brenda's voice jarred me from my trance.

Devon looked at her, and then at me and cleared his throat.

"I'd like Keri Ann to serve me, please. So if she has a section, I'd like to be in it."

I swallowed. Brenda looked confused for a moment and glanced back at me. "You're leaving aren't you, Keri Ann?"

I was saved from having to answer as the door at Devon's back opened again, and Colt stepped around them and strolled toward me. "Ready to go, sweetheart?" he asked. I glanced at him but couldn't answer—I still needed to find my voice—and then back at Devon, whose face had just gone altogether unreadable.

"You know what?" Devon said to Brenda, his eyes still on me and now Colt. "I don't think I need that table after all."

"Oh, okay," Brenda said, obviously confused. I was too. Did he want to talk to me, is that why he asked to sit in my section? There was almost too much going on here to process. Devon turned to leave. I realized how Colt's endearment must have sounded. But why should it matter? Unless . . . unless he thought we were together, but even so . . .

"Keri Ann!" Colt's voice called out after me as I bolted out the door Devon had just exited. I didn't stop.

"Devon," I called. He paused in the dark courtyard. The same courtyard where I first saw Jack.

"What?" he asked, turning around, his hands shoved in his pockets. My heart pounded so loud in my head it was making me dizzy. I didn't know why I'd run after him. I didn't know what to say.

"Did . . . did you need to speak to me?" I sounded breathy and awful.

"Keri Ann?" Colt's voice was behind me again.

Damn it!

Devon's eyes cut over my shoulder. "Your boyfriend?"

"No!" I yelled vehemently. God. Colt heard that. I turned around to his shocked eyes, but I couldn't do this right now. I needed to know why Devon was here. "I'm sorry, Colt. Please go on without me, I'll be home when I'm done talking to Devon."

"Fine," he said through gritted teeth. "But I'm not leaving. I'll wait inside. Come get me when you're," his eyes flicked up and down Devon, "done here."

But Devon had turned and started walking again. "Wait, please." My voice caught over the last word.

Devon stopped and turned back. "I don't think *he* knew he wasn't your boyfriend."

I shook my head. "It's not like that. I mean, I know he likes me, but he's also just a friend. I don't . . . I can't . . ." Why were we talking about Colt, when I wanted to talk about Jack? And I did want to talk about Jack. I'd chased Devon out here because, before my head could catch up, my gut had instinctively reacted to my last lifeline walking out the door.

"Please. Is Jack . . . Is he . . ." God, I didn't know where to start.

Devon blew out a deep breath, and then nodded his head toward the closest table and chairs. We sat down in the dim lamplight. I shivered slightly in just my t-shirt and no sweater. I folded my arms across my chest, willing Devon to just start talking so I didn't have to figure out what to ask. He did.

"Jack's messed up," he said quietly. "I don't know if you read about it. The shit's been all over the fucking Internet already."

I swallowed and tried to recall all the stuff Jazz had been trying to tell me that I didn't want to listen to.

Devon looked at me as if trying to work out what to say.

"Jack and Audrey are definitely over. It was a nightmare. Even Andy's been fired. His agent." I nodded. I knew who Andy was. "Something . . . something happened. Audrey and his agent deceived him about something pretty big. They totally blindsided him."

I knew how few people Jack felt he could trust, and my stomach flipped over for him.

"I . . ." My voice was scratchy. I tried again. "I didn't read the story, a friend tried to explain today, but I didn't believe it. Is . . . is he okay?" My heart hurt.

Devon shifted forward, and resting his elbows on his knees, scrubbed a hand down his face. "Jack was devastated. We were all sitting around at their house when Andy just let slip— shit, I can't tell you anything else. It's not my place. But my God, the look on Jack's face . . . I mean I know he's been acting a little *off* but," Devon let out a rough breath, "I've never seen anything like it. It was eerie as shit."

"Poor Jack," I said, pained. God, I couldn't imagine what a shock that must have been to learn your girlfriend and your agent were conspiring against you and treating you like some puppet. And for what? For money? I didn't know what they could have done, but for Jack to fire his agent and break up with the mother of his baby, it must have been huge.

Jack and Audrey had clearly been back together for real. That Devon had said '*their house*' wasn't lost on me. I was glad I was sitting down, because my body was having trouble dealing with all of the reactions I was having to Devon's words. I felt nauseous, weak, and again that feeling of dread was spreading through me like an oil slick.

"What did you mean, Jack's been acting a little *off*?" While Devon was here, I felt like I needed to get as much information as I could. It was idiotic, I knew. I had avoided any news about Jack for so long as a way to try and get past him, and now I was doing the exact opposite. It didn't make sense. And why was Devon here? "And why are you here?"

Devon looked up at me long and appraisingly. "I really shouldn't be having this conversation with you. I haven't told you anything you couldn't have read about, though. To be honest, I'm not sure why I came. I was curious, that's all."

"Curious? About what?" I twisted my fingers, nervously.

Devon's eyes dropped to my hands, then came back up to mine. I had the feeling he had just edited what he was about to say. "I was curious about whether Jack would come back here."

My breath left me, involuntarily. "Why . . . why would you think he would come back here?" I tried really hard to take any kind of emotion out of that question, and it only left a whisper.

Devon was looking at me hard, as if trying to answer that for himself. It made me uncomfortable, and it made me feel like . . . less. He took a deep breath as if reaching a decision.

"Jack left right after he fired Andy. He could have been here by now." He looked at me straight in the eyes. "This is where I heard him tell Katie he needed to go." My heart hammered harder. "And, based on some of the things he's shared with me, this is where I expected him to go."

I hadn't realized how tightly I was wound until Devon said those words, and a small sob tore out of me. I took a deep, unsteady lungful of air and tried to blink back the tears pooling in my eyes.

Devon immediately grabbed my hand and hung on, squeezing tight, as I breathed through it and brought myself under control. "Shit," I blew out another breath. "I'm sorry."

"Don't be. I needed to know it wasn't one-sided. That it was real for you. And I think you've just set my mind at ease."

I could feel the elation, the confirmation I had meant something to Jack, trying to spread its rays through me, but the scared and terrified dark part of me I had been fighting with since Jazz's text this morning wouldn't let go.

What if it wasn't enough? What if *I* wasn't enough? It was one thing to fixate on a girl you thought embodied all you felt like you were missing in your life. Especially when you were trapped there. But when all the bars had gone, and all the steel doors had been unlocked, did you really need the girl? What if she was just a symbol of hope and not a destination?

"But he didn't come here, did he?" I asked Devon.

He looked at me, sadly, and my heart plummeted. "No, he didn't. Not yet, anyway. But, Keri Ann—" he seemed to struggle with what to say or maybe how to say it. "I feel pretty sure he will."

I swiped at my eye. "How?" How on earth could Devon be sure? Or was he just trying to spare my feelings? If Jack was coming right away, why wasn't he here yet?

He let out a deep chuckle. "Well, now I've met you, I guess. I don't know how I know. I just do. And the fact that, when I told you about the shit that went down, your first reaction was compassion for Jack and not happiness he was free, means you have definitely earned *my* trust. I . . ." He stood up and I followed suit. "I hope you two manage to work it out somehow. I can't imagine it's going to be easy."

Well, it wasn't a ringing endorsement, but it was more than I'd had when I woke up this morning. I held out my hand. "We've never formally been introduced. Keri Ann Butler.

Waitress slash soon-to-be art student. I hope. And friend of Jack's."

Devon gave a half smile and took my outstretched hand and shook it. "Devon Brown. Producing, for now, while I figure out what I want to be when I grow up. And friend of Jack's."

"Nice to meet you, Devon."

"Likewise, Keri Ann." He gave a small nod.

"Okay, well, I better go and get Colt. I'm late for my own birthday party." I grinned sheepishly.

Devon's eyebrows raised. "It's today? Well, happy birthday. I hope you get everything you want this year."

"Me, too," I said. I really did. "And, Devon? Thank you."

JACK

I saw a diamond road
And I took it
I made a lot of friends
But they were crooked
A cold hand reached out
And I shook it
I made so many mistakes
Now it's too late
To put 'em right
In the high twilight

—Lyrics from 'High Twilight' by Daniel Isaiah

CHAPTER THIRTY-SEVEN

I'm good at compartmentalizing. You have to be in my profession. As long as the cameras are rolling, you are someone else. Living like someone else, thinking like someone else, reacting like someone else. I've learned how to convey a thousand conflicting emotions without uttering a single word. I can also hide a thousand conflicting emotions in a lead-lined fortress, while chatting amiably with whoever needs a piece of Jack.

Right now, I'm sitting in a chair in a back room at True Tattoo while Nick Parker uses his needle and ink to pry me open. Nick and I were a two-pack of trouble on the streets of New York before we decided to stop giving our mothers short trips to early graves and move to L.A. He was the only one who knew about my father. Now, he is one of two.

And he won't fucking shut up.

"So Loggerhead Turtles are mostly native to the Georgia and Carolina coasts, did you know that?"

I don't grace him with an answer as he shades away at the scutes on my foot.

"And you know after they are born there, it doesn't matter

how far and wide they swim and for how many years, they go back to the same freaking beach?"

"What the fuck is your point, Nick?" I say, focusing on his wall display so I don't see the beach in my mind's eye.

"Nothing, man. It's just interesting you've chosen to put a tiny sea turtle on your foot. Not a big old Pacific Leatherback either." He shifts his angle slightly, and I wince as the needle moves over a particularly sensitive tendon.

I breathe out and fold my arms over my chest. I have a ton of shit to do today, including having seventy people over to my house for a final thank you as we wrap up the Erath tour. I must have been crazy to try and slide in and out of Nick's space without his irritating questions. My head is aching behind my eyes. All I want to do is get shit-faced.

Nick creases his brow in concentration that doesn't synch up with his leaking opinions. "After they hatch, they can get distracted by bright and artificial lights and instead of meeting their destiny, they are lured to their deaths."

"Jesus, Nick. What the hell is your problem?" I am pissed off. "Are you done yet?"

He smirks. "Not even close. Do you need her initials on it, or what?"

I grit my teeth. "No, Nick, I don't," I say calmly. Even though I do, actually. I'm not sure why. It's not like I won't be reminded every time I look down. Or any time at all. I quickly stick to my original plan. "Actually, yes. Do it. Hurry up about it, and let's go next door and get a drink."

"Okay, man. I just can't work out whether you're supposed to be the turtle or she is. It's bugging me."

"For the last time, shut the fuck up."

My phone vibrates in my pocket. Ignoring Nick's no cell phone rule, I pull it out gingerly, trying not to move.

Devon Brown.

"Hey, D. You're still coming tonight, right?" I greet him with the question, knowing full well he'll be there. *Erath* was his puppy after all. I just need the reassurance. I can't stand these industry backslapping events. The fact that Audrey offered to do it at home, instead of some restaurant, just shows how far apart she and I are these days. I need someone there on my side.

"Of course. Where are you? I want to talk to you about a new project and won't be able to do it tonight."

"Nick's giving me another memento. We're about to go next door and get a drink. Join us?"

"I'll never understand your obsession with permanent ink. It's a nightmare for makeup. I'll be there in twenty." He hangs up.

I realize I've been drinking a lot lately, but I can't seem to muster the energy to care. I can write it off to jetlag most of the time, but Audrey knows. We have done about seventeen countries in the last thirty days. At times, I feel like we are getting back to the friendship we used to have before it all became so complicated. I know she wants us to be more again, especially for the baby's sake. I'm trying.

"I'm done. The initials are designed into the scutes on the shell so you can't really see them unless you know they're there," Nick says, scooting his stool backward. I look down at the creature on my foot. It's tiny and beautiful. Nick is an artist. It doesn't make me feel better. But then again, it is more to remind me every day how easy it can be to take advantage of someone, so that I never do it again. Maybe it's so that I can focus on providing my son or daughter some sense of honor. Honor that I don't have.

I stand at the railing of my house, looking out over the valley to the Pacific Ocean as the sun sets. A glass of champagne dangles from my fingers. I'm tense but trying to look relaxed. Voices and laughter of mingling sycophants swirl around behind me, every sound another bar on this clichéd cage of mine. I drain the glass and let it slip out of my hand. It satisfies me to see it shatter on the rocky scrag of the hillside below. I'm wallowing. It doesn't become me.

I mentally prepare, and school my features, getting ready to turn around and become the carefree, successful, and handsome host once again. It has been a tiring evening, the last five minutes the only ones I've had to myself. Hopefully, this is one of the last parties for *Erath* I'll have to do now that the promotional tour is reaching its end. Endless photo-shoots, interviews, and staged outings with Audrey are finally slowing down.

It was Audrey's idea to host the party for Andy and some of the studio executives who had first championed the *Erath* script. It isn't that I'm not thankful and grateful to these people, but I also know that they depend on me just as much, if not more. Especially now. Inviting them all into my home is too much of an invasion for where my head is.

Audrey wasted no time moving back in here after I pulled the house off the market. I know she needs to show everyone things are fine between us.

I try to stay engaged with her when we are in public, and the effort is exhausting. And I know I have to start trying harder when it's just the two of us, especially for the baby's sake.

It helps that I can still pretend it was her public indiscretion that is taking me some time to get over, especially after the tabloids spun my drunken brawl in Savannah as me dealing with my heartbreak. How close they were . . . just the wrong girl.

Only Audrey knows the real reason for that incident, and she wastes no time being the perfect, fawning girlfriend. It is nauseating, but I feel sorry for her.

I think of my mother trying to bring me up alone, and I know Audrey is trying her best to repair the damage before the baby comes. I don't fault her for it. I admire her. It's a baby. Who wouldn't do their absolute best to create a perfect environment?

At any moment, I expect Audrey will start the argument that it's time to make a public announcement. I'm dreading it. I know it's necessary, but—and I don't like my mind going there—it will be national and international tabloid news that won't miss Butler Cove.

"Hey, man." My agent's voice accompanies his hand clapping down hard on my back, making me jump.

"Hey, Andy." I affect a friendly grin; it is what I do best, after all.

"Great party, my man. The latest numbers are in, they're making an announcement in a moment, come on."

Andy, dressed in a light gray suit and white shirt open at the collar, highlighting his ruddy complexion, manages to look like a perfect mix of managed stress and competence like he's just been working his ass off to secure my latest success. Slightly balding, he wears his hair buzzed close to his scalp and stands about a foot shorter than my six-foot-two frame.

"Ja-ack!" Audrey's voice lilts from behind us. We turn. She is beautiful in a sheer white dress with a small modest slip beneath, her hair flowing in dark waves over a shoulder. For a moment, I'm reminded of a certain white bikini cover-up that didn't really cover anything up. I flinch under the memory and swallow, and then I lean in for a kiss.

"You look beautiful, and we're coming," I say. I take her hand, and the three of us walk inside to hear the latest gross earnings from the movie that has just been released in three eastern European countries. There have been numbers announced after each opening weekend and there will be many more releases, although no more requiring a personal appearance from any cast members, thank God.

There is a lot of backslapping and raising of glasses as the numbers are announced. It should make me especially happy since I agreed to a royalty payment structure, instead of a one-time payment back when hardly anyone believed in the success of the project. It was Devon who advised me to take that route, and it has been the best financial decision of my career.

Devon comes up to me as the announcements and toasting subsides. "Jack, good to see you, man. How's the foot?" He gives me a brief hug like he didn't just see me four hours ago. Devon is the only person, apart from what little Nick knows, that I have confided in. Not much to either of them, but some. It was Devon's friendship and generosity with his beach house that allowed me to get away in the first place. It is also in Devon's best interest with Peak Entertainment to keep Audrey's and my relationship on the rails.

"Fine."

Devon shrugs. "Anyway, we need to talk about scheduling for the Dread Pirate Roberts project. I'm so psyched you agreed to take the role. I told Monica you wouldn't take it, and then when you accepted today—you realize you owe me a blowjob. Right?"

"What?" I laugh. It feels good.

"Yeah, man. That's what I said I'd give up if she was right."

"Ugh. Please don't talk to me about your sex life." I shudder dramatically. Devon roars with laughter.

We banter a little more as the party winds down, and people leave for other invitations and appearances. It helps that I capped the alcohol and don't let anyone do drugs at my house any more. That pretty much assures an early evening by L.A. standards. Before long it's just Devon, Monica, Katie, my assistant, and Andy, who is anxiously texting, sitting around the littered living area while two hired servers pick up around us.

Audrey has gone upstairs to lie down. I know that pregnancy is tiring so I don't begrudge her. She is growing a whole new human being, for Pete's sake. Now that the touring is done, she needs to take it easy, and I need to call and tell my mother. I haven't called home in a while, not even when I was in London for the premiere. I'm a shitty son.

"Isn't this great, man?" Andy sighs, finally putting his phone down and getting comfortable. "I knew if you just got back here, it would all sort itself out."

I nod. Andy has said this about a hundred times since I came back to L.A. with Audrey.

I've forgiven Katie for ratting out my location. She owned up to going out for a lunch date one day and letting Audrey stay at her desk under the guise of just needing somewhere to sit and write out some notecards. Audrey writing out notecards should have been a clue, but mistakes happen, and Katie was devastated and convinced I was going to fire her. There was no love lost between Katie and Audrey to begin with, and now it's even worse. It's actually quite comical to watch them in the same room together like two grown female cats in a circling dance of avoidance, interspersed with occasional hissing.

Andy sits back smugly and takes a sip of his scotch. "It was a gamble, man, but it paid off. Andy always knows best."

"What paid off?" asks Devon, vocalizing my exact thought.

"The pregnancy, of course." Andy laughs indignantly. "I mean, what else could have galvanized our tragic hero here to get back to reality?" He leans forward, shrugging off his gray suit jacket, oblivious to the four faces staring at him, nonplussed.

"What do you mean?" I try to ask, but whisper. My face and lips feel tight, like there is no blood left.

Devon stands up at that same moment and leans dangerously over Andy. "You better fucking explain yourself, and fast, because if you just said what I think you did, I'm going to fucking kill you."

I'm staring at Andy, waiting for his response to Devon's question. My tongue feels like a sack of cement.

I vaguely notice Monica grab Devon's sleeve. "Devon," she murmurs, and then glances toward the staircase where Audrey is gliding down, a large smile on her face, her eyes unnaturally bright. Clearly not napping. She stops dead when she sees the strained scene.

Audrey looks at me with confusion and then glances at Andy. I see the exact moment when she realizes. It is the exact moment when I see the truth in all of its soul-stripping agony.

I don't know what she sees on my face, but I know she is suddenly rushing toward me, her hands open in supplication, and I am moving to put as much furniture between me and her as possible.

"Please, Jack. Just wait, let me explain. I didn't know what else to do." Her words and her breath are choppy. "I knew I'd messed up, but we both had a contract to fulfill and we were happy, weren't we? I mean before? I just needed you, I mean us, to be together, so I could make it right." Audrey tries to round the couch to where I'm standing, my back to the wall. She looks panicked.

I find my voice but it's a snarl. "Stay where you are. Don't fucking come near me!" I am still in complete shock and not sure I'm processing the enormity of the lie.

Her tone takes on a high, pleading note. "Please, Jack. I'm sorry, it was for your own good, so you didn't break your contract, you would have forfeited half your royalties." Her eyes are wide and begging.

"So you thought you'd make up a *baby*?" My eyes swing around. "Who else knew, was it just you and Andy? Who came up with it? Wait, do I even care whose idea it was?" It's true, I don't care. Not yet. There are too many other things right now. I can't believe there's no baby. I haven't been sure how I feel about the concept, and now there is nothing. I don't like this either. I'm empty. There has to have been a mistake, a misunderstanding.

I turn to Devon as if he can answer this for me, even though I know he can't. I am finding it difficult to breathe for some reason. "God, it's not true, is it?"

"We didn't know," Devon manages. His voice is rough with emotion as he looks at my face. Monica squeezes his hand. Her elegant face is transformed into sadness and concern. Devon's look also smacks of pity, and I think of the throbbing skin on my foot. I think of the might-have-been that this lie has cost me.

I know, right in that moment, that I would give it all back.

I would trade all of this and all of these people and every royalty I've ever earned to get one moment of the peace I experienced for the first time in my life. It is so clear to me that I wonder why it has taken me this long to see it.

My eyes fly to Katie, who winces at what she must see in my expression. "Can you fix it?" I bark. "I mean, can you get me there? I can't go commercial, I'm a wreck, can you get a plane to Hilton Head? I think it's the nearest private airfield. See who has a pilot available."

I don't know what I'm saying. There is no way I can go back there. Not after all of this. After what I did and the way I left.

But Katie nods, wordlessly, and fumbles to pull her laptop out of her messenger bag. "I'm so sorry, Jack," she says again for the thousandth time in two months.

My skin feels hot and tight, and I am slightly nauseous.

"God, you're not going to *her*, are you?" Audrey says, her voice pouring acid all over me.

I hate her. My look must tell her everything I feel right now, because she flinches as I turn her way.

Rage rumbles from deep inside me, erupting as I turn and blindly punch a huge hole right through the wall behind me.

Fuck, it hurts.

Everybody is frozen.

"You can't be serious," Andy's caustic tone grates over my already shredded nerves. "Dude, that cheap waitress you messed around with, *that's* what this is all about?"

I grind my teeth together, and taking a deep breath, finally turn to him.

My hand is throbbing and it stings. I cradle it. Blood, I'm sure, is pooling in the skinned divots. The pain helps me focus. I wonder who this man is, who I have blindly trusted for the last six years. Just what he would do for his next paycheck.

After several moments, where even Andy must suddenly know better than to offer anything else, I say what I should have said to him sooner. "You're fired. Get. The. Fuck. Out."

EVERSEA PLAYLIST

'She Sells Sanctuary' – The Cult
'In the End' – Snow Patrol
'Steal Your Heart' – Augustana
'Only the Young' – Brandon Flowers
'Silenced by the Night' – Keane
'Hearts on Fire' – Scars on 45
'High Twilight' – Daniel Isaiah
'Run Dry' – Civil Twilight
'Hold On' – Alabama Shakes
'Madness' – Muse

Special thanks go to Daniel Isaiah for giving me permission to quote the lyrics from 'High Twilight' (Secret City Records).

Don't miss out on what happens next for
Keri Ann and Jack.

Read on for a sneak peek of

forever, jack

KERI ANN

CHAPTER ONE

Five Months Later . . .

$\mathcal{I}$ rolled up the windows in the pickup as I glanced nervously at the heaving pregnant gray bellies of the clouds above me. It was just in time, too. The first fat raindrop splattered over the windshield, followed by a deluge, as the cloud waters broke.

I flicked on the wipers, peering ahead at the bright sunshine that shone up the road and shook my head. Nana always used to call this *A Monkey's Wedding*. I had no idea what that meant, still didn't, but there'd be a heck of a rainbow in a few minutes. I'd have to look out for it. The April showers were incessant this year.

A shrill ring emanated over the loud roar of the heavy drops hitting the truck, and I felt around blindly on the seat next to me trying not to take my eyes off the slick road.

"Hello."

"Hey, sweetheart. You almost here?" Colton's deep voice comforted me.

I tucked the cell under my chin so I could keep two hands

on the wheel as the road got trickier to manage. "Yeah. Almost. I hate driving in the rain. Did you miss it?"

"Just. I wish you'd let me drive you."

"I know, Colt. But surely you have other stuff to do besides take care of your best friend's baby sister 'cos he's too freaking busy to come home. This way you can get on with your day after you help me unload this stuff."

There was a beat of silence on the other end of the phone. "Colt?"

"Yeah." He cleared his throat. "I'm here. I'm parked at the service entrance. When you get to the front of the Westin, drive to the left around the building." The line went dead.

I let the phone slide down to my lap and pursed my lips as I squinted through the water-distorted view. It was dumb to make the baby sister reference again. But it was Joey who was supposed to help me drop these pieces off for the exhibit. He was the one who called Colt when he couldn't make it. Setting me up again.

"Shit," I muttered. I shouldn't have agreed to go out with Colt when my heart wasn't in it. He was such a nice guy. Well actually, several girls in Savannah would probably disagree with me, but he was nice to *me*. Too nice. I was leading him on, and I knew it. Even though I'd told him, repeatedly, I wasn't ready for a serious relationship.

But a month ago, I'd capitulated. Well, I had agreed to go out to dinner with him. Like a date. *One dinner*. That had turned into a couple of other dinner occasions, taking me for lunch after I went to drop something at the admissions office at SCAD, going to a few movies, kayaking trips on Saturday mornings, and heck . . . we were basically dating. Or at least *special-friending* as Mrs. Weaton, my elderly tenant, called it. I snorted and rolled my eyes. I felt bad. It was exactly why I hadn't asked him to help me out today.

The rain finally eased up as I turned off William Hilton Parkway toward Port Royal Plantation and made my way under the canopy of curvy live oaks that lined the main driveway.

"Is that it, then?" Colt asked as I brought the last piece, a base for the sculpture I had made, from the truck. His dark hair was cropped short, making him look a little like a marine.

I nodded. "I just have to do the install on a few pieces. This, for example," I said, heaving my load up slightly. "Thank you so much for helping, I know you probably have to get going."

He rocked back on his heels and stuffed his fingers into the front pockets of his distressed khaki jeans. "I'd like to stay and watch, if that's okay?" He looked at me questioningly.

"Uh, yeah, sure."

"Then afterward I can buy you an early dinner at View 32." He paused, trying to sound innocent. "Since we're here and all."

I shook my head as I laid down the piece I was holding, but I was smiling. He never gave up. "You don't have to buy me dinner, but food would be good."

He smirked with satisfaction and came close, sliding a hand around the back of my neck and depositing a kiss onto my forehead. And I swear, *I swear*, he inhaled just a little.

Pulling away, I elbowed him jovially in the ribs.

I worked fast, and then checked in with the events coordinator, Allison, before heading back to find Colt. I'd met

Allison at my opening at the Picture This Gallery back in December. She'd invited me to be a part of this exhibit. Soon I'd be back here on Hilton Head Island for a black-tie cocktail party, with me as one of the star guests. It seemed totally surreal. And all my sweet friends in Butler Cove were raiding wedding rental companies for formal attire. Who knew what I was going to wear? It sent me into a flat panic every time it crossed my mind, so I tried not to let it. Now the party was just around the corner, and I was still dress-less.

Colt wasn't where I left him, so I headed to the walkway deck then looked over the pool area and followed it toward the restaurant. I found him leaning on his elbows overlooking the beach and the ocean beyond.

"Hey," I said coming up beside him and resting my arms next to his.

"Hey you," he returned softly, bumping my shoulder.

We both fell silent watching the shadowed pool area as the sun lowered somewhere behind us. White ribbons tied to some wooden chairs near the beach flapped haphazardly in the sea air, the remnants of a wedding celebration.

I had yet to attend a wedding in my adult life, although I remembered going to one when I was nine with my parents in West Virginia. My mom's high school best friend was getting married. My parents fought for the entire car trip there about something my young mind didn't think to retain. They were stone cold silent for the entire ride home. I was looking forward to seeing some of my friends tie the knot in the years to come, happier occasions they'd be, I was sure.

Colt breathed in a loaded breath, bringing me back to the present. "This is a huge deal, Keri Ann. I don't want to sound patronizing, but I'm so proud of you and what you've accomplished." He angled his head to me.

I smiled self-consciously. "Thank you. It's pretty cool, huh? I can't quite get over it, really. I mean, I know this is just a hotel and not a New York Gallery, but this island gets over two million visitors a year, and I think they are promoting the heck out of this exhibition all summer long." I shrugged my shoulders and felt the beat of heat in my cheeks.

Colt grinned. "Come on, let's go get you fed."

I watched him turn away to walk toward the restaurant entrance. "Colt?"

He turned back, eyebrows raised above bright blue eyes. "Yeah?"

"Thank you." I clasped my fingers together nervously and looked away as I spoke. "It was good to have a friend here. *You* here," I quickly amended and glanced at him. "Helping. Today was kind of a big day for me."

Colt took an almost step toward me, then halted, like he'd purposely stopped himself. He shook his head and blew out a breath. "You're welcome."

The heavens opened again as soon as we were on the way home, this time with huge gusts of wind. I slowed the truck as the visibility went from bad to worse and checked the rearview mirror.

Colt's dark BMW followed, as well as a smattering of other cars. It seemed he'd decided to follow me. I really appreciated that, but wondered whether I'd have to invite him in, or if he was just seeing me home. Ugh. This whole *special friends* thing was driving me nuts. I didn't know what was expected of me, or scratch that . . . what *he* expected of me. Was I supposed to kiss him and let him think this was something more out of some warped sense of duty? I didn't think so. I wouldn't. But spending time with Colt had given me a whole new understanding of the general dating scene. It was an ocean of unspoken expectation and misunderstanding. And pressure. Some real and some imagined. There was also undoubtedly a lot of frog kissing on the way to the prince. Not that Colt was a frog . . .

No, this was Colton Graves, my brother's best friend and friend of mine. And I had definitely made myself clear, both by explicitly stating I wasn't ready for a serious relationship, and with my endless comments about friendship. Then again, I had agreed to go out with him. Several times.

I glanced nervously in the rearview mirror again just in time to see the blue tarp I'd strapped down to cover all my pieces earlier rip clear off one side and flap wildly over the edge of the truck bed.

Damn!

I slowed and put the blinker on to pull over. I hated to stop on the side of a highway, but I risked a certain accident if the tarp got caught in the wheels. Just as I rolled to a stop, I thought I felt it do just that. A ripping sound emanated from behind me and the truck shuddered.

Wrenching open the door, I climbed out into the warm and driving rain that had me soaked within nanoseconds. I bent to inspect the wheel then heard Colton's door slam and looked up as he approached, holding a dark windbreaker over his head that he extended over me, too.

"It's jammed. Dammit," I yelled over the gusts of wind and passing cars, kicking the tire with my wet sneaker.

"We'll probably have to take the wheel off like we're changing a flat."

I nodded at his yelled words, just what I was thinking. "I have a jack in the truck bed."

Turning to go get it as Colt did what he could to pull the tarp away from the wheel, I saw a silver Jeep Wrangler slowing down and pulling onto the hard shoulder ahead of us. Then it reversed closer. I was glad I wasn't out here alone. No one got out right away. I caught Colt's eye and we both shrugged.

I was soaked and getting more chilled from the wind by the second. Grabbing the iron and the jack, I went back around the truck in time to see the door on the Jeep open. A long denim-clad leg ending in black biker boots, the kind that were etched in my memory, like forever, swung out the door of the Jeep and hit the pavement at about the same time my stomach did. And perhaps given the loud clang, the tire iron, too.

This was not happening.

My eyes traveled upwards over an olive green button-down shirt that was not only rapidly turning dark khaki in the rain but was also plastering to the body beneath. Then I looked up over a familiar roughly stubbled jaw to the shadow of a ball cap, where eyes I couldn't see, but could certainly feel, should be.

"You've got to be fucking kidding me," I heard Colt say harshly next to me.

My eyes tracked back down to the boots, and I watched as they headed toward us. I willed my mind to work. Hadn't I thought of this scenario a thousand times? Okay, maybe not on the side of a highway, but hadn't I rehearsed what I would say, over and over, and pathetically, over again?

But, *nothing*.

Nothing came to mind as the boots approached. The boots I remembered sitting by my fireplace after a rainstorm like this one. And as the water poured, streaming rivulets over me, I couldn't look up. I just stood there.